THE NORTH

SEAN CUMMINGS

SEVERED PRESS
HOBART TASMANIA

THE NORTH

ISBN: 978-1-925493-32-0

On open ground, I would keep a vigilant eye on my defences.
On ground of intersecting highways, I would consolidate my alliances.

On serious ground, I would try to ensure a continuous stream of supplies.
On difficult ground, I would keep pushing on along the road.

On hemmed-in ground, I would block any way of retreat.
On desperate ground, I would proclaim to my soldiers the hopelessness of saving their lives.

Art of War by Sun Tzu

Nominal as at 5 November 1400 HRS ZULU

Binns, Robert – Dead
Bosworth, David – Dead
Czerini, Martin – Dead
Collings, Stephen – Dead
Consworth, Denise – Missing on July 9th, presumed dead
Cruze, Pam – Ark Two Commander, Group 2IC
Dale, Mitchell – Dead
Dawson, Kate – Ark One 2IC
Dixon, Melanie – Ark Two 2IC
Dorn, Gregory – Dead
Binh, Mandeep – Dead
Eves, Dale – Dead
Falton, Geoffery – Missing on August 31st, presumed dead
Ferguson, Bonnie – Dead
Finnerty, Michael - Dead
Finnerty, Robert – Dead
Gainey, Terrance – Infected, Quarantined
Graves, Mona – Missing on August 31st, presumed dead
Green, Robert – Dead
Holowaychuk Alex – Dead
Howard, Kenneth – Ark Two Driver
Jeffers, Calvin – Dead
Jiwa, Anil – Infected, Quarantined
Manybears, Doug – Ark One Driver
Rogers, Pam – Dead
Sawchuk, Willie – Missing, presumed dead
Simmons, David – Ark One Commander, Group Leader
Simmons, Jo – Ark One
Singleton, Bryce – Dead
Switch, Dale – Dead
Toomey, Sid – Ark One Gunner

THE NORTH

H-Hour Minus Thirty-Six:

We stood in silence around Sgt. Green's mangled body. In his right hand was the three-foot long steel pipe he'd carried as a weapon for the past six months. It saved on bullets, he'd told us, and he was right. It just didn't save him.

Maybe if he'd used his sidearm, he might have stood a fighting chance against the trio of creeps that tore him apart, but they'd cornered him in a storage room with no possible exit other than the doorway where the monsters now lay still as a stone, each with a bullet fired into the back of its head. We heard his screams – we just couldn't reach him in time.

"Those three had been hiding their fucking infection!" snarled Pam Cruze as she shouldered her still-smoking carbine. "Jesus ... are we going to have to strip down to our skivvies so that each of us can check one another for bites? This shouldn't have happened."

I clenched my jaw tightly as I gazed over at the three monsters lying on the floor. They used to be like us ... they used to *be* us until they turned.

Sid Toomey, a giant sixteen-year-old Newfoundlander fished a cigarette out the breast pocket of his combat jacket and lit it with a quick flick of his Zippo lighter. "Cal Jeffers was a pussy ... he wouldn't have volunteered that he'd become infected if you'd held a knife to his throat. Bonnie wasn't showing any signs of illness when I talked to her yesterday morning and Bosworth? That fucker was a secretive bastard at the best of times."

"We've got to burn the bodies ASAP," I said, as I stepped over Sgt. Green's mutilated remains and placed the barrel of my carbine against his head. "Cruze ... would you go to the kitchen and tell Dawson to grab Kenny and bring a stretcher. We need to move fast

… it's getting dark outside, and the creeps will swarm the fence in the parking compound as soon as the sun goes down."

"Alright, Dave," she said, still eyeballing the horrific scene. "Fuck … what are we going to do now."

"Figure out our next move," I said, as I squeezed the trigger.

CHAPTER 1

Journal Entry: 12 November 22:15 HRS ZULU

I'm on sentry duty in about fifteen minutes, so a quick note. There are only eight of us left now that Sgt. Green is gone. Sid Toomey is now the oldest person in a group ranging in age from eight years old to seventeen.

Mom is dead. I should be mourning her loss, but I've given up on the idea because there's just no point anymore. Maybe in the madness of the days and weeks following the siege, Mom fell into the inescapable blackness of depression over our hopeless situation or maybe her mind simply wouldn't accept what her eyes bore witness to. Anyway, it probably doesn't matter now because part of me believes that nobody will survive. I haven't told Jo that I found a gun lying next to Mom's body or that the right side of her head was missing.

But I took the gun.

Death prowls in clusters of ten or twenty that can sometimes grow as large as a small army if the creeps ever catch a whiff of your scent. Their outstretched arms and claw-like hands drip gore onto the pavement, and their shuffling feet can be heard to echo in the distance when the night is clear and cold. When they swarm you; their inhuman voices will cry out, screeching, raging and animal-like, and it's only a matter of time until they burst through the barricade of your hiding place wherever it might be.

I'm all that Jo has left; it falls on me to save her life and perhaps my own, though lately, it's near impossible to believe that any life can be saved when the sun hasn't shone in more than six months. The sky is a flat grey canvas that blankets the burning cityscape like a body bag, and the air is tainted with the smell of smoke and blood and putrefying bodies because the dead surround us. We can't stay here in the armoury. We need to get out of the city.

Somehow.

I took the first sentry shift at 23:00 along with Melanie Dixon. She was sporting a do-rag, and she's recently shaved her head. That Pam Cruze had also shaved her head and wearing a do-rag had me thinking the pair might be an item, not that I or anyone else left alive gave a damn. If Cruze and Melanie had found something resembling happiness in this hell-hole new world, even temporary satisfaction, then good on them. We stood atop the north tower and gazed out over the blocks of overturned and smashed-up cars and trucks that clogged the streets surrounding the armoury. Less than a hundred yards away shambled small groups of the monsters, tripping and stumbling through the debris of a city that had transformed into a nightmare world where the dead don't fucking stay dead, and the living are just meat. Four stories below us in the parking compound a fire blazed furiously, fuelled by the bodies of the creeps and Sgt. Green.

He kept us going. He kept us alive even though our numbers whittled away in the weeks and months after Day Zero, the day when the old world ended.

"It doesn't seem right to burn his body along with the monsters," said Melanie as she wiped her nose on the sleeve of her combat jacket. "We should have known those three were infected."

When she said "we," what Melanie really meant was that *I* should have known. I was Sgt. Green's 2IC, his second-in-command. I had only a year under my belt as a militia soldier, but I'd shown a knack for organizing the team, and the wily old Afghanistan war veteran picked me to be his back-up. That was two months ago.

"I don't know what we could have done any differently, Mel," I replied, as I spotted a creep trip emerge from a debris-filled alleyway and fall flat on its face. It slowly got back to its feet and continued stumbling mindlessly down the middle of 9th Avenue. "They probably became infected when the creeps breached to fence two days ago. It was dark, and we couldn't exactly start shooting the fucking things because gunfire is an open invitation to swarming."

She shrugged and leaned over the parapet. "Maybe ... or it

might have been before that. We've had people carry the infection for up to seven weeks without showing any signs of illness only to drop dead while on sentry or taking a dump. Anyway … I'm not blaming you, so get that out of your head. Got it?"

"Yup," I said quietly.

A sharp gust of wind pushed the flames of the bonfire in our direction, and the smoke from the bodies filled my nostrils. The sickly sweet smell of burning human flesh is something we'd become accustomed to over the past six months, though even admitting this fact made me feel like the David Simmons I used to be never once existed. The old me was just a hapless weekend warrior who'd spend Saturdays and Sundays marching around a parade square dressed in combat fatigues just to make a few extra bucks.

I didn't have a freaking clue back then, and I sure as hell don't have a clue now – none of us do. We'd been fighting and dying by inches for months, and if we didn't come up with a new plan for survival, none of us were going to make it through to the end of the year.

My mind flashed back to my first encounter with a creep. We lived in a three bedroom upper floor of a small house in Forest Lawn. It was a crummy part of town before the end came, and we'd been the victims of three break-ins – not that we owned anything worth stealing. When she wasn't liquored up, Mom worked at the doughnut shop next to a Ford dealership and took the bus to work each day. It was a Friday morning, and I'd just turned on the TV only to see the emergency broadcast beacon on all the channels. Mom was passed out on the couch – pissed again as usual – and Jo was packing her lunch for school.

Only there wasn't going to be any school that day – or ever again. I listened closely to the emergency instructions telling everyone to stay in their homes – to lock all our doors and to stay off the phones so that we wouldn't jam the lines for emergency services. Ignoring the warning, I grabbed my cell phone and called up the orderly room at the armoury to see if the King's Own was about to be mustered. The orderly sergeant didn't answer, but Sid Toomey did. What he told me next sent me reeling – it was too unbelievable to be true. Even now, six months after the siege, I remember the madness in his voice.

"Dave!" he shouted into the phone. "We're bugging out – get your shit in gear, and I'll be at your place as quick as I can to pick up your family!"

I kept my eyes peeled on the Emergency Broadcast System symbol on the TV. "What the hell is going on, Sid? Every channel on the television is showing the same emergency warning! I can't even get the news online – the website is overloaded!"

In the background, I could hear shots being fired. *"Fuck!"* Sid roared. I heard a loud clunk and then the sound of screaming. A series of hard, wet thuds filled my ear followed by Sid screaming in an inhuman voice.

"Fucking die!" he thundered.

Another series of thuds and then Sid returned to the phone, breathless.

"What the hell is going on?" I shouted as my heart raced. *"Sid ... Sid!"*

"There's a shit storm blowing into town that's too fucking unreal to be true – no time to explain!" he panted. "Dave – grab a baseball bat or a pipe or anything that's long and sturdy. If one of these things attacks you, bash its head in. That's the only way to stop them! Keep your mother and kid sister close because ..."

"Bash them in the *head*?" I nearly spat out the words. "What the hell are you talking about?"

And then I saw who was standing behind my little sister in the kitchen. It was our elderly downstairs neighbour, Martin Kessler. Only he didn't look right. His movements were jerky, and his hair was flat and matted.

"Get the hell out of here, Martin!" I shouted. "I don't know what makes you think you can just walk into our place but ..."

The old man opened his mouth to reveal a set of yellowing teeth rooted into blackened gums, and I thought for a moment he was going to say something, but no sound came.

Not a single freaking sound.

He looked more animal than human, his face was the colour of ash, and his eyes were just lifeless orbs set deep inside his skull. His shirt was stained with blood and chunks of what looked like meat, and he wasn't wearing any pants or underwear.

"Jo ... run!" I barked. The monster reached out with a pair of arthritic hands streaked with blood and gore, missing her hair by inches. She raced to my side and wrapped her arms around my waist for dear life.

Any other day, I'd have been able to kick the living shit out of the old man, but his sharp, almost feral movements belied the fact that he was a senior citizen. He lunged at me, and I grabbed him by the wrists as he snapped at my face.

Martin Kessler's skin was ice cold. In that wild moment, I didn't even try to contemplate how a dead man could have come back to life. I was holding him at bay, and the only sound I heard outside of Jo and Mom's shrieking was the sound of the old man's teeth snapping together.

Mom raced into the kitchen as I fought the creature. She came back brandishing a butcher's knife, and she thrust it hard into Kessler's back.

He didn't even flinch. Not once. He pushed me back against the wall, as Mom pulled out the knife and stabbed it into the side of Kessler's neck. Blood oozed out of the wound when there should have been arterial spray, and even that didn't slow him down as he tried to take a bite out of me. In that moment of adrenaline-fuelled terror, it dawned on me that Martin Kessler wasn't just another crazy senior who forgot to take his meds. His skin was cold, his eyes bore right through me, and he had a butcher knife sticking out the right side of his neck.

Martin Kessler was dead, and I'd be dead too if I didn't think of something. I placed my right foot into his chest and pushed with all my might. Kessler's grip released, and he toppled backward over the coffee table, landing flat on his back.

"Jo ... get my baseball bat out of my bedroom!" I shouted as Mom raced down the hall with Jo in tow. I stood in the doorway leading to the hall as Kessler slowly got back to his feet. The monster's lips folded back into a snarl, and he lunged at me again, so I gripped the top of the door frame with both hands and swung my feet into his chest sending him careening backward until he smashed into the wall a few feet away.

"H-Here!" said Jo shakily as she handed me my aluminum baseball bat.

"Stay down the hall, Jo," I ordered. "And close your eyes. You don't want to see what's going to happen."

She did as she was told, and I moved into the center of the living room gripping my bat tightly in both hands. Kessler lunged at me again, and I swung the bat hard, connecting with the top third of the monster's head. There was a loud crunch as the bat struck with enough force to leave a dent in his skull, and Kessler dropped to the floor like someone had cut the strings from a marionette.

I stood there, bat in hand staring at the creature. In the background, the sound of the emergency broadcast beacon on the TV filled the room. Kessler didn't twitch. He just lay there with his dead eyes staring up at the ceiling, his crushed head frozen in a pool of blood that was as black as tar. I'd just killed a man, only it wasn't murder. The thing that attacked me wasn't any way human. Now I understood the horrific sounds that I heard when I'd called Sid Toomey.

"W-What happened, David?" my mother gasped, her breath stinking of whatever she'd been power drinking into the middle of the night. "Why did Martin attack us?"

I shook my head. My stomach pitched and heaved, and it was everything I could do to keep myself from throwing up right there on the carpet. "You won't believe me if I told you. All I know is that we need to pack some stuff and get the hell out of here. Sid Toomey is coming from the armoury to get us."

"We'll do no such thing!" she barked. "We're going to have to call the police and let them know that Martin Kessler attacked you – we have to report this."

I pointed to the TV. "You won't get the police. That emergency broadcast signal is on all the stations and ten bucks says you won't connect to the Internet."

"But ..."

I grabbed my mother by the shoulders and gave her a hard shake. "Listen to me ... Martin Kessler is dead, Mom, and he was dead when he came up the stairs – that's all I know. The safest place for us to be is at the armoury. There's food, and medical supplies and ..."

It was at that moment the TV shut down. I grabbed the remote control and tried turning it on and off but the power was out.

"Shit … the grid just freaking died. Look, Mom … let's just get some stuff together and head to the armoury, okay? Sid is on his way."

We spent the next few minutes stuffing everything from toiletries to undergarments in a small overnight bag. Sid arrived as promised. I gazed out from behind the curtains over the living room window to see an armoured personnel carrier ploughing through a trio of cars that were blocking access to our front yard. It stopped on the lawn, and I spotted Doug Manybears' head sticking up through the driver's hatch. Seconds later, Sid leaped out the back door, carbine in hand. We raced down the front steps and straight to the back of the carrier. The air was filled with the sounds of hundreds of car alarms and honking horns. Across the street, I saw to my horror a person shrieking in an inhuman voice as a trio of monsters dug into his torso, each one pulling out a handful of shining, bloody organs which they promptly began feasting on.

"Unreal," I whispered, unable to take my eyes off the grisly scene. *"This can't be happening."*

"Dave!" Sid shouted as a foursome of monsters, each one shuffling just like old man Kessler, stumbled and tripped around from the side of our house and marched Sid's way. He raised his carbine to his shoulder and fired a series quick well-aimed shots that dropped them.

"Hurry the fuck up!" Sid roared again as he covered us. He kept his carbine at the ready as we climbed in, then he jumped in the back and pulled the door closed, locking the combat locks for good measure.

He pulled a carbine off the weapon rack and handed it to me. "Here. You provide cover from the rear hatch, and I'll crew command back to the armoury. These … these *creeps* are everywhere. If any of those things get too close, fire single shots right at their heads. It's the only thing that will stop them."

"We were attacked by our downstairs neighbour, Sid," I blurted out. "Mom stabbed him, and it didn't do anything. I finally stopped him by caving in his skull with a baseball bat. A fucking dead guy attacked me – his skin was freaking cold, man! And across the street! They were … they were eating a guy! What is this? What the hell is happening?"

"Hell on Earth, Book of Revelations, End of Days … who the fuck knows?" he replied. "Get your ass up in the hatch and single shots, okay?"

I pulled the carbine to my shoulder and nodded.

"Dave … you with me?" Mel said as she batted me in the back of the head. "What's our next move?" She spun around on her heels to look at me, and I hoped she wasn't expecting me to bark out orders like Sgt. Green would do, because for the life of me, I didn't have anything to offer. I wanted to throw her a glimmer of hope, something she could cling to that would get her through to the end of our sentry shift or to first light. I wanted to pull a genius tactical move that would save our lives, but what could I offer that would have been better than Sgt. Green's plan of hunkering down in the armoury and waiting things out? There was nothing left to wait for in a city that's little more than a creep-infested husk.

The man pack radio we'd kept on sentry had been silent for weeks. We'd monitored daily to keep track of any military movement in the vicinity and mostly in a desperate hope that maybe a helicopter would be dispatched to get us the fuck out of the city, but the army as we knew it was dead.

It occurred to me that other survivors somewhere might have access to the short-wave band – the frequency that ham radio operators used.

"Mel … flip that radio over to short-wave. I want to try something."

She nodded and pressed the toggle with an index finger as I started switching through the channels. A spray of radio static spat out of the speaker with each turn of the knob, so I continued to switch channels in hope of hearing something … anything.

"You think there might be military assets broadcasting?" she asked.

I shrugged. "Probably civvies. I mean, if we're alive, there have to be other people out there somewhere. If they have a radio, they'd be using shortwave to contact others – the signal carries all over the globe."

We spent the next half hour flipping through the channels one at a time, listening for a few minutes and then switching to the next one. I was about to switch back to the military frequency when I finally heard something. It was barely audible amid the background hissing, so I fiddled with the squelch knob.

NODUFF. THIS IS SANCTUARY BASE CALLING. SANCTUARY BASE AT 53.200 NOVEMBER 105.7500 WHISKEY. ALL CLEAR NOW – I SAY AGAIN – ALL CLEAR. SANCTUARY BASE. NODUFF. ALL CLEAR. NODUFF. NEXT CONTACT AT 0630 ZULU.

Mel threw me a look of shock or surprise, I couldn't tell which. "Noduff? They're military, Dave. They're using army voice procedure."

I pursed my lips tightly as I scribbled down the message on my field message pad. It was broadcast three more times and then ended abruptly. "Yeah … maybe."

"Someone else is out there, finally!" Mel said through a wide grin. "We've got to tell everyone what we heard. We've got to contact these people."

I wanted to agree with her, but we didn't have a clue who sent the message and what it meant. "Mel … don't, okay? Not yet. We need more information before we get everyone's hopes up – I need to talk with Cruze. She's the only qualified signals person we've got. If there's anyone who can verify the message, it's her."

"Everyone should know, Dave," she said sharply. "They have a right."

I couldn't pull rank on Melanie Dixon because she'd probably kick my ass, but I had to reel her in. "Look … let me talk with Cruze, okay? Just trust me on this, Mel, can you give me at least twelve hours?"

"They're broadcasting again at 0630, Dave. We might miss something. That's seven and a half hours from now."

I exhaled heavily and said, "Then give me seven and a half hours. We'll let everyone know what to do at first light. It's what Sgt. Green would have done. He'd take the cautious approach."

She turned and then leaned over the parapet and pointed to the fire. "Yeah, well he's dead … and we're going to be dead if we don't come up with a plan."

"Just keep quiet about it, Mel," I warned.

She didn't reply, and instead, she just gazed out into the darkness.

Perfect.

CHAPTER 2

A message on short-wave radio from a place called Sanctuary Base and some possible map coordinates along with the words "all clear." For all I knew, those coordinates could be on the other side of the world. I stared at the hastily scribbled message on my field message pad and rubbed the back of my neck as I wandered down a hallway lit only by tea light candles. We'd made lanterns out of tin cans, and the tiny candles threw heavy shadows on the walls, each one shifting and stirring amid the soft ambient glow.

I needed to talk with Pam Cruze, because if we couldn't come up with a way to present news of the broadcast to the team, the shit could hit the fan. We'd managed to cobble together some measure of military discipline, but that was all under Sgt. Green's leadership. The only thing scarier than the prospect of being ripped apart by creeps was to wind up on the receiving end of one of his patented blasts of shit. I'd seen him make Sid Toomey cry without even raising his voice, and Sid was a good foot taller than our now deceased section commander.

We'd spent nearly six months hunkered down in the armoury; a four-storey brick and sandstone fortress that was built after the First World War. It looked like a throwback to medieval times, a weathered old castle surrounded by glass-encased skyscrapers and million dollar condominiums. But it was a defensible position with four towers, each with a commanding view. All the windows were secured with iron bars, though the creeps had broken through the main level windows on the north side in a skirmish that cost us ten lives. There was a thick oak door at street level reinforced with a two-foot thick wooden brace. Inside, there was the parade square with two fully functional armoured personnel carriers, offices and billets on the second floor and a kitchen, not that it was of much use given we'd run out of gas and electricity months ago.

"We can't stay here forever," I whispered.

I poked my head inside the room I shared with my kid sister, Jo. She was sound asleep on a folding cot buried beneath a pair of thick grey wool blankets. On the wall above was a gun rack - the same kind we'd screwed into the wall above everyone's cots. It was Sgt. Green's idea. He'd said that personal weapons are useless if they're not within arm's reach and that we'd have to scramble if the alarm went during the silent hours. If that cowbell rang, everyone would know that creeps had somehow managed to get inside the armoury.

And Jo knew how to use her carbine; I'd made sure of that as early as three weeks past Day Zero. Even at eight years old, my sister knew how to double tap when shooting at a creep all the while making sure to count the remaining bullets in her thirty-round magazine.

Across the room was the now empty cot where my mother used to sleep. All of her belongings were stuffed into a duffel bag that lay atop the cot, and in the darkness, its outline could easily be mistaken for a person sleeping. Jo had made that mistake two days after Mom died, and I knew that deep down inside, my little sister was still reeling from losing her. We did what we could for Jo up to and including lying about why Mom killed herself. We told Jo that Mom had become infected and that she took her own life. We said nothing about the suicide note she'd left in the breast pocket of the old combat coat she'd been issued.

And there are only so many lies I can tell.

Jo was the only family I had left next to the people still holding out in the armoury. We'd all lost family members, we'd all stared death in the face every single day since we bugged out – we all counted on each other. And those times when things looked their bleakest, Jo would lift everyone's spirits by somehow, miraculously, still managing to resemble the person she used to be. She always helped out, never once complaining. She could still smile, even though there was little to smile about anymore. Even though I'd seen her shoot creeps from the north tower of the armoury, or when she'd insist on taking part in night sentry duties, Jo still somehow managed to remain an eight-year-old kid. She did chalk drawings on the floor all the while singing in a voice so sweet that even big burly Sid Toomey would get choked up.

"Sleep well, kiddo," I whispered as I shut the door. I took a breath and shambled down the hall to Pam Cruze's room. The door was wide open so that meant I could come inside. She was hunched over a map of the city on top of a metal desk, and she was dressed in a faded blue T-shirt tucked into her combat pants. Her do-rag was folded neatly over a chair, and in her left hand was a large plastic up with a scratched up 7-11 logo. She took a sip and then placed it on the table.

"You can come in, Dave," she said, not even looking up from the map.

"How'd you know it was me?" I replied as I walked into the room.

"You've got a heavy left foot. It's a little louder than your right foot, and that's how I know it's you. Kenny's heels click on the floor, and Dawson glides when she walks – an amazing feat when you consider she's wearing combat boots like the rest of us."

"Pretty cool trick," I said. "How can you tell if it's Sid?"

She glanced at me through the corner of her eye. "Two reasons. One, he smokes cigarettes so I can smell them on him and two, he likes to announce his presence by farting."

I chuckled and made a sour face. "Yeah, there's something wrong with that guy's guts, man. What are you looking at?"

She pointed to our location on the map. "Obstacles and odds. We're going to have to make some difficult decisions."

I bent over and examined the map. The armoury was on the western edge of the downtown core in a city that once had a population of more than a million and that meant there were probably a million or so creeps waiting to rip us apart. To make matters worse, our location was in the geographic center of the city. The Bow River flowed in from the mountains and was located just a few blocks north of us, and the roadways were jam packed with abandoned and burned-out vehicles as far as the eye could see.

"We should have bugged out of town five months ago," I said. "This old armoury might be a fortress, but every fortress throughout history has been breached. I can't see how this one would be any different."

Cruze made a grunting sound and said, "No shit on that one. How are you and Jo doing after what happened to your mother?"

Anger bubbled up in the pit of my stomach as my mind flashed to the suicide note. It was just four sentences long. Four rambling, drunken sentences and not even the word goodbye written down anywhere. Just a lot of "I'm sorries."

"We're fine," I said coolly.

Cruze snorted. "No, you're not. Christ, I know it took me weeks after ..."

"After your parents were attacked," I said, finishing her sentence.

Cruze lost her mom and dad in those mad first weeks after Day Zero when the world began to burn amid wave after wave of monsters. A detachment from the King's Own somehow managed to get Cruze and her parents to the armoury alive. They were attacked while they slept by a member of the Combat Support Section who'd turned in the night. Cruze was on night sentry and heard noises in the small dorm room her parents were assigned to when she saw their wounds. She killed the creep and then put a bullet in both her parent's heads – that left her pretty much catatonic for days. She'd lie on her cot staring at the ceiling. She refused to eat, she didn't wash. Cruze was simply frozen in place – her mind fused to that bloody moment in time.

We all took turns caring for her, and I'd spend my nights reading from Pierre Berton's book *Niagara* to kill off the silence. I wanted to get her talking, and I was willing to do anything that would snap Cruze out of reliving the hell of shooting her own parents. The fact that both were dead the moment they'd become infected or that she killed them before they transformed did nothing to diminish the sheer totality of her loss. It took some a couple of weeks, but Pam Cruze came back to us – this time with a fire in her eyes and a desire to mete out payback to the monsters that destroyed her family.

"You got me through the death of my parents, and I want to help you get through this, Dave," she said. "Jo needs you – we all need you."

I took a deep breath and kept my eyes fixed on the map. Cruze was only trying to help, I knew that, but Mom abandoned us. She gave up and shot herself because she couldn't cope. She stopped caring about survival, and because she'd killed herself, I couldn't place her in the same category as those who'd died through no fault of their own. Cruze's family were victims. Sgt. Green was a victim. Anyone who survived an attack from a creep and became infected as a result was a victim. Mom could have hung on. She could have at least talked to me about how she was feeling and maybe we could have done something to help her. She betrayed Jo and me when she chose to end her life at the very moment when everyone else was fighting a daily battle just to draw their next breath.

"I don't want to talk about it, Cruze," I said, my voice shaking.

She gave me a small shove. "Yeah, well, maybe you should *start* talking about it, because if your Mom's death has been hard on you, it's a hell of a lot worse for Jo. You're her only blood left, Dave. If you can't sort out your feelings, then how the hell is your own sister going to learn how to heal?"

"I'll protect her," I said trying desperately to maintain my cool. "I've been protecting her for the past six months. And healing? What the hell does healing have to do with anything anymore?"

"It has everything to do with it," she said sharply. "Nobody knows what caused Day Zero, and here we are six months later. We're fighting for our freaking lives, Dave, but if we're going to survive this, we also need to remember who we once were. Part of being human is allowing one another an opportunity to grieve – you showed me that."

"Just stop, okay?" I half-growled at Cruze.

"No, I won't stop," she shot back "You can't protect Jo from the truth of this world. And you can't save her from the creeps all by yourself, now listen to me. We all rely on each other, and you need a clear mind if you're going to be of use to anyone. Just talk about how you feel, can you do that? Talk to me, talk to Dawson … hell, even talk to Sid Toomey for all that's worth."

She wasn't going to let this go, so I simply nodded and put on my best "I'll be fine" face. "I'll get through this," I said flatly. "But right now, there isn't time … I need you to look at something we picked up on short-wave not more than an hour ago."

I flipped open my field message pad and handed it to her. She read the message aloud and stepped back, taking a seat on her cot.

"Wow … um, close the door," she said.

I did as instructed and then pulled the chair away from the desk, taking a seat with my arms resting on the back. "It could be a military unit out there, somewhere," I said. "Those coordinates aren't six-figure grid references, though."

"Nope," said Cruze. "It's longitude and latitude. As a matter of fact, it might not even be that far from here."

I blinked. "How do you know?"

"Because the border with the U.S. is the 49th parallel. The message says it's the 53rd parallel north – that's what NOVEMBER means. It's phonetic voice procedure. 105.75 WHISKEY is the longitude. Here in the city we're at 51 degrees north and 114 degrees west, so this Sanctuary Base is northeast of us. I'll need to go down to the OPS room and look on the map to confirm the location for certain, but yeah ... I'm thinking about a thousand miles east."

"Outside of Wainwright, the only military base northeast of here is at Dundurn, and that's awfully close to a built-up area. The message says they're all clear, but clear of what? Creeps? That's impossible – there are creeps everywhere."

She tore the page out of the field message pad and stuffed it in her pocket, tossing the pad on my lap. "They broadcast again at 0630, so we need to listen to see if the message has changed. It would be nice if we could send a reply, but those radios don't have the range."

"That's what Mel wanted to do. She also wants to let everyone know about it, but I asked her to hold off on telling the team until I had a chance to consult with you."

Cruze emitted a heavy sigh. "We should do a briefing as soon as that broadcast comes through."

"They'll want to break out of this place when we do," I said ominously. "Probably within an hour of hearing the news if this message checks out."

Her eyes narrowed sharply. "Then you put them in their place. You're in charge now that Sgt. Green is dead. They'll listen to you because they've been listening to you for the last three months."

It's true that I was Sgt. Green's second-in-command and that he picked me over everyone else, but I hadn't seriously considered that I should take over now that he was dead. I just figured we'd pick Cruze – she'd have received my vote in a heartbeat. The funny thing is that I don't recall ever once aspiring to lead anyone. Sure, I tried like hell to keep everyone's spirits up and yes, I did have my nose in the books on soldiering and field craft, but that's because I wanted to make sure all the angles were covered. I wanted us to have an edge.

"You actually want me to be in charge?" I asked. "Christ, we've reached rock freaking bottom then."

Cruze cocked an eyebrow, and I hoped that she didn't think I was fishing for a vote of confidence or a compliment or anything stupid like that.

"Take your self-pity and shove it up your ass, Dave," she said flatly. "We're at war. When a section commander is killed, it's his or her 2IC that takes over. Everyone will accept you because that's what they've been trained to do. Look, I need to go to the OPS room, and you need to get some sleep."

My face flushed with embarrassment and I said, "Okay … give me a shake when you verify that location. And maybe you should be the one to try and connect with whoever these Sanctuary Base people are at 0630."

She hunched over the map a final time. "We're running out of time, here. We can't stay."

"And we need a plan," I replied. "Soon."

CHAPTER 3

I wanted to sleep, but my brain wasn't having any of it.

Sanctuary Base: it sounded tranquil enough. Too tranquil.

We'd been talking about breaking out of the armoury now for more than a month while towns and cities burned, and the stuff of nightmares clawed at the barred windows on the ground level of the armoury. But that was simply chatter between team members. We'd all kept our opinions to ourselves when Sgt. Green was in earshot because he'd have clamped down on that notion immediately. He wanted us focused on just getting through the freaking day alive.

We weren't exactly going to starve in our location. The armoury had at least a year or more worth of rations in the company stores. We had ammunition, lots of it, and weapons. We could rain death onto the creeps at a murderous rate any time we wanted to, but even with our guns and ammo, we'd still lost more than 90 percent of those who'd made it to the armoury when the call out came. And there was also the matter of fresh water. We'd filled two storage rooms with plastic Jerry cans of fresh water in the days after the siege began. We kept filling them until the municipal water supply finally shut down. But we all knew we'd eventually run out, and the closest source of fresh water was from the Bow River – a death sentence for anyone wishing to venture even two hundred feet from the safety of our position.

Surely Sgt. Green had to have realized that we couldn't stay here forever. I sat up in my cot and glanced at Jo. Her stringy mop of red hair covered her face, and I listened to the sound of her breathing when the sheer magnitude of Sgt. Green's death hit me like a brick thrown in anger through a shop window: I could no longer defer to an adult's wisdom. None of us could – we just didn't have that luxury anymore.

"We're going to figure something out, Jo," I whispered as I climbed out of my cot and grabbed my flashlight. I snuck out of our room and crossed the hallway into what was Sgt. Green's billet. On the floor across the room was a half-open sleeping bag on an air mattress. His helmet and fighting gear were laid out neatly next to his ruck sack, and it looked like he'd just crawled out of bed to take a leak and would return minutes later. Only that wasn't going to happen.

I shuffled across the room, placing my flashlight on the floor next to his gear.

"He must have had a plan," I said quietly as I started fishing through his kit. I found his trusty field message pad stuffed in a pocket of his webbing and started flipping through the pages. There was a list of everyone's names dating back to Day Zero, most with a line struck through them. I saw a detailed list of rations from the company stores along with a count of ammunition, each one listed by its NATO nomenclature.

I tossed the pad onto the sleeping back and pulled out Sgt. Green's junior general kit, an olive drab cotton duck-covered portfolio containing maps, plastic-coated sheets to write on and china markers. I tore open the Velcro fastener with a loud rip and flipped through the pages. There was a detailed drawing of potential routes of access away from the armoury along with a series of scenarios he'd written under the heading THREAT ASSESSMENT.

And then I saw a page with the heading SIMMONS – READ THIS.

I arched my eyebrows and flashed my light on the page.

Simmons:

Congratulations, you found my OPS kit and that means I've bought the farm so guess what, kid? You're in charge now. Before you start protesting that someone else should take command of what's left of the King's Own, dig through my ruck sack and look for the ball peen hammer. It's there for you to club yourself in the head with for being a moron. I picked you as my 2IC because you've got a tactical mind and you get shit done. More importantly, I chose you because out of all the survivors of the King's Own, you have the most to lose and by that I'm talking about little Jo. Your kid sister is going to be the catalyst for a hell of a lot of tough decisions. Because of her, you'll make the hard choices – the ones that twist your stomach into knots because you know deep down inside that you're ordering someone to their death or to take a life. That's the burden of leadership, kid. It's not pretty, but there it is.

We can't stay here. By my estimation, we've got enough fresh water left to last us until Christmas, and after that, we're fucked big time. So we have to conduct a breakout, got it? You have to get out of the city, and then after that, it'll be a matter of finding a secure position with a reliable source of fresh water and game for you to hunt because those rations aren't going to last forever either.

On the following pages, you'll find a detailed plan. I've given it an operational name for now – call it PLAN Z.

We have two fully functional fighting vehicles and enough Jerry cans of diesel to refill the tanks once, and that's it. The quick and dirty is pretty basic: use both APC's to break out of the armoury and head out of the city. West – preferably to the mountains where there's lots of game and hundreds of streams with fresh water that will keep you all going. You'll have a hell of a fight on your hands just getting out of the downtown core, and any number of things can go wrong. The carriers are old but serviceable. They each have a cruising range of about 700 KMS in optimal conditions. Use them until your fuel runs dry, and depending on where you've made it to, you'll have to scrounge for diesel. You might have to abandon them, which would be a shame, because once the combat locks on each carrier are engaged, nothing can get you, so they'd each make a solid last line of defence. They're the Alamo.

You could all pile into one carrier, but I recommend taking both because if one breaks down, you've got spare parts. You should split the team into two squads, each with a squad leader and a 2IC. Kate Dawson should be your second, and Pam Cruze should take the other carrier. Sid Toomey will give you push back, and you'll need that for sober second thought. Doug Manybears and Kenny Howard are both qualified drivers and Mel Dixon is a damned fine shot, not to mention being machine gun qualified. Put her in the turret of one carrier and Toomey in the other. Once you're out of the city, keep an eye on your fuel levels and try to stay on relatively even ground because you can't afford to throw a shock absorber or blow a tire. Fix a toboggan and tent group onto each carrier because you'll need them for shelter when the snow flies. It's the middle of October right now, who knows when the snow will hit us. Pack as much naphtha as you can for the stoves and lanterns.

Pack light and medium anti-armour weapons, a 60 MM mortar for each carrier as well as rounds to spare. Bring pyro. Para-flares and trip flares. You'll need smoke for the dischargers on each vehicle and bring M1 frag grenades – there are five cases in the company stores.

I wish I could offer you something better than this. Maybe light at the end of the tunnel or a beacon of hope, but I got nothing, kid. I don't know what caused Day Zero and at this point, I don't want you or anyone else wasting a minute thinking about the why's of your situation. The only thing that matters is staying alive. Now, a warning: once you're on the road, the creeps aren't going to be the only threat. You can deal with creeps if you keep your wits about you. The real danger will be other survivors. They'll do whatever it takes to get your food, fuel and weapons. They'll drag you into the weeds and cut your throat just for the boots on your feet, got it? Trust only in the team, and if you come into armed conflict with survivors, wipe them the fuck out and take their shit because that's what they'll be planning on doing to you.

I'll close off this letter for now. I'm sorry about your mother, kid. She hit the wall hard and couldn't deal so try not to hate her for what she did. Take that anger you've got bottled up inside and put it to good use – by fighting to survive.

Soldier on, troop.

Greenie.

I started at the letter as a wave of nausea threatened to flatten me. *Wipe them the fuck out?* Kill other survivors? Holy shit!

Sgt. Green had never talked to me about breaking out of the armoury, but I knew him well enough to know that he'd have simply ordered both APC's to be loaded with gear, and he'd have delivered orders to everyone with the expectation that our team would follow his plan to the letter. He was a regular forces infantry sergeant – the mere fact that he wore three chevrons on his sleeves absolutely demanded obedience. But now he was dead, and I'd have to fill his shoes. But how the hell could I even hope to get the team to follow me in the same way they did with Green? I wasn't even the oldest member of the King's Own. I didn't have enough time in to command even the tiniest amount of respect and obedience from everyone else. And what if I presented his plan and just read the letter to everyone? How would Sid Toomey react to Sgt. Green appointing me as his successor?

Cruze said everyone would follow me, and maybe she was right. But follow me to where? Green said head to the mountains, but what if we actually managed to break out of the city and headed northeast? If the place was creep-free, they must have implemented some damned good security procedures to deal with them. Or maybe the base was secluded enough that creeps hadn't stumbled onto the place yet.

"Well, we're fucked if we do and fucked if we don't, aren't we, Sarge?" I said to the letter. "But you're right. We're going to die if we stay here."

I stood up and grabbed my flashlight. I glanced at my watch, it was 01:15: a little more than five hours until the broadcast from Sanctuary Base. Cruze was trying to figure out the location whoever sent the message, and I decided that come hell or high water, in the next twelve hours, we'd make a decision. Whether we headed west or east: the most important thing was to get out of town alive.

Plan Z was Sgt. Green's plan. Now all I had to do was sell it to the team.

CHAPTER 4

Kate Dawson and Kenny Howard were on sentry. Overhead, a moonless sky only amplified bleakness of the smouldering cityscape. I longed for the constant hum of traffic or a police car's siren; any one of those million or more noises that used to be the soundtrack of the city seemed like they never existed at all. Silence was our best defence, and when we talked to one another, it was always muted or hushed whispering – if we could have willed ourselves to become invisible, we would have.

A light wind from the south carried with it the sharp stench of death mixed in with the smell of countless fires in a city ruled by the dead. Somewhere out there were other survivors. Somewhere, people like us were clinging to one another, fighting to see another morning or draw their next breath. I imagined that most would emerge from their hiding places in the same way a mole or a ground squirrel would come out of its den to search for food. Always moving quickly. Always keeping a sharp eye for predators. Always looking for anything that would give them a continued shot at survival.

Hope probably hadn't even occurred to other survivors.

I threw the pair a wave as I climbed up the staircase and strode through the tower doors. Kenny was scoping out the area around our position with a set of night vision goggles, and Dawson was poking through a foil ration bag with a plastic fork. She was wearing a thick black hooded sweatshirt that hung loosely over her combat pants. Around her waist was an olive drab web belt containing a holster with a 9 mm automatic, a water bottle and the large pouch she kept her first-aid kit stored in. Her auburn hair was tucked underneath a Boston Bruins ball cap, a thick ponytail hanging down onto her shoulders through the back.

"Hey," I said with a wave. "Anything weird out there tonight?"

Dawson gazed up from her ration pouch and nudged Kenny in the ribs. "I got nothing ... what are you seeing, Kenny?"

He pointed to the parking lot of what used to be an office supply shop about a block and a half away. "If you count the pack of feral cats attacking that creep across the road as weird, then yes. Cats are fair game for the living dead, so you'd think they'd have high-tailed it out of here long ago."

"Cats are hunters," Dawson said, shovelling another mouthful of what appeared to be ravioli into her mouth. She glanced up at me. "If feral house cats are attacking the creeps then I'm all for it. You should be in bed, Dave."

"Go team mittens," I said with a snort. "Also, I can't sleep, so I checked on Jo and then decided to see how you guys were doing. Anything on the radio?"

"You mean anything from Sanctuary Base," said Dawson. "We know about it, and before you decide to flip out all over Mel, she'd left the radio on short-wave, and we heard a series of beeps – like someone keying a handset or something. She got all excited because she thought it was this Sanctuary Base, and so naturally, Kenny and me asked her what the hell she was talking about, so she told us. You were in the can."

I made a disapproving grunting sound. If Kenny and Kate knew about the radio broadcast then there wasn't any point in keeping it under wraps. "Shit … anyone else know about it?"

"Sid and Doug are asleep until their shift at 0400," said Kenny. "We should tell them so that we can figure out our next move. It's something, right?"

Kenny Howard had a shock of bright red hair on top of his head that seemed to glow in the darkness. The pale skin on his face was dotted with freckles that climbed down from his cheeks onto his skinny neck. He was wearing an army-issue sweater with rolled-up sleeves and a pair of combat pants that were worn away at the knees. His carbine was slung over his right shoulder, and there was a plastic coffee cup dangling from a belt loop on his waist. On his right forearm was a homemade tattoo that Mel had done for him using the ink from a Bic pen and a sewing needle. It was comprised of two words done in a reasonably fancy font and wasn't half bad for an amateur job: "Still Alive."

"Yeah, it's something," I answered. "I told Cruze – she's in the OPS room trying to see if she can find the place on a map."

The fire in the parking compound had died down to little more than a pile of glowing embers that drifted into the air. A pair of creeps was pressed against the fence, their gaping mouths hanging loosely as if on hinges. Two creeps didn't pose a threat, but at least four times a week, groups of up to ten threatened to push the fence down, so we'd launch a smoke grenade into the abandoned lot behind the armoury using a makeshift slingshot, and the monsters would stumble toward the billowing blue or red smoke. Two months ago, we reinforced the perimeter of the fence line with rolls of double concertina razor wire. It was Sgt. Green's idea, because if the fence ever did come down, the monsters would wind up snagged in the wire buying us time to muster our defences. Not that it would have mattered much, because if the creeps did get through, it would be due to a massive swarming of hundreds that we'd have less than no chance of killing without taking major casualties of our own.

Dawson opened her vacuum bottle and poured a cup of coffee into her plastic cup. She handed it to me, and I took a swig. "We're going to have to reorganize the team," she said as she screwed the cap back on and stuffed the bottle into a thermal sleeve.

"Or what's left of the team," added Kenny. "Kind of timely that broadcast came through what with Sgt. Green winding up getting killed. It's time to get the hell out of the city."

"Maybe," I said, handing the cup back to Dawson.

"Maybe?" Kenny said as he spun around and looked at me like I'd taken leave of my senses. "There were fifty of us six months ago, and there are eight of us left now. If we'd blown out of town at the start of this shit, we could have headed for the country – or maybe linked up with other military elements."

Dawson raised a hand. "Just chill, Kenny. What we should have done then doesn't matter anymore. What we do next is the most important decision we're ever going to make. I think everyone would agree that we're going to have to make a break for it."

I grabbed the night vision goggles from Kenny and slipped them over my eyes. I didn't want to respond to Dawson's statement, not because I disagreed with her, but because if we were going to conduct a breakout, then it would have to be a single plan that everyone could get behind. We couldn't afford to get into a pissing match between personalities, because when you're at war, the tactics and decisions can't be negotiation points. And there was still a decision to be made that loomed large: go west and take our chances in the mountains or head toward a place called Sanctuary Base that we knew nothing about.

I scanned a dark alley about two hundred feet from our position and spotted a creep feasting on what looked like a large rat. Another creep stumbled out of the shadows and lumbered up the alley when another pair of feral cats launched themselves at the creature's head with two deafening screeches. The monster clawed at its face in vain and tripped over an overturned garbage can, landing hard on its back.

"I agree with Kate," I said, handing the goggles back to Kenny.

"On getting out of town?" he replied.

"About feral cats being on our side," I said.

"What's the plan?" the pair asked impatiently. My cat joke didn't even register.

I took a deep breath and said, "We're going to get out of here. But first, we need to listen to the next broadcast so we're in a holding pattern. We can't contact them on this radio; the range is only a few miles. We need a base station for that, and the one in the armoury needs electricity. The grid conked out after Day Zero, and we don't have any back-up generators."

"You're thinking we should head there?" asked Kenny.

I shook my head. "Maybe once we know where they are – but we need to look at other places we can take refuge. We have to careful because we know absolutely nothing about those people yet."

Dawson sipped at her coffee and threw me a wary look. "It could also be a set-up. An invitation for other survivors to get themselves killed while the people at Sanctuary Base take their supplies."

I thought of Sgt. Green's cryptic warning about other survivors and shuddered. "You're not wrong about that, Kate."

There was a clattering sound from the park behind the armoury, and the pair of creeps at the chain-link fence slowly canted their heads in the sound's direction and then stumbled off into the darkness.

Dawson took another swig of coffee and said, "You're going to be in charge then?"

I handed Kenny the night vision goggles, which he promptly slipped onto his head. My eyes drifted from the scene in the alley to Kenny and then over to Dawson. "Is that a request or an assumption?"

"More of a statement of fact," said Dawson. "If you want, I mean."

I looked a Kenny. "What do you think?"

He adjusted the focus on the goggles and stared out into the night. "Better you than me, brother. At this point, I'd even take Dawson in charge if she can get us the fuck out of the city alive."

"Thanks a lot, Kenny," she said sourly.

I allowed myself a mild chuckle, and then I gazed up at the night sky. The city had been blanketed by cloud cover day or night for months –it was as if the sun, the moon, and the stars had turned their backs on us.

"Snow will be hitting us soon," I said glumly. "If we're going to make a move then we have a narrow window of opportunity. We need to think about supplies for when we get out of here."

"In the morning, I'll check on the tent groups and the toboggans then," said Kenny.

"Check on the carriers, too," I suggested. "Maybe do a fitness inspection and see if there's anything we need to fix."

Kenny's lips arched up into a grin. "You're thinking we use both APC's to break out of here, aren't you?"

I nodded. "Something like that – we'll discuss in the morning, okay? I'm going to try and get some sleep."

Dawson put a hand on my chest. "Dave ... do you actually *want* to be in charge?"

I looked down at her hand and sighed heavily. "I want to protect Jo. And if that means that I have to hatch a plan to get out of the city to protect her, then I'm going to do it. Sanctuary Base will be broadcasting again at 06:30 – might as well inform Sid and Doug when they go on sentry."

"And then what?" she asked.

I started walking toward the doors and the stairwell. "I'm still trying to figure that one out."

CHAPTER 5

I lay atop my cot and flashed my light on Sgt. Green's letter. If only he'd just ordered us to load up the carriers and fight our way out of the city – even if he'd done it twenty-four hours ago, he'd still be alive, and I wouldn't have to worry about stepping into his shoes.

Across the room, Jo stirred and then yawned, stretching her arms out of the sleeping bag. She unzipped it halfway and kicked her body out of the down-filled cocoon, sticking her feet inside a pair of rubber boots. She clumped across the room and then climbed onto the edge of my cot. I didn't bother trying to hide the letter from her as she poked her head over to see what I was reading.

"Whatcha looking at?" she asked as she pulled a shock of hair away from her eyes. "Is that ... is that a letter from Mommy?"

There was a tiny, almost hopeful sounding lilt to her voice. I had Mom's goodbye letter – Jo didn't know about it. She'd never know about it. Ever.

I flipped the letter over and showed it to Jo. "It's from Sgt. Green," I said very business-like. "He left us something to help us survive."

Jo seemed to shrink a little. She was wearing a T-shirt that was more nightgown than anything. Across her narrow chest were the words CHARLIE COMPANY.

"So many people are gone now," she said quietly. Her eyes drifted away from the letter, and she gazed at her rubber boots. "Is Sgt. Green going to come back? Is he going to become a creeper?"

I shook my head. "He won't. We took care of it."

"Nobody else is 'fected, right? Nobody else is going to turn, right?"

"We're all good to go, Jo," I replied. "And we're all going to keep you safe. Got it?"

She nodded but kept her eyes fixed firmly on her rubber boots. "We're not safe, David. The creepers got Mom ... they'll get all of us."

I folded up the letter and dropped it on the floor, and then I leaned forward and gently placed both hands on Jo's face. I turned her head and rested my forehead against hers. "Jo … I'm your big brother, and I'm going to protect you. We're getting out of here – we're going to go somewhere safe. That's what Sgt. Green's letter was about. He put together a plan for us to get out of the city. We're going to get as far away from civilization as we can get. We're going to start over."

"But there's so many creepers – they're everywhere. We'll get swarmed and then …"

I lifted her chin and stared hard into her eyes. "Jo … we've got lots of ammunition. We've got food and supplies. We've got each other – we're a family."

She pursed her lips together tightly, and I allowed her a few moments to absorb what I'd just told her. I wanted her to hope even though hope was always something we'd tried to keep at arm's length. If the last six months had taught us anything, it was that hoping would always come back to bite you in the ass. But Jo was eight, and she needed something to believe in.

"How are we going to get out of here?" she asked as she bent down and grabbed Sgt. Green's letter.

"The armoured personnel carriers," I said calmly. "When we're hatches down in those things, those monsters can't touch us. We can blow right through them like bowling pins."

"But where will we go?"

I brushed her hair away from her eyes. "We've gotta figure that one out still. Sgt. Green said we should head to the mountains where there is fresh water and game for us to hunt, but there's another place … maybe."

"Where?"

I told Jo about the radio broadcast from Sanctuary Base. I told her that it was about a thousand miles from the city and that it was supposed to be zombie-free, and all the while Jo nodded silently. She didn't smile. She didn't jump up and down on my cot to celebrate that we were going to be leaving. She was processing the information the best way she could, and what she said next took me by surprise.

"They might be bad guys," she said coldly. "They might be trying to trick us. They could be getting people to go there and then they might kill them and take their stuff."

Wow. Six months of living in hell had given my kid sister a brutally practical outlook on our new reality. I didn't know whether to bust out bawling that an eight year old was talking like a combat veteran or to hug her for having the sense to recognize a very real threat to our survival.

"It's possible," I said, matching her tone. "We need more information. We need a backup plan, and we need to make a decision as a team."

"How much longer will we stay here?" she said with a hint of anticipation in her voice. Her eyes flashed over to her carbine fixed against the wall above her cot.

"Not much longer," I said quietly. "Keep this to yourself for now. We're going to have a team meeting, and I'm going to simply tell everyone what has to happen."

She gave me a big hug and then she flashed me a toothless grin. "Good – you should be in charge."

Her vote of confidence lifted my spirits. Jo believed in me when I was having trouble believing in myself.

I glanced at my watch; it was 04:10 and the broadcast from Sanctuary Base would be in a little more than two hours.

"Okay, kiddo … you're part of the team. We'll gather around the radio on the sentry tower, and we'll hash out our next move. And Jo?"

"What?"

"Thanks for believing in me."

She gave me another hug and then planted a big wet kiss on my right cheek. "You're my brother, dummy. Of course I believe in you."

***

Cruze gave me a hard shake. "Dave, get up … we need to talk."

I'd been dreaming about pizza of all things. A nice, thick wedge of George's Pizzeria pizza loaded with extra cheese, onions, bacon and pepperoni. It almost broke my heart to open my eyes.

"What's going on, Cruze?" I said, yawning as I glanced at my watch. It was 05:45, and I'd probably been asleep for less than an hour.

She shut the door to my room and nodded toward Jo who'd back into her sleeping bag and was sound asleep.

"She knows," I said. "Everyone except for Sid and Doug know about the broadcast."

"You told Kate and Kenny?"

I shook my head and handed her Sgt. Green's letter. "Mel did … have a look at this."

She opened the letter, and I gave her a moment to read through Sgt. Green's final instructions. Cruze made a grunting sound a few times and then handed me back the letter after she was finished.

"Interesting," she said.

"What?"

"Green said we should head to the mountains, and I've sort of plotted out a spot where we could go to if we decided against heading to Sanctuary Base."

Cruze dropped to one knee and pulled a map out of her pants pocket. She unfolded it on the floor, and I swung my legs over the edge of the cot and leaned in to take a look. It was a map of Western Canada, and Cruze had marked off a red star to show our location and a blue X just that was smack dab in the middle of a forest. I leaned closer and saw the words PRINCE ALBERT NATIONAL PARK printed in black ink just above where she'd marked the X.

Cruze had been busy. There were small red X's scratched over the cities of Airdrie, Red Deer, Wetaskiwin, Camrose and Edmonton, which made sense as those were built-up areas, and if we were going to head northeast, we'd want to avoid them. I looked on the western side of the map and saw a series of blue lines that meandered through secondary roads leading into the mountains, and she'd drawn a big red circle around Lake Louise, a tourist destination for skiers in the winter time.

"So yeah … Sanctuary Base is secluded enough, but according to the coordinates in the radio message, they're in the middle of a freaking forest … they could anywhere in that park."

"The middle of a forest!" I groaned. "Not exactly the best place for line of sight defence."

"The mountains are nothing but forest," she said, pointing to the big circle at Lake Louise. "But a ski resort is the high ground; I mean you're on the top of a mountain. It would be harder for creeps to get up there, and we could pick them off if it came to it."

I nodded. "High ground matters. But assuming we made it there, we'd be completely on our own. Sanctuary Base sounds military, they'd be well-armed. There's strength in numbers, right?"

Cruze exhaled heavily. "Or it's a trap."

"That's what Jo said, too."

"Smart kid. Look, Dave ... there are risks associated with both places and about the main benefit to Lake Louise is that it's only a couple of hundred miles from here. Sanctuary Base is a hell of a lot further away."

I glanced at the map. "Yeah ... our carriers wouldn't make it so we'd have to go scrounging for fuel or alternate transportation. There would be enough fuel to get us to Lake Louise for sure."

We sat in silence and just stared at the map. I was leaning toward Lake Louise, but the lure of attaching ourselves to another military unit seemed too good to be true. There might be medical care and better organization. They could have set up a ton of defensive traps in the woods, and more importantly, there would be a rigid chain of command to follow. There would be real full-time military leaders with way more experience than a bunch of weekend warriors.

There was also the issue of selling a move to a secluded spot in the mountains to the team. We'd be well and truly on our own if we managed to get out of the city. We'd have to learn how to hunt, how to trap and how to survive in the bush. Sure, Sgt. Green had recommended we head to the mountains, but he didn't know about Sanctuary Base. I wondered if he would have recommended we head there had he been the one to hear the radio broadcast.

I gave Cruze a pained look. "Jeez ... I don't know what to do here. There's risk any way you look at it."

She folded up the map and stuffed it back into the pocket of her combat trousers. "If it helps, Dave, I'm going to say the risk is equal on both counts. And we're going to have a hell of a time just getting out of the city to begin with."

I glanced at my watch one more time. It was 06:00 and the

broadcast would be in half an hour.

"Okay, Cruze," I said, climbing out of my cot and stuffing my feet into my combat boots. "Would you get Jo up and gather everyone up at the sentry post for the broadcast. I'll brief Sid and Doug. I'm going to read everyone the letter from Sgt. Green, and we'll decide something ASAP."

Cruze patted me on the shoulder. "Smartest thing you've said all week. Okay, I'll get everyone, and Dave?"

"Yeah?"

She folded her arms across her chest and said, "We're fucked if we do, and we're fucked if we don't. Just make the call."

"Yeah," I said grimly. "I'll make the call."

CHAPTER 6

Doug Manybears was scanning the area around the armoury for anything that might be a threat to our defenses while Sid was leaning over the parapet, flicking ash from a burning cigarette every few seconds.

"We need to talk," I said, mustering a bit of firmness in my voice.

"Sounds serious," said Doug, a spindly Sarcee from the Tsuu T'ina nation. He was the improviser of the team. He'd lost not only his family, but also his entire Indian band in the weeks after Day Zero, and somehow, incredibly, he managed to fight his way from the outskirts of the city into the very heart of creep-infested territory. We found him under the cover of darkness in that same parking compound where we burn the bodies. He was cut to ribbons and ensnared in the razor wire after he'd scaled the chain-link fence. It took us a month to mend his wounds and bring him back to full strength – all of us marvelling at the mere fact that he somehow survived against incalculable odds. That Doug survived gave all of us hope that we too might survive, even though we were losing people every few days.

"It is serious," I replied.

Sid leaned onto one elbow and dropped his smouldering cigarette butt on the cold cement walkway, stubbing it out with his heel. "We know about Sanctuary Base, so spill. What do you know?"

Sid lost his father during the opening days of the siege. He'd been an only child: his mother died bringing him into the world, and on the few occasions when I'd hang out over at Sid's house, there was a layer of tension between Sid and his dad that was so thick, you'd need an industrial cutter to slice through it. Standing at six foot four, and with hands the size of dinner plates, he was brawny and utterly fearless during the dozens of terrifying breaches of our security. We'd fought side by side, and he was ready to lay down his life to protect my kid sister, Jo. We all were. I just hoped he was going to back me on what I was going to say next.

I read Sgt. Green's letter and filled the pair in on the broadcast from Sanctuary Base. I told them about bugging out to Lake Louise or heading Northeast Prince Albert National Park, and the entire time, both listened attentively, each throwing me the occasional nod.

But then came the inevitable question – the one I'd been hoping to avoid, and unexpectedly, it came from Doug Manybears instead of Sid.

"Who gets to lead this thing?" he asked. Sid lit another cigarette and cocked his right eyebrow as he looked me over.

"We're going to fight our way out of the city," I said, deciding that a matter-of-fact approach would buy me more goodwill than say, for example, my raising a shaky hand and offering myself up as a volunteer to be in charge. "We're taking both APC's. Sid ... I want you in the turret for my carrier. Doug, you'll be our driver, and Kenny will drive the other one. Cruze is the unit 2IC and will be in charge of the other carrier. Kate Dawson will be my second while we're mobile. Mel will be the gunner in Cruze's machine, and Jo is coming with us. We're going to break out of the city and head northwest until we're clear of town."

I'd been expecting push-back from Sid, and surprisingly, it didn't come. He looked at Doug and then back at me and said, "About fucking time we're out of here. I'm good with being a turret gunner so consider me a second set of eyes. As for Dawson ... whatever. She's usually got her shit together."

"Good," I answered as I glanced at my watch. I could hear the sound of approaching footsteps from the stairwell leading back into the armoury.

Doug opened the cotton duck accessory bag for the radio and reached inside. "I'm going to put the ten-foot whip antennae on, maybe that will make the broadcast come in clearer."

"Not a bad idea," said Sid as he slipped the night vision goggles over his head.

It was still dark outside as everyone gathered at the sentry post. A strong breeze pushed the ten-foot whip antennae Doug had secured on the radio back and forth with each little gust, the mast tapping against the parapet every few seconds. Doug had also just installed a fresh battery into the bottom of the man pack and cleaned the connections for the handset and small speaker that was no bigger than a saucer.

I gazed at each of the last survivors of The King's Own. Every single one of them wore a look of expectation mixed with quiet desperation – well, everyone except for Sid. He'd lit another cigarette and was keeping his eye on the streets surrounding our position. I looked at my watch – it was 06:28.

"Everyone keep quiet," I said as I flipped the radio to short-wave. "When the broadcast comes through, just listen closely. Dawson, write down every word you here because I want to compare it to the original message in case they've altered it."

"Will do," she said she fished her field message pad out of the pocket of her combat jacket.

I set the knob to the frequency of the original message. A haze of static penetrated the silence of the early morning, and nobody said a word. Nobody even breathed for fear of jinxing ourselves. In the distance, I could hear a series of throaty, lifeless groans – the sound you hear when the creeps catch a whiff of you. It was too far away to be a threat to any of us, and I decided that maybe the creeps were giving payback to the feral cats that had attacked them.

The static abruptly stopped, and a male voice filled the air:

NODUFF. THIS IS SANCTUARY BASE CALLING. SANCTUARY BASE AT 53.200 NOVEMBER 105.7500 WHISKEY.

There was static for ten seconds and then:

NODUFF. THIS IS SANCTUARY BASE CALLING. SANCTUARY BASE AT 53.200 NOVEMBER 105.7500 WHISKEY.

Jo stood next to me and took my hand. Her palm was clammy and cold. More static filtered through the speaker for another ten seconds and then:

NODUFF. THIS IS SANCTUARY BASE CALLING. SANCTUARY BASE AT 53.200 NOVEMBER 105.7500 WHISKEY. ALL CLEAR NOW – I SAY AGAIN – ALL CLEAR. SANCTUARY BASE. NODUFF. ALL CLEAR. NODUFF. NEXT CONTACT AT 12:00 ZULU.

"Fuck this," Mel Dixon snapped as she grabbed the radio handset and squeezed:

"Sanctuary Base this is, I spell, KILO INDIA NOVEMBER GOLF SIERRA OSCAR WHISKEY NOVEMBER. Our unit has received your message, over!"

There was more static and silence for about five seconds as Mel tried again:

"Sanctuary Base this is, I spell, KILO INDIA NOVEMBER GOLF SIERRA OSCAR WHISKEY NOVEMBER. Our unit has received your message. Radio check, over!"

I took the handset from Mel and shook my head. "They can't hear us – they're too far away."

"Shit!" she hissed as she kicked the accessory bag in frustration.

Sid exhaled a plume of smoke and said, "Nice fucking move … anyone with a short-wave receiver in the area would have heard us. You just told them the King's Own is alive and well, you twat."

Mel threw Sid a venomous look. "Fuck you, Sid."

He shook his head and chuckled to himself, muttering the words "split arses."

Dawson took a threatening step forward until she was less than an inch from Sid's face. *"What the fuck did you say?"*

He took a drag on his cigarette and deliberately blew a mouthful of smoke in Dawson's face. I saw her clench both hands into tight fists, and if I didn't step in, there was going to be a dust-up that could tear the team apart.

"Enough of this shit!" I snarled as I stepped between the pair. I gave Sid a hard shove that didn't even move him from where he stood. It was as if his feet were encased in cement. "We're on the same side so get it together."

"Fucking prick," Dawson spat.

"Kate!" Cruze snapped. "Raise your voice again, and we'll be swarming with creeps. If Green was still here, this little outburst wouldn't have happened."

"Yeah, well, he's not here," Sid griped.

I needed to say something so there would be no doubt in anyone's mind as to who was in charge. And surprisingly, I didn't flinch. I didn't feel like I was going to throw up. I didn't do anything more than look at my kid sister whose eyes narrowed sharply. She threw me a single nod, as if she was telepathically giving me a vote of confidence.

I drew in a deep breath and growled, *"Everybody down on one knee now!"*

The team complied with my command. Instantly. Even Sid.

I shut the radio off and let everyone kneel in silence for a few moments. I wanted them to hear the sound of the monsters shuffling around our position. I wanted them to breath in the scent of death and decomposition. To suck the poisonous air of a city ruled by the dead into their lungs.

I pulled Sgt. Green's letter out of my pants pocket and read aloud in a voice that was little more than a whisper. And I didn't give anyone a chance to say a word about it when I'd finished.

"Dawson, you're my 2IC," I said firmly. "Sid and Doug are with us – and Jo, too. Cruze is taking the other carrier with Mel and Kenny. I want both machines packed with everything we need to survive. I want rations stripped down. Section level weapons. Mortars and H.E. I want the guns mounted in both turrets. Two toboggans lashed on the sides with full tent groups. Camouflage nets for winter and summer. Check the med kits … check fucking everything and then double check it. We're getting the hell out of here, people. Unit-O-Group at the carriers – 18:00 tonight."

Then I stood up and took Jo by the hand. Together, we walked through the stairway and disappeared into the armoury.

I didn't bother looking back.

CHAPTER 7

I stared at the show of hands. The interior lights beamed with a dull red glow that cast shadows onto the thin armour plate walls behind their heads. I scanned everyone's faces for any sign of dissent or disagreement, and all I saw was the faces of a bunch teens that looked like they'd aged twenty years in the span of a few months. We'd fought side by side for months. Each of us was ready to lay down their life to protect Jo.

"Plan Z," I said slowly, "Isn't my plan. It's Green's. We're going to put it into motion."

"It's cool," Doug grunted with a slight nod. "Listen, brother … you've got skin in the game. Jo believes in you, and that's good enough for me."

I threw Doug a firm nod.

"You were closest to Sergeant Green before the creeps took him down," said Dawson as she cleaned the barrel of her carbine with a push-rod. "I'm sorry about this morning. Won't happen again."

"You didn't start it," I said as glanced over at Sid. "It won't happen again, right, Sid?"

He nodded and said nothing. That was good enough for me.

"*I* want you to lead this thing, Dave," said Cruze, her filled with resolve. "We're going to break the fuck out of here and head for Sanctuary Base, and we're going tomorrow at first light. It's decided."

"Jesus … *tomorrow?*" I nearly spit out the words. I hadn't expected to go within hours.

"It'll be winter soon and tomorrow is as good a time as any," said Mel Dixon. "We can't collect snow and melt it for drinking water. The sky is poisoned – we've all seen the rain. It's fucking oily – who the hell knows what's in the rain when it hits the ground."

Sid snorted. "We'd probably freeze to death in this place too. We've got tents and plenty of naphtha, but that will eventually run out."

"You have my support, Dave," Kenny Howard added. He ran a

freckled hand through his shaggy mop of red hair and then pointed to the crew commander's hatch behind him. "We've all decided, and it's unanimous. Green picked you. He knew that you were always the guy with his nose inside *Infantry Section and Platoon in Battle*."

There it was – the unanimous vote of confidence I was hoping for. I could have thanked everyone. I could have tried to improvise some bullshit speech that was designed to motivate and inspire, but I knew they would see through it. And there was still a major decision to be made that couldn't come as a directive from the team leader.

"Sgt. Green said we should head to the mountains. If we'd have never heard that broadcast, we'd break out of here and push through to Lake Louise. But we know about Sanctuary Base. It's a thousand miles from here, and these carriers will get us maybe a third of the way if we're lucky."

"We're going to need a shit pile of luck," said Cruze. "When we burn out the last of our fuel, we're going to be on foot and hauling the toboggans – we're not even sure of their specific location."

"But the closer we get, the better the chances are that we can hail them on the radio," said Doug as he took a sip of coffee from his plastic cup. "They must want people to join them otherwise they'd be on radio silence."

"There's probably close to a million creeps in this city," Dawson said with no shortage of gloom in her voice. "Once we're clear, there's every reason to believe we might even find a better place than Sanctuary Base – you never know, right?"

"Good point, Kate," I said as I studied everyone's faces. There wasn't even the tiniest flicker of doubt among them.

"This is an escape," Sid Toomey interrupted. "This city is a prison. I don't give a shit where we go, as long as we're moving."

"Alright then, tomorrow at first light," I said firmly. "Kenny and Doug – are these carriers going to fail us?"

The pair looked at each other and then Kenny said, "They're serviceable as far as we can tell. Once we're on the road, who knows?"

"This is like Noah's Ark!" Jo chirped. "We're gonna escape just like Noah and his family."

I gave her a big thumbs up as my lips arched into a wide grin. "Then my carrier's call sign will be Ark One. Cruze's will be Ark Two."

"YES!" Jo shouted as if she'd won the lottery.

"Alright … alright," said Cruze. "Radio frequencies should be fifty-one twenty for day travel, fifty-one sixty for night time."

"Agreed," I said as I pointed to the map on the floor of the carrier. "If you look at the map, you can see that we should be no further than 500 meters away from each other once we get out of the city."

Mel leaned forward and squinted as she focused on the map. "Yeah, but we won't have line of sight, so if we get in trouble, we're going to have a hell of a time making it over to you."

"Listen for the shooting," Sid chuckled.

"What happens if we run out of fuel before you guys?" asked Kenny. "I mean … we can't expect you to come and get us … so we're on our own then, right?"

I shook my head. "We're all we've got, so nobody gets left behind. We'll need to radio our fuel levels periodically during the day. We'll also set firm rendezvous points before nightfall in case we get separated or so we can share whatever we scrounge up. If you come across a fuel tank on a farm or some equipment we can siphon from, then you need to radio a grid reference, and we'll RV before investigating. Nobody goes it alone … we clear? You don't leave your APC without covering fire from the other section."

The group bobbed their heads in agreement as Kenny pulled out his water bottle and gulped back a mouthful. Mel leaned over and pointed to the map. "500 meters between two APC's – man that's a hell of a distance to cover if anyone gets in trouble."

I clenched my jaw and ran a finger along the route I'd traced on the map with a china marker. "And that's why you hit the combat locks on the doors and stay hatches-down until we can get to you."

"Fair enough," said Kenny. "But if the carrier is swarming with creeps, I'd appreciate if someone would divert them away with their personal weapon and not the turret guns – the hulls on these carriers can't stop ammunition bigger than 5.56 MM. The turret guns are way bigger than that."

I nodded. "No freaking doubt. The creeps are attracted to noise, light and movement – that much we know."

"Yeah, just like any predator," Cruze said grimly. "Except these ones don't exactly have critical thinking skills."

"Oh yeah … Kenny can totally relate to that," Mel chortled, as she nudged the bony redhead in the ribs.

Kenny stuck his index finger in his mouth and then drove it into Mel's left ear. "You just say that because you're secretly hiding the fact that you're into me."

"Ugh … I'd rather make out with a walking corpse!"

"Well take your pick, Mel … there's a jillion of them just outside the main doors!" Kenny said with a snort.

"Look, guys," I said ominously. "The creeps are just one of the obstacles."

"What are you saying?" asked Dawson.

I took a deep breath. "Think about Green's warning. Other survivors are going to be out there – people like us, people with guns. We're a unit, and we need to stay that way. Now, between us, we've got plenty of food and ammo, and it's *ours* – got it? We lose any of that stuff to other survivors then it means less for us."

Kenny gave me a nudge. "Yeah, we're a unit – we gotta guard our stuff and each other with our lives."

"And we might have to kill to protect it," said Cruze in a cold voice. "We need to lay down some rules right freaking now so that when we're on the move there's no second-guessing – we don't have that luxury."

Kate Dawson grunted. "I wish we weren't heading north. Aren't there warmer places to start over?"

Doug raised a finger. "There were three hundred million people in the U.S. before Day Zero and millions more the further south you go. We only know about one city they nuked before the Internet crashed – for all we know, three-quarters of the country could be a radioactive wasteland. That means on top of the nuclear hot spots, there are probably three hundred million creeps that would love to make a meal out of you – simple math, Kate. Sanctuary Base said they were all clear – that must mean they've got a handle on creep control. Maybe the colder temperature slows the creeps so it makes sense that they'd freeze come winter.

They're just dead flesh walking and nothing more."

Doug's matter-of-fact observations seemed to have hit the spot with everyone because nobody said anything for the next few minutes. We all just studied the map, and if anyone was contemplating our chances for survival, they were keeping it to themselves. The team wanted to go at first light. They accepted my leadership, and it was clear they were leaning toward Sanctuary Base. I just needed to confirm it.

"Okay, listen up. Plan Z – do we head to the mountains? Raise your hands?"

Nobody raised their hand. It was unanimous.

"First light then," said Cruze.

"Wait … what about the main doors?" asked Kenny. "Whoever opens them is gonna get their ass chewed off by the creeps."

I shook my head and tossed a stick of C-4 to Kenny.

"No, they won't," I said menacingly. "We've got high explosives."

CHAPTER 8

"Mount up!" I shouted, as I waved my left arm overhead in a circular motion. The parade square was thick with the acrid stench of diesel, and I coughed heavily as I raced to the main gate with Sid Toomey in tow. I could hear the loud clank of the hatches on the APC's, and I glanced over my shoulder to see the headlights blinking from both vehicles, confirming that everyone was accounted for and ready to go. We'd placed five shaped explosive charges on the door, designed to detonate outwards – we'd have sixty seconds from the time we pulled the ignitors until the charges would blow, one every ten seconds, so we'd have to haul ass back to the carrier.

I blinked a few times and drew in a deep breath as I pulled the small sliding hatch on the main door to the right and peered outside to see what we were in for once the charges detonated. To my front, no more than ten feet from the peep-hole, was a small gaggle of creeps. The one closest was shirtless. The dull grey skin on his torso was pulled tight – like the skin itself was receding back into the creature's skeleton. A massive gash stretched from its left shoulder down to its right nipple exposing the rotting layers of tissue beneath, and I could make out its ribs through the wound.

I was about to close the hatch door when the monster slowly looked up at the peep-hole. A thick, cloudy blue-grey film gave its eyes an unearthly appearance. It was like staring into the eyes of a statue; cold, empty and forever lifeless. The skin on its face was puffy, and I noticed a thin stream of yellowish liquid dribbling out of a wound on its right cheek.

Even through the thick wooden door, the foul stench of decomposition filled my nostrils, threatening to cause my breakfast to wind up being spewed across the door. The monster lurched forward, followed by a small gang of rotting husks, so I placed the barrel of my carbine into the viewing port and fired off three quick rounds that tore the top of the creep's head clean off. It dropped like a wet sandbag.

I closed the sliding hatch and then glanced back at my APC as I gave a thumbs-up – Doug Manybears, my driver, gave me one in return and pulled the driver's hatch down over his head. The plan was that Doug would plow through what was left of the blasted doors as soon as I took my place in the crew commander's hatch. Sid would climb into the turret and open up with the .50 calibre machine gun and the smaller GPMG. Both guns fired in tandem through an electronic solenoid, and the barrels were bore-sited to fire at whatever Doug saw through his visor-mounted scope.

I slipped my left index finger into the pull ring on the first ignitor, and then glanced back at Sid.

"You ready for this?"

"Are you done daydreaming? I thought I lost you there for a minute," he said, nervously, as he dropped to a kneeling position and cocked his rifle.

"Yeah, I'm good. Here goes nothing," I said, and pulled.

My nostrils filled with the pungent smell of burning powder as the safety fuse hissed and spat flaming embers and melted plastic onto the floor. Quickly, I pulled the rings on the other four ignitors and ran like hell to the back of my carrier. Sid dove in after me, and we pulled the doors shut, slipping the combat locks over the door handles. I crawled over the other three people in my carrier and grinned at Jo as I climbed into my crew commander's hatch.

"Cover your ears!" I shouted as I glanced at my watch. "Ten, nine, eight, seven, six, five, four, three, two, one ..."

The vehicle pitched sharply as the first charge exploded, followed shortly by the other four. I peered through my periscope as I adjusted the microphone on my helmet, and saw a minivan-sized hole through a plume of smoke and burning wood. But that was nothing compared to what I saw next.

It was like we'd opened a door into hell. No sooner had the smoke from the explosive charges cleared when a huge swarm of the monsters poured through the opening like water through a spillway. Sid opened up with a series of controlled bursts from the turret guns, and the inside of the carrier quickly filled up with the smell of cordite and burning gun oil.

I grabbed the radio switch dangling from my helmet and pressed the push-to-talk button.

"Go! Go! Go!" I roared into the mouthpiece.

I felt the vibrations of the engine revving up behind the engine panel beside me and then our APC lurched into gear. I grabbed hold of my periscope handle and pushed my face into the rubber-coated visor as the ten-thousand-pound armoured fighting machine barrelled through the door, smashing through the monsters like a wrecking ball. We bounced heavily as the eight twenty-two-inch tires bounded over rotting bodies and debris. My carrier was clear of the building.

"Hard left!" I shouted, spotting a clearing between a pile-up of smashed cars. The carrier swung sharply, and our bodies tilted to the right as Doug made the turn.

My radio hissed and squawked in my ears. "Ark One, this is Ark Two – we're clear of the building and right on your tail, over!"

I pressed the push-to-talk button. "Ark One, Roger. Keep a distance of twenty meters behind me. You're weapons free in controlled bursts, but only if we become surrounded. Stay within your prescribed arcs of fire left and right of my position. Over!"

"Ark Two, Roger that!" the radio hissed.

Smashing out of the armoury was the easy part. We still had to navigate through streets filled with monsters and the burned husks of automobiles as far as the eye could see. The carrier pushed on, and I swung my periscope left and right to survey the war zone that had once been the very heart of the city. The office buildings stood like towering sentinels, lonely reminders of wealth and power from a time and place that was still fresh in our minds.

The explosion was attracting the attention of hundreds of creatures, shambling menacingly through the twisted metal. Their mouths hung open, dripping gore and offal onto the pavement. They could surround our fighting vehicle ten deep for all I cared. We were safe inside, and there was nothing they could do to get at us. The powerful engine would push us through the sea of creatures as easily as a plow pushes through the snow after a blizzard.

I glanced at my map of the downtown core. We'd decided on a route that looked reasonably clear of obstacles back at the armoury, but that was from my vantage point on the northwest tower. I hailed Sid Toomey on the intercom. "Sid! We gotta get to Third Avenue, and it'll be smooth sailing onto the bike paths.

There's a wall of creeps blocking our route out of here – at least a hundred of them. Can you spot another way out? I don't want to burn out your gun barrels."

"Roger – clogged up, Ark One. I'll swing the turret around and see if we can ... HOLY SHIT!"

I spun my periscope around to take a look at what Sid was seeing. Dozens of the monsters were hurling themselves from the office building in front of us. The carrier backed up a few feet as I watched monster after monster plummeting to the earth from smashed windows more than ten storeys above us.

"Hard right *now,* Doug!" I shouted into the microphone. "Get us the hell away from this building – I don't want one of those things landing on us!"

"Roger that!" Doug replied in my earpiece as my body pitched sharply to the left and I grabbed onto the engine panel for support. Within seconds, we were barrelling across a green space littered with decomposing bodies. Some moved but most didn't, and the ones that did move – well, Doug Manybears took great pleasure in grinding them to pulp underneath the wheels of our APC. I caught a glimpse of Cruze's carrier to my left. She was keeping the prescribed twenty-meter distance from me, so I swung my periscope to the twelve o'clock position and gazed out in hopes of finding a clear path to the river. I was just about to swing the periscope right when everything went black. Doug hammered down on the brakes as a monster dressed in a tattered police uniform slid off the front of the carrier and onto the ground. Doug tromped on the gas pedal, crushing the zombie beneath us.

"Where the hell did *that* thing come from, Sid?" I shouted into the microphone.

The radio squawked loudly in my earpiece and then Sid made a grunting sound. "It probably crawled across the hull to the front of the carrier when we stopped a few blocks back. I must have missed it. Hey, I see a clear path to the river, Dave. Do you see it?"

"No – it's pretty much obscured from where I'm at," I shouted back. The vibration from the engine made my voice sound like I was a robot. "What have you got?"

Sid was silent for a moment. I could hear the electric motor of the turret engaging the driving gear behind me, so I knew Sid was spinning left and right to get a clearer view.

"If we keep going straight for another five hundred meters or so, we'll hit another green space that looks like it leads to the south side of the river. I can't tell what's past that – it's all low ground, but I'm pretty sure there's a railroad track down there. Does the map show anything in the low ground up there?"

I tapped Doug on the head and told him to stop as I switched on a lamp and stared down at the map. I ran a shaking finger ahead of where I thought our position was to the green space that Sid was talking about. The Canadian Pacific Railway line cut right through the low ground, just as Sid said, but it was an area thick with woods and undergrowth. Also, the railroad track was a big obstacle for an eight-wheeled vehicle – each rail had to protrude a good five inches above the wooden railway ties, and there would be a sharp embankment on either side of the track. Our vehicles' independent suspension might get wrecked if we hit the tracks too hard, and there was also the possibility that we'd wind up with a flat tire.

I peered through my periscope to get a real-time view of the route ahead. Six months' worth of uncut grass waved in the breeze, and I could see countless pillars of smoke towering up into a blackened sky. Not a bird could be seen anywhere in the distance, and I thought for a moment that if I popped open the hatch, the air itself would poison my lungs.

I grabbed the radio handset and clicked the toggle. "Ark Two … how's your field of view?"

The radio hissed for a second and then I heard Cruze's voice. "If you swing left, you'll see the fourteenth street overpass. We can't go through there – it's filled with smashed-up cars."

"We're just in front of Millennium Park. Can you see if there's a way to cross over Sixth Avenue? If we get past that, we'll avoid the train tracks, and we can cruise along the river bank until we hit the spot to ford the carriers across."

"One sec," she shouted back. The sound of the rumbling engine filled my ears, and I glanced back over my shoulder to check on Jo. She was huddled in a corner against the back door with a poncho liner draped over her tiny frame, and she threw me a wide-eyed smile along with a big thumbs-up. I gave her one back, and then turned to look out my periscope again.

The radio squawked. "Dave, just swing left, and you'll be directly in line with Sixth Avenue. From what I can see, it's a hell of a mess of smashed cars, but I think we can push through."

Cruze's view was better than mine. I tapped Doug Manybears on the shoulder and yelled into his ear. "Swing left and then straighten your wheels. Go slow as hell – we're going to try to push through to Sixth Avenue. After that, just follow my lead, and we'll be on the paths alongside the river."

His helmet bobbed up and down, and the vehicle lurched forward. The smell of diesel and engine oil clung to my nostrils as I slid the periscope left and right, all the while keeping a sharp eye for obstacles that wouldn't be in Doug's field of vision. In minutes, my APC was crossing Sixth Avenue with the riverbank no more than a two-minute ride away. I felt a .50 calibre shell casing hit the back of my neck as the twin guns in the turret opened fire in a short burst of loud pops that I could feel in my fillings.

"What are you shooting at, Sid?" I shouted into the headset.

"Just a trio of creeps in the bushes along the river, no probs."

"Conserve your ammo! Three creeps aren't a threat to this boat, and we have to take the long view. You're our eyes and ears – you've got a three-hundred-sixty-degree traverse. Can you see Cruze?"

I heard the turret spinning and then Sid said, "About thirty meters behind us – they're being chased by a mob of about two dozen."

"That's not a problem," I said, eyeing the river bank. "The current is pretty damned fast, and the rocks are slippery as hell. Once we ford the river, they'll be swept downstream."

"Roger that," said Sid. "We going to head to the crossing we'd planned? There's a few good spots I'm seeing about ten degrees to the northwest. The north bank of the crossing is just crab grass and dead brush."

I glanced down at my map. We were about two kilometres short of our planned crossing site and the contour lines for the north bank showed a gradual slope that stretched west for about four kilometres. We'd have little problem climbing the forward slope and then we could coast westward until we were out of the city, assuming there weren't any major obstacles.

It looked too easy, and that gave me a slightly sick feeling in the pit of my stomach. Still, it was a way out of the city core, and it didn't vary too much from our original plan. I tapped Doug Manybears on the shoulder. He glanced back at me, and I signalled to drive another hundred meters. He gave me a thumbs-up, and I pressed the PTT switch.

"Ark Two – we're going to halt on the forward bank of the river – prep your section and seal up the back doors and firing portals with gun tape. The river should be shallow enough to cross without going into amphibious, so keep your props off and use your trim-vane only if necessary."

"Roger, Ark Two," Pam Cruze replied.

I removed my headset and then climbed to the back of the APC. Jo was still hunkered down in the corner with her poncho liner pulled up over her chest.

"All eyes on me!" I shouted as the APC came to a squealing halt. "Seal up the doors and firing ports, we're going to cross the river as soon as you're done."

Kate Dawson immediately went to work, pulling long strips of dark green tape off of a pair of rolls that had to weigh about five pounds each. She stretched each strip across anything that looked like it might let in water as Jo scrambled across a case of ammunition to get out of her way. I motioned for Jo to come up to the crew commander hatch, so that she'd be clear of Dawson, and then I crawled around the turret and sat down in my crew seat. Jo hopped onto my lap and threw her arms around me.

"How are you holding up, kiddo? Do you remember what your job is for now?"

She nodded amiably and said, "I'm in charge of bullets for Sid an' Kate. Oh – an' I'm in charge of passing out water and food."

"And what are you *not* supposed to do?"

"Leave the carrier or go anywhere by myself," she said flatly. "Don't worry too much cuz I know you have other stuff to take care of, but I do have a question."

"What's that?"

Her face turned beet red. "What if I have to pee?"

Well, crap. How could I have forgotten something as simple as that? I hadn't taken into account how long we'd be hatches down as we exited the city. It could be as long as a day or more until we'd be out in the open where we could actually get out of the vehicles and stretch our legs.

"Um – canteen cup, Jo," I said, as my own face reddened.

"But I can't go if people are watching!" she protested loudly.

I smiled at her and nodded slowly. "Remember that poncho liner?"

"Yeah."

"Just throw it over yourself so that nobody can see you. And don't spill any on you, okay?"

She nodded. "What if it's number two?"

"Do you have to go number two?" I asked, hoping like hell her answer was going to be no.

She shook her head. "I went before we left the army."

"Armoury," I corrected. "Good then. And Jo, that was a really smart thing to ask me. I'm sorry I didn't think about it before we left."

She kissed me on my right cheek and then gave me another hug. "That's why you have me here – to help you think about stuff you never thought about. I'm going to go back to my spot now."

I lifted her around the turret cage. "And don't stick your hands outside the firing ports, Jo. I mean it!"

"Okay, David!" she shouted as she crawled back over the ammunition case and into her corner.

Doug Manybears emitted a loud grunt from his driver's compartment. "That was real sweet, Dave. I'm getting all misty over here."

I smacked him on the back of his helmet and peered into my periscope. "She's eight," I said, as I looked down on the river. "I can't even conceive of how all this is registering to her ... oh, my God. This can't be real!"

I thought six months of battling the living dead had prepared me for anything, but clearly I was wrong on that account. The river was full of bloated bodies. Some were decomposed beyond recognition, their bony limbs reaching skyward to a God that had forsaken them, while others were fresh kills. Their torn corpses reanimated, only to find themselves swept away by the rushing current.

And this was where we were going to cross the river.

Sid Toomey's voice squawked in my headset. "I wonder where they're all coming from."

I pressed the talk button. "Somewhere ... everywhere. The city, the outskirts ... Cochrane and the foothills. Maybe they thought that creeps couldn't swim, and they used the river as an escape route."

"Yeah, well, they didn't make it, did they?" said Doug Manybears.

I clenched my jaw tightly as Ark Two's nose appeared out of the corner of my eye. The trim vane, a six-foot-long sheet of armour, slid up from beneath the nose, so I reached over and pulled the switch for ours. I could hear the hydraulic pump inside the engine panel humming away as the trim vane popped up, blocking my view.

"Okay, Sid," I shouted into my microphone. "You're navigating – I can't see past the trim. Please get us across in one piece!"

The turret spun to the twelve o'clock position. "I'm on it. Doug! The forward slope is about forty degrees – take it down at crawl speed."

The nose of the carrier pitched sharply. I held on tight and glanced back at the rest of the crew. Dawson peered out of her firing port as Jo dug her feet into the crew seat to keep herself from sliding forward. In seconds, we'd levelled off, a sign we were in the cold water of the Bow River. At this point, Dawson closed her firing port, choosing instead to sit quietly, her eyes staring blankly at the floor of the carrier. The look on her face speaking volumes, too. She'd seen what I'd seen only moments earlier.

"There's so many of them," she said. "They're all dead – everybody is freaking dead!"

I looked back at Kate and gave her a slight nod. "Keep it together, Kate. Can you do that?"

"I'll try," she said, wiping at her eyes with the sleeve of her combat shirt.

"Good," I replied. "Take a look out the back and see where Ark Two is."

She scrambled to the viewing ports on the rear doors and peered out to the rear of the carrier. "Cruze is in the water – about fifty feet behind us."

"Right on!" I shouted. Just then, Sid Toomey's voice flooded my headset.

"Hang tight – we're going out of the water in about ten seconds and then we're going to head up the river bank. Doug, lower your trim vane – my job is done."

I spun my periscope back to the twelve o'clock position and pressed the talk button. "You're not done yet, Sid. Have an eye for obstacles on the top of the river bank because you'll be the first one to see them."

"Roger that!" said Sid.

In seconds, the nose of the carrier pitched up sharply, and I held on to the front of Doug's driving seat. The engine protested loudly as we crawled up the embankment, but only for a short moment as we levelled off on what according to the map was flat terrain. We pushed on for about fifty more feet until I heard the radio hissing in my ear.

"Ark Two is clear," said Sid. "Give me a minute while I do a three-sixty so I can get my bearings."

"Take your time." I poked my head into my periscope. Waves of heat from the engine rose over the hull, giving everything a blurry appearance. The ground was carpeted with acres and acres of fallen poplar leaves, only they weren't yellow and gold, they were black and brown, probably poisoned by the poor air quality or low-level radiation.

Sid gave the crew commander seat a small kick, so I turned around to see his head poking down below the turret. "There's a pretty big gaggle of creeps bearing down on us," he said grimly.

"How many?" I asked.

"Hard to say," he replied. "There's a ridge up ahead, and I'd peg it at maybe fifty or so. Want me to open up on them?"

We had a good supply of ammunition, but I remembered Sgt. Green's first rule of combat: don't waste a single bullet. At the same time, I didn't want the carrier to get bogged down with the monsters as we climbed to higher ground. Then an idea came to me. We knew that the creeps were attracted to sound, light and movement. We had five crates of smoke grenades and six grenade dischargers on the sides of each carrier. Rather than waste bullets, I decided to create a diversion

I pressed the PTT button. "Ark Two, fire three smoke grenades onto the riverbank. I have a hunch the creeps will be attracted to the smoke, and it should clear them off the crest of the hill."

"Will do," Pam Cruze replied.

Sid spun the turret to his left. "Smoke's on its way!" he said. "Good call, Dave. The creeps are following it."

"Thanks," I said. "Give me a boot as soon as the area is clear and we'll move on."

"Yup."

I glanced back at Kate, who was keeping close watch on our surroundings from the safety of her viewing port. Jo was hidden underneath her poncho liner but reappeared after a short moment with a canteen cup full of pee. She gave me a helpless look, so I crawled between the turret cage and the engine panel into the back of the carrier.

"I'll take that," I said as she happily handed me the canteen cup. I opened a firing port and carefully dumped the contents out of the carrier, then wiped out the cup with a rag.

"Thanks, David," she said, her face beet red. "I didn't want it to splash on me cuz it's like a rollercoaster back here when we're moving."

"I know," I said, as I tightened a bungee cord around the cases of small arms ammunition just above her head. "I want you to wear your helmet back here at all times, okay? It's going to get even bumpier and stuff always falls onto people when you're going cross-country in these things."

She nodded as she placed the SPECTRA helmet on her head,and I allowed myself a small chuckle when I saw that it came down past her nose.

"I can't really see anything," she said.

"Good," I replied. "The less you see of what's out there, the better, kiddo. Trust me."

Jo put a dirt-smeared hand on my knee and exhaled heavily. "I've already seen lots of bad stuff. How come we're stopped?"

"We're just checking out our route and then we're going to get moving," I lied, not wanting to tell her about the wall of creeps on the ridge ahead.

She pushed the helmet up to her forehead and her eyes narrowed. "I know what's outside, David," she said fixing me with her gaze. "Sid was doing a lot of shooting, and I know that you have to shoot them in the head. Did he get them all?"

My heart sank a little at her question. Jo was eight years old and thin as a twig. Her red hair hung limply onto her shoulders, and her heavily freckled face was smeared with dirt and grease. She should be playing with freaking Barbie dolls and experimenting with makeup and costume jewellery, not sitting in the back of an armoured personnel carrier surrounded by bullets and grenades. She shouldn't have to live in a world that had been transformed into a living nightmare – none of us should.

"I want you to listen carefully to Kate, okay?"

Jo nodded, the helmet bobbing up and down her forehead. "Don't worry, I know the rules."

"And what's the number one rule?" I said with a note of warning in my voice.

"Don't ever get out of the carrier by myself," she said with a groan.

"What's rule number two?"

She rolled her eyes. "Don't stick my arms out of the firing holes."

And rule number three?"

She blinked. "What's rule number three?"

I leaned over and wrapped my arms around her bony shoulders. "Your brother is never going to leave you. Ever." I whispered in her ear.

She hugged me back and said, "That's what big brothers are for, aren't they?"

CHAPTER 9

My idea for a smoke diversion worked surprisingly well. The three canisters landed on the river's edge, and nearly all of the creeps plodded down the riverbank and out of sight. Only a handful remained on the top of the ridge, and we smashed through them like they were crash test dummies.

Thank God zombies don't have any reasoning ability. If they did, we would never have made it past nightfall on Day Zero.

We'd been gone from the armoury for more than two hours. It wasn't nearly as far as we'd have hoped and that presented a problem. The last thing we wanted to do was to fuel up the carriers with our Jerry cans while we were inside the city limits. Creeps were on our tail, and the risk of winding up being overrun was too great if we stopped. But damn it, I'd told everyone we'd be clear of the worst of things within a couple of hours, and clearly, I'd called that one wrong. Both carriers crawled along at less than twenty clicks an hour, and that was eating our fuel.

The radio hissed. "We should have covered more ground, Dave," said Cruze. "If we keep moving at this pace, we'll be fuelling up in a built-up area. We'll be exposed."

"Don't think that hasn't been worrying me too," I replied. "We'll go hatches up. That way we can gun the engines, and we'll have all eyes providing security."

"Alright," she answered. "I'll get everyone ready."

It wasn't a bad idea to go hatches up. We needed to air out the stench of diesel and motor oil from inside our carrier, and I'd be able to orientate my map to the ground without having to rely on the pale yellow lights inside my hatch and the restricted field of view through my periscopes. Even though the sun hadn't shone in months, daylight was still something we all craved. Terror lived in the darkness and night was when we'd had our most vicious skirmishes with the creatures.

We'd made it as far as Edworthy Park on the southern tip of Sarcee Trail. To my left was what used to be the Trans-Canada Highway, heading west to Banff, and to my right was the entire northwest of the city. That meant suburbs full of walking corpses.

The smartest thing to do was to avoid the entire area, but that meant that we'd have to ford the river again and hug the tree line along the eastern edge of the woodland that led up to Olympic Park. But even though it might have been a smart move, there was still an element of risk. The ground would be uneven, there were sharp culverts, and of course, any number of the monsters could come teeming out of the woods and swarm our carriers.

I glanced down at the map and ran my finger along the river's edge. We could simply drive along the river bank, but we'd be exposed to the southern tip of the community of Montgomery, and that meant possible swarms, too. I dropped back down and lowered the hatch door over my head. Kate was carefully removing the gun tape from around the doors and gun ports while Jo held a small garbage bag.

It was dumb luck that had allowed us to make it two-thirds of the way to the western edge, and I decided that when push came to shove, it probably didn't really matter which route we took – there was always going to be an element of risk. I pressed the talk button on the radio. "Ark Two, we're going to alter our route. Stay within twenty meters and keep your turret peeled to the right. The best way to go is along the forward slope of the Bow River, over!"

"Roger, Ark Two," Cruze replied. "Um … you do know we're going to be exposed from the high ground."

"I know," I said grimly. "And if we have to, we'll gun the engines and race along the riverbank like we're on a combat run. But the sooner we get to the western edge of the city, the better. Keep your weapons primed – we don't know what we're driving into."

"Will do, Dave," said Cruze. "We'll have an eye for creeps and obstacles, too."

I squatted on my crew seat and leaned into my periscope. "All right, Doug – keep along the bank," I said into the intercom. "Sid, you're our eyes on this again, and you're weapons free if shit hits the fan!"

The engine groaned as we pushed through a tangle of broken trees and brush. I could hear the turret spinning left and right behind me as I swung my periscope to the right just in time to see a shopping plaza come into view.

Dozens of charred bodies and skeletons lay strewn about the sidewalk. The only proof that it was ever a plaza was the Safeway grocery sign at the entrance to the parking lot. I decided that survivors must have barricaded themselves inside the store – that's where the food was. Judging from the smouldering shell of the building, they'd either been overrun or fought a pitched battle against other survivors to get at the goods. In the end, it didn't matter, because there was nothing left.

We edged along the uneven ground at a decent clip as I surveyed the now dead community. Burned houses dotted the landscape, their foundations poking through the blackened ground like gravestones. Bowness Road, once a main artery into the city core, was filled with debris and abandoned cars. I spotted small clusters of the monsters turning their heads toward us as our two APC's passed by.

"Ark One, they've caught wind of us," said Cruze into her radio. "I don't know if you can see them, but there's creeps coming out of houses and burned-out shops. Want me to open up on them?"

"Hold fire for now," I said into the radio. "The ones behind us aren't a threat. If there's a few hundred in front of us, then we're in the shit. Keep going straight, Doug!"

The APC crawled over deadwood and debris along the riverbank. I tapped the fuel gauge with my index finger, noticing that we'd burned half of a tank of diesel.

Damn. We should be out of the city by now.

The temperature gauge showed that we weren't putting any major strain on the engine, but this was just the first day. What about tomorrow? What about when we'd eventually break down or when our Jerry cans were empty?

The cool breeze brushed against my face, and the air carried the stench of death and smoke. I glanced to my right and nodded to Cruze, who was standing in her crew commander's hatch with her weapon at the ready.

"What are you seeing up ahead, Sid?" I shouted

"Hang on," he shouted back as he gazed into a pair of binoculars "Dave, you *gotta* see this!"

I motioned for Sid to climb down. He slipped off his helmet –

his face was practically gray.

I pointed to the crew commander's hatch, and Sid handed me the binoculars. He grimaced as he made room for me to climb up into the turret. In seconds, I was poking my head up through the hatch and gazing through the binoculars.

"What the hell?" I whispered.

It wasn't the hundreds of creeps now stumbling and tripping along the riverbank behind Cruze that had worried Sid. It was the small front-end loader on an overpass about a thousand meters in front of us that was pushing smashed-up vehicles and human remains over the railing and directly into our path. I spun the turret left and right and saw the loader had built a wall of smashed-up cars and trucks on the east side of the overpass.

Then things went from bad to worse.

Cruze's panicked voice on the radio filled my ears. *"Ark Two contact, over!"*

I whipped the turret to the reverse position, just in time to hear the sharp clang of bullets ricocheting off the hull. Then Sid's voice filled my headset.

Sid's head appeared through the crew commander's hatch. "Holy mother, Dave! – They're trying to create obstacles for us – they want to slow us down!"

"That's not the only thing they're doing," I shouted. "We're taking fire!"

I spun around to see Ark Two being chased by a rigged-up Brinks armoured car with a ten-foot-long spiked I-beam welded to the front bumper. The makeshift tank barrelled through the wall of creeps behind Cruze, smashing them to grease under its wheels. A male figure dressed in coveralls and a hockey helmet with a face cage popped up from a hatch in the roof and hurled a flaming Molotov cocktail at Cruze's vehicle, narrowly missing the rear end by a few feet. It exploded in a burst of orange light, spilling liquid fire across the tinder-dry grass.

"Cruze!" I shouted into the radio. "You've got someone on your tail."

The radio hissed loudly. "No shit, Sherlock! If we get hit with one of those fire bombs, we're screwed!"

"Roger that!" I replied as I spun the turret around and cocked the .50 Calibre machine gun. "Hit the brakes and hold fast, Doug! We'll give supporting fire to Cruze!"

A series of well-aimed shots, like large hailstones hitting a tin roof, bounced off the lid of the turret and the only thing on my mind besides providing support to Cruze was protecting the Jerry cans of diesel lashed onto the hull of our APC.

I dove out of the turret and into the back of the carrier. Jo had awoken from her nap and gave me a worried look, but I didn't have time to offer any reassurance.

"He's gaining on me!" Cruze's panicked voice blared through my headset. "Give me the word, Dave, and I'll open up the turret guns!"

"Hold your fire!" I replied, as I climbed back into the crew commander's hatch and peered through my periscope.

"Holy shit!" Doug choked as a blinding flash filled my entire field of vision. The ground shook beneath us, and the APC pitched sharply to the right as the blast from an exploding car swept over us like a rogue wave. I ground my knuckles into my eyes, and within seconds, my vision returned. I gazed up to see three men with hunting rifles in the kneeling position, their weapons aimed straight at us.

"Dave, if they knock out our tires, we're going to be SOL!" Doug shouted into the intercom.

"They're shooting at me, Dave!" Cruze barked. "And they're going to try to ram us if they get enough speed going!"

I looked over my shoulder at Jo, who was just about to peer out of the rear viewing port, and made my decision.

"Weapons free!" I roared into my microphone.

CHAPTER 10

A series of explosions ripped through the air. Shock waves smashed our carrier one after the other, rocking us inside like we were marbles in an empty tin can. I squinted through my periscope to see the three figures on the overpass tossing home-made bombs. One landed no more than ten feet from the nose of the APC and exploded, sending fragments of high-velocity shrapnel into the hull of our machine.

"Sid!" I shouted into my microphone. "Two hundred meters, overpass, watch and shoot!"

"On it!" Sid answered as the turret spun to the twelve o'clock position.

A pair of loud pops filled the carrier with the stench of cordite. I watched two single tracer rounds tear across my field of view like laser beams. I spotted a bright red spray of arterial blood splatter across the side of the front-end loader, and a body slumped over the edge of the cement barrier.

"One down, two to go!"

"Roger," I replied. "One of them ran behind the loader, but I can't see the other guy. Ark Two, how are you holding up?"

The radio hissed loudly. "Just pulling in beside you," said Cruze. "The Brinks truck from hell decided to stop."

"Keep your guns trained on him while we take out the two remaining shooters on the bridge," I said, eyeballing the overpass.

The .50 calibre machine gun fired off another series of single shots, and I watched as a second man fell over the edge, slamming into the ground.

"That's two," said Sid. There was an edge of anticipation in his voice.

It was only a matter of time before Sid took out the third shooter. I wondered for half a second whether the guy would actually try to surrender. I hoped not – we weren't in any position to take prisoners.

"Holy shitbirds!" shouted Sid. "He's got four creeps bearing down on him – where the hell did *they* come from?"

"Probably one of the vehicles they used to barricade themselves on the overpass!"

The intercom hissed for a few seconds and then Sid said, "Christ ... they're all over the guy. Poor bugger."

"Is he still in your field of view? If you can see the guy, shoot him ... you'll be doing him a favour."

"Yeah ... I guess you're right," Sid replied grimly.

A few seconds later, I heard one loud pop from the machine gun, and Sid informed me that it had been taken care of. I peered into my periscope to see a small army of monsters stumbling and plodding across Bowness Road, no more than six hundred meters from our position.

I was just about to order that we press on, ignoring the Brinks truck, when a flash of light to my left temporarily blinded me. The radio squawked, a sharp, piercing screech followed by Cruze's panicked voice.

"More Molotov cocktails, Dave!" she roared. "Two guys just popped up through a hole in the roof, and they've got some kind of big-ass jerry-rigged slingshot!"

"Back your carrier the hell away from here, Cruze!" I shouted. "Have an eye on the creeps but don't start shooting unless they get within one hundred meters of your position. We're going to take out that Brinks truck!"

"Roger, Dave!" Cruze replied. I spun my crew commander seat until it faced the rear of the carrier.

"Dawson!" I barked. "How many M72s do you have packed away?"

She quickly poked her head underneath the large olive drab tarp that covered the floor. "A dozen."

"Get one primed and ready. As soon as it's cocked, get your butt topside and take down the target – it's about two hundred metres directly behind us."

Her eyes narrowed for a short moment, and she gave me an uneasy look. Dawson wasn't stupid. She knew that as soon as she popped her head through her hatch, she'd be exposed to everything from a sniper to a creep that we might not have been able to see through the periscope. I felt a gnawing sense of unease about taking down yet more survivors, but I reminded myself that they attacked us and not the other way around. They could have chosen to simply let our two carriers pass without firing a single shot.

I gave Dawson a firm nod to show her that I had confidence in what she was about to do, so she clenched her jaw tightly and nodded back as she reached beneath the tarp and pulled out the rocket.

My eyes moved to Jo, who was fighting a losing battle against her helmet. I threw her a half-smile and motioned for her to come up to the crew commander hatch, so she threw off the helmet and scrambled across the back of the carrier like a mouse in an obstacle course.

"We bein' attacked, huh?"

"Yeah, squirt ... and it's about to end, in less than two minutes."

Her eyebrows arched. "Survivors like us? Trying to get us?"

I sighed heavily. There wasn't any time to get into an age-appropriate discussion about survivalist nut jobs bent on killing us and taking our supplies. Instead, I decided to deflect the discussion.

"Look, Jo, you get to be in charge for a few minutes, okay?" I asked.

She beamed at me as I picked her up by the armpits and placed her in my crew commander seat. "Does that mean I get to tell Doug where to go?"

Doug Manybears cocked his head back and said, "I got something better for you – I want you to keep an eye on the engine gauges, Jo. Can you do that?"

She nodded as I put a hand on Doug's shoulder. "Thanks, brother," I said. He understood that I didn't want Jo looking outside of the carrier.

I gave my baby sister a thumbs-up as I crawled to the rear of the carrier, grabbing my carbine off the stowage rack. I pulled back the cocking lever and then positioned myself beside Dawson, who now had the M72 fully extended and ready to fire.

"You didn't think I was going to let you do this alone, did you, Kate?" I said as I disengaged the combat lock on the hatch door. "*I'd* fire off that rocket, but you hit every target at the anti-tank range in Suffield last year. I can't hit the broadside of a barn with one of those things. Don't worry – I've got your back."

She grasped the hatch lever tightly and nodded. "Just make sure you whack anything that isn't breathing and eats meat."

"Count on it," I said, exhaling nervously. "You ready?"

"Ready."

"On three then … one … two … *three!*"

We popped up from our hatches like a pair of gophers poking their heads out of the ground. I quickly oriented myself and caught a glimpse of the small army of creeps shambling along about a hundred meters to our rear. I did a quick scan of Cruze's APC to see that she hadn't taken any damage from either creeps or home-made explosives, and then I followed Dawson into a firing position behind our turret. A flash of movement out of the corner of my eye immediately sent a wave of panic through my stomach as I glimpsed at a creep tangled up in our tow cable on the right side of the carrier. Its sunken eyes gazed up at us, and then it flung its one good arm up onto the top of the hull, narrowly missing my combat boots. I stomped on its blackened fingers, crushing the bones beneath the heel of my boot as I lined up the barrel of my carbine with the creature's forehead. I squeezed off a single shot, and the monster's head snapped back violently, sending a spray of bone and brain matter splattering onto the grass. It slumped back, sliding off the top of the hull, and I spun around to cover Dawson, who was lining up the sight on her M72 with the Brinks truck.

I could see two figures readying another volley of Molotov cocktails in their slingshot. "Don't waste any time, Kate! Hit those pricks *now!*"

"I'm on it!" she shouted, as her fingers dug into the trigger bar. There was a flash of light, followed quickly by an intense wave of heat, as the sixty-six-millimetre rocket jetted across the open field. It hit the Brinks truck right through the improvised armour-plating covering the driver's windshield, and the vehicle lit up in a ball of fire. To my horror, the pair of figures standing through the hatch in the roof simply *disappeared*; their bodies vaporized in a mixture of blood and gore and burning metal that shot fifty feet into the air. We scrambled across the roof of the carrier and dropped back down through the rear hatches. We slammed down the hatch doors with a deafening clank and hit the combat locks.

Dawson closed the now empty firing tube and replaced the end caps, securing them with a pair of cotter pins. She stared at me blankly. "They didn't stand a freaking chance," she said. Her voice was hoarse.

"They were going to kill us, Kate," I said firmly. "If we hadn't fought back, one of those fire bombs would have hit its target."

"The creeps are the enemy," she said flatly. "I hate this. I freaking *hate* this!"

I handed Kate my water bottle. "It's good that you feel lousy taking them down, Dawson. It shows that you're still a human being. You did your job, and that's all that matters right now. Are you going to be okay? – we've got to keep moving."

She nodded. "Yeah – I'll get past this."

"Good," I said, as I crawled back to the crew commander's hatch. Jo threw me a toothy grin and then wrapped her arms around Doug's shoulders.

"Thanks, Dougie!"

I motioned for Jo to head back to the rear of the carrier, and then slipped my crew commander helmet over my head. She climbed back across my lap, the heel of her shoe digging uncomfortably into my groin, and gave me a high five.

"Doug's going to teach me how to drive!" she announced.

I snorted, and peered through my periscope. The creeps were bearing down on us fast. "Cool – but tell me about it later, kiddo. Right now we gotta jet. The creepers are getting a bit too close for comfort."

"Okay, David," she shouted as she wedged her frame around the turret cage and then back to her spot by the rear doors.

The radio hissed loudly in my ears. "We have to pull out now, Dave!" said Pam Cruze.

"Roger that," I answered. "Doug ... get us the hell out of here!"

He raised his thumb over his shoulder as the carrier raced forward until we'd resumed our place in front of Ark Two.

Two and a half hours since we'd left the armoury, and already we'd been in a fight for our lives. I could only hope that there weren't any other human-made surprises in store as we pushed on. But it would be only a matter of time until we ran into a smarter, better-armed group of survivalists who'd kill their own mothers to take our two carriers and all our supplies. I just hoped like hell that we'd keep our wits about us when the time came.

Were we murderers because of what we'd just done? A large part of me felt like a murderer, even though we'd have been dead if they'd had their way. Can you be a murderer when law and order are distant memories and the only things you can count on are the bullets in your gun and the people in your tribe?

And that's what we were, as our APC's rumbled along the riverbank. A small, heavily armed nomadic tribe.

At least, with the living dead, we knew who our enemies were. I decided that if we were going to survive, then we'd have to somehow learn about our other enemy – the ones that looked like us.

Kate was right, this sucked.

Big time.

CHAPTER 11

Journal Entry: 14 NOVEMBER 1800 HRS ZULU – Breakout Complete.

Ten hours have passed since we broke out of the armoury, and we're having a quick break to eat. I honestly didn't think we'd be in a fire fight with other survivors. I thought they'd see our two APC's and run like hell, but I was wrong about that. I can only hope that we aren't wrong about making it to Sanctuary base.

The noise from our APC's has attracted every creep within earshot – that small army we encountered back in Montgomery has morphed into something the size of a brigade. Cruze has been sending me a situation report every ten minutes, and she figures there has to be easily a thousand or more of them – but they're a few kilometers behind us, thankfully. Who knows, maybe they've found some other survivors to swarm.

Back at the armoury, I had no idea how bad things were in the outside world. Every burned-out house and boarded up gas station we passed had a few creeps lurking around. Sometimes we see a lone monster shuffling up the middle of the thoroughfare opposite the riverbank like a stray animal. Sid, with trademark black humour, has decided to call monsters that cluster in tiny groups happy wanderers.

Dawson and Sid have been snapping at each other off and on all day. I don't know what's going on with those two – ever since Kate threatened to flatten Sid, they've been bickering about the stupidest crap in the world. The good news is that Doug has gotten us clear of the city, and we're going to be in open country soon. I've just radioed Cruze to see how her team is handling things – Mel is pretty shaken up about our close call with that Brinks truck. Hell, we're all pretty shaken up.

Tomorrow, I'm hoping we can make a hundred kilometers or better. It's wishful thinking, but right now, that's all we've got.

***

We crossed Bearspaw Dam Road. We were far enough from built-up areas that I decided it would be safe to go hatches up – but only after we'd circled one another to do a visual inspection for cling-ons. Not the Star Trek ones.

I decided to poke my head up first to have a look around, carefully opening my hatch door after Cruze gave me the all clear. The first thing I noticed was the *slightly* fresher air. The stench of death and decay was more pronounced in the center of the city; on the outskirts, it simply lingered, like when you catch a whiff of road-kill skunk from about three miles up the highway.

According to my map, we were at least a thousand meters from Lynx Ridge – a collection of million-dollar homes on one acre lots with expensive views of the river valley. Our vehicles were exposed, being on low ground, but ahead were foothills that rolled out before me like a carpet. We're safely outside the city now, but only by inches on a map, and there was still that army of monsters splashing through the swift-moving current of the Bow River somewhere behind us.

I glanced at my watch. We had about an hour of daylight left, and my carrier had already burned half a tank of fuel. I didn't want anyone setting foot outside once darkness fell, so it was on me to identify a relatively secure spot on the map, with an easy way out in case we wound up getting swarmed.

"Okay," I said into my radio. "It all looks clear from my vantage point. It's safe to go hatches up, but I think we should all be carrying their personal weapons and keep your eyes peeled for anything that looks like the tiniest of threats."

"Roger that," Cruze replied, as our carrier slowed down to a crawl. I glanced down to see Doug Manybears flip open his hatch and take a huge gulp of fresh air.

"Remind me again why I wanted to be a driver?" he shouted.

"Because you haven't rolled a vehicle yet," I said jokingly, patting him on the shoulder. "We made it out of the city, and it's an hour until last light. We're going to have to fuel up soon, I think."

"Yeah," he said grimly. "We're gonna want to go scrounging sooner rather than later, I bet."

"We will, but not today. We're still too close to the city – we can scrounge once we hit a rural village. A smaller human population means fewer creeps."

Ark Two pulled up beside us in a cloud of dust. I noticed the sides of their vehicle were relatively free of zombie gore, which was better than I could say for ours. Streaks of black slime stretched from the trim vane all the way to the front tires, and I spotted a hand stuck in the camouflage net to the right of the driver's hatch. Cruze opened her hatch and emerged with a look of determination on her face. She pulled off her crew commander's helmet, and I noticed a pair of black smudges just below her penetrating blue eyes. She was about five foot eight, a couple of inches shorter than me, and it was hard to tell if Cruze was a male or a female in her baggy crew suit. She grabbed a rag out of her back pocket and wiped her face clean and stuffed it inside her helmet.

"What are you gawking at?" she said, arching an eyebrow.

"Nothing," I answered, feeling slightly embarrassed.

"I see ... well, the creeps are a good distance back," she said with a huge stretch. "God, I am so glad to straighten my legs. I'm all cramped up."

Sid Toomey emerged from the turret and fished a cigarette out from the breast pocket of his combat jacket. He flipped open a Zippo lighter with a flick of his wrist and lit up, taking in a deep haul.

"We made it, huh?" he said, eyeing our surroundings.

Dawson waved her hand in front of her face to blow away Sid's second-hand smoke. "We don't need to worry about the creeps killing us. Disgusting habit, Sid."

He shrugged his broad shoulders and blew a mouthful of smoke in Dawson's face. "Meh – it's the end of the world. I'm gonna smoke. Deal."

In seconds, all the hatches on both vehicles were wide open. Everyone kept a close eye on their prescribed arcs of fire as Cruze hopped over onto the hull of Ark One to discuss our next move. Dawson reached down and lifted Jo up onto the hull. She grabbed a rag from her back pocket and gently wiped away the dirt collecting around my little sister's eyes. "Just sit tight on the hatch door, Jo," she said. "I don't want you falling, okay?"

Jo nodded and emitted a loud yawn. "I will, Katie. Um, anything I can do to help you out? You look pretty tired."

Dawson threw Jo a warm smile. "Wait a minute … you're taking care of me? I thought I was supposed to be taking care of you. See, this is what happens when you hit thirteen, Jo. Your mind starts to go."

Jo snorted as her eyes slid in my direction. "We all take care of each other! That's one of *my* rules."

"That's a good rule, Jo!" I shouted. "Thanks for taking care of everyone. You get to be our social worker."

A chill breeze blew in, carrying a hint of precipitation, as Cruze and I hunched over my map. She peeled the wrapper off a granola bar and took a huge bite off the end.

"How are your people, Cruze?"

"A little shaken up," she said, between chews. "At least back at the armoury, we had a defensible position. Out here, not so much."

"No freaking doubt – but everyone knew the risks when we decided to break out … at least I *thought* we knew the risks."

She pointed to the map. "Everyone knows we couldn't stay there, and we've made it more than twenty-five kilometres today. That's a hell of an accomplishment when you think about the fact that we had to fight our way out. If you're bummed about those guys back at the overpass, don't be."

I nodded. "I know … the rules have changed. Yadda-yadda."

Cruze pursed her lips tightly. "The rules are that we're making up rules as we go along, but you want to know something?"

"What's that?"

"Even before Day Zero, every single person living on the planet was facing their own deaths every day, only it wasn't creeps they faced; it was drunk drivers or some mentally disturbed guy going postal at work or cancer or any of the bazillion other things that kill people. The only thing that makes this shit feel worse is the fact that we're not the top dogs anymore."

I nodded. "We're the hunted now instead of the hunters."

She slapped my shoulder and then cocked her carbine for effect. "Yep … but who says any one of us still breathing has forgotten how to be a hunter. There might be more of them than there are of us, but I can shoot a round up the backside of a gnat from a thousand meters away. The creeps? All they can do is stumble and swarm, and that's it. If we keep working as a team, we can beat the bastards back, no question about it."

Now *that* took me by surprise. There I was thinking that I had to keep strong for everyone in our group, and I hadn't once considered that someone might be trying to keep it together for me. I felt the tiniest spark of hope deep inside my chest at Cruze's very practical outlook. She was right. Zombies were just another form of dying that we could add to a growing list. Human beings had faced down any number of calamities in the past; Day Zero was just modern man's cataclysmic event. Six hundred years ago, the Black Death wiped out nearly sixty percent of humanity in Europe and human beings managed to bounce back. Time was actually on our side if we lived long enough. The creeps were just walking cadavers, each one slowly decomposing with every passing day.

I folded up the map and stuffed it in the pocket of my combat trousers. "Thanks for the pep talk, Cruze," I said.

"No problem ... let me see the map again."

"Why?"

"I just need to check something, alright?"

Feeling slightly annoyed, I pulled the map out of my pocket and handed it to her. Cruze unfolded it across the hull and pointed to the spot I'd chosen to go to ground.

"What is it?" I asked as she placed her index finger and thumb on the distance scale, moving quickly to the black dot I'd picked for our crew to go to ground for the night.

"I think we're still too close to built-up areas, Dave. The place you've picked isn't far enough from Airdrie. The creeps will hear our vehicles ... that or a repeat performance of what we dealt with in the city."

"Well, I'm not the world's greatest navigator, Cruze, but the area is heavily wooded, and it's the highest feature on the map for miles. There's a utility road in and out in case we need to leave in a hurry."

She grunted and pointed to another high feature about an inch away from where I'd plotted our route. "I think you mean this one here," she said, tapping the other hill with an index finger. "Are you sure you picked the right spot because I'm not convinced."

"Geez ... you go from giving me a pep talk to questioning my route?" I said with a tinge of sarcasm in my voice.

Cruze spun around and pointed the map in the opposite direction from our route. She ran a finger along the shaky black line I'd scrawled onto the map as we broke out of the city and then lifted her head and gazed out on the horizon.

"You know what? Never mind," she said finally. "I don't like the place you've picked, but we voted you in charge, and the last thing we need is a disagreement because we all have to support each other. If we get knee-deep in the shit, we can pull out in a hurry."

I glanced at the map and then shifted my gaze to Cruze. "Well … we could still go to the high feature you picked, but we'd burn more fuel getting there."

She slugged me hard in the arm and then deftly jumped over to her APC. "Don't sweat it. Anyway, we probably wouldn't make it to my spot with any daylight left to scout the area. We also don't need the others to see us disagreeing on anything. Team cohesion and all that shit. So what's the plan?"

I gazed out at the rooftops dotting Lynx Ridge. "We fuel up to three-quarters of a tank and press on until we're in open country."

"Fair enough," she said, turning on her heels. "Mel, get out the horse cock and dump one Jerry can in the tank. Kenny, put together a sentry list for tonight. We'll stay inside with the combat locks on until first light, and then we'll press on in the morning."

Kenny and Mel both gave Cruze a thumbs-up as I turned my eyes to my section. "Same thing for us. Sid, throw in one can of diesel and Kate, get the sentry list going. We pull out in ten minutes!"

CHAPTER 12

The crest I'd chosen to go to ground was surrounded by eight-foot-high scrub brush, providing excellent concealment for both carriers. Doug and Kenny parked back-to-back; the APC's facing east and west to give both turrets a 360-degree field of vision for our night sentries. We couldn't open the rear doors without the interior lights spilling into the darkness and giving away our position, so any interaction between Arks One and Two would have to be via radio. The swarm following us had to be more than 15 km behind us – we'd gunned our engines to about 30 km/hr, and we'd driven cross country for 45 minutes after we fuelled up. I estimated that there was little chance they'd catch up to us by first light – we'd still be about three or four clicks ahead, and that was a conservative estimate. The ground was uneven, and there were cattle fences stretched out across former farmland, as well as a host of other man-made obstacles.

But that didn't mean we were going to kick back and relax. Each one of us was determined to stay vigilant. One thing that you learn when you're a soldier is the reasons why things are seen: shape, silhouette, shadow, spacing, texture, light and movement. There's also the other issue of noise. Sound travels farther at night, because you don't have to compete with every other living thing that might be awake during the daytime, though since Day Zero, cities and towns had fallen silent. The only sounds we'd heard from the safety of the armoury were the creeps shuffling around the city and sporadic gunfire in the distance. Now that we were in open country, we'd have to invoke stricter discipline during the silent hours.

We'd pulled blackout covers over all the viewing ports in the carrier, and the interior of our machine was now bathed in red light, which took everyone a few minutes to adjust to. White light can seep through blackout covers and draw attention to your position, but red light is far less noticeable.

I sipped on a drinking box of orange juice with my back to the rear doors while Kate brushed Jo's long red hair, trying not to tug the small hairbrush too hard every time she encountered a knot. It was shortly past eight o'clock, and we'd been out of the armoury now for more than fourteen hours.

"How's everyone holding up?" I asked as I watched him dole out foil packages of rations from the simmering pot of water over a portable mountain stove.

He sniffed loudly as he pulled a hunting knife out from its sheath; slicing open a steaming hot bag of corn beef hash. "I'm good ... all things considered," he said, poking his knife around the contents. "MMMM ... corn beef hash. This is just like Christmas dinner."

Dawson slipped the hairbrush back into her rucksack and then began to braid Jo's hair. "We're going to have to cut your hair one of these days, Jo. It's getting pretty long now."

Jo flashed me a toothless grin as I opened her pouch of ravioli and blew inside to cool it off. "Maybe I could get my hair chopped like Pam. Or maybe a Mohawk!"

Sid snorted. "Then we could count the freckles on your scalp, squirt. Or maybe play connect the dots with 'em."

Jo threw him a sour look. "I don't have freckles on my scalp, and even if I did they'd be beauty marks, right, David?"

I took a swig on a cup of instant coffee and then sliced open my ration pack. Naturally, it was the one containing the dreaded ham omelette. "I'm not taking a position on the matter of freckly scalps, Jo. I like your hair the way it is. But then it's not me that has to brush the knots out every day."

The radio squawked in my earpiece. "Ark One, we're finishing our rations and will be going to ground shortly. Radio checks every hour, on the hour?"

"Roger that – We'll be going lights-out in about twenty minutes. Doug will be doing the first night sentry followed by Kate, me and then Sid. I'll have a route established for first light and will radio it to you during my sentry shift. Over."

"Ark Two, Roger over," the radio hissed.

"Hull drains to dump out the ... well, you know?" asked Sid.

I grimaced. Everyone would have to go to the bathroom at some point, and I'd already relieved myself in an empty bottle. It was easy for a guy to urinate, but not so easy for a girl, and while Jo could hide behind a poncho liner to do her business, I felt sorry for Kate. I didn't bother asking her how she'd been going all day – she wasn't exactly pleased when Sid whipped it out and pissed off the side of the carrier two hours earlier. Also, nature would eventually call for all of us to defecate, and we sure as hell weren't going to do it inside of the APC, for obvious reasons. Back at the armoury we had folding toilets that resembled a small stool; you'd simply tie a blue back underneath the seat and do your business. The bag would then go into an oil drum in the middle of the parking compound, and we burned our waste every day. We still had a folding toilet on board, but really, we'd just have to exit the carrier and squat over a log, just like infantry soldiers had been doing for thousands of years. Only, in this case, the person going would have someone providing security because it has long been every soldier's worst nightmare to get killed while taking a dump.

"Yep ... hull drains it is," I said. "Pour out your waste and everyone washes up during their shifts tonight. One bottle of water each, got it?"

The team all nodded in unison as I turned my attention to Jo. "And you, baby sister. You get to wash up before you go to sleep – you can use the leftover water in the cooking pot. And I want you to brush your teeth."

Jo nodded as she scooped a mouthful of ravioli into her mouth. Dawson tore open her pouch of chilli with her teeth and then dumped a handful of ground up soda crackers inside.

"How far did we make it today?" she asked, as she stirred the contents with her spoon.

"About fifty kilometres," I said. "Maybe we can do fifty tomorrow ... who knows?"

Sid scraped the inside of his pouch of corn beef hash with his hunting knife. "Scrounging tomorrow, right?"

I shrugged. "Maybe. Possibly. It'll depend on what's out there."

"It'd be nice if we could all be together at night," said Dawson. "Everyone from both carriers."

"What do you want everyone to be crammed in for?" said Sid as he crumpled up his foil bag. "This is the problem with having chicks in combat roles – always wanting to freaking socialize."

Dawson flashed a fiery glare his way as she edged forward on the jump seat. "You know what, Sid?"

"What?"

"Get bent," she said angrily. "That's what."

Sensing a possible scrap, Jo dropped her foil pouch of ravioli and scrambled over Kate's lap, standing in the center of the carrier to separate the pair. She threw an accusing glare at Sid and said, "I'm a girl, and I've shot a creep, Sid. You were there ... you told me I was a good shot *and* a good soldier. Well ... I'm eight and Kate is fifteen. She's twice as good as any boy."

Sid snorted and poked at his ration pack in an attempt to avoid Jo's gaze. "Yeah, kid ... you're a good soldier. I'm just old fashioned is all."

"You're a knuckle dragger," Kate griped as she leaned back against the wall of the carrier and relaxed a little.

I swallowed a mouthful of ham omelette, doing my best not to gag. Jo climbed over my lap as I gave her a hug and whispered in her ear. "Good, job on that. You put Sid in his place."

She hugged me back and said, "I know."

Doug Manybears spun around in his driver's seat to face us. "Kate's right – it would be good to be together even if it's not as tactically sound as Sid would like."

"Once we run out of fuel, we'll have to abandon one carrier, and siphon all the fuel from either Ark One or Ark Two," I replied. "Then we'll all be piled into a single vehicle. If anything, it'll be crammed tight."

"And that could be tomorrow for all we know," Sid grunted. "Still ... I mean we might find an abandoned car or truck or even a minivan or something. There's no shortage of them."

Dawson crumpled her now-empty pouch of chilli and tossed it in a garbage bag we'd taped to the turret cage. "I'm going to crash, seeing as how I'll be up again before midnight. Two-hour sentry shifts, everyone. Nobody falls asleep during your turn, or you'll have my boot in your ass, got it?"

"I believe you'd do it, too, Kate." I tossed my pouch in the trash. "At first light, we'll do a check on fluid levels, and I want the tire pressures checked, too, Doug. In the meantime, everyone should catch a bit of kip while they have the chance. We're safe in here from the creeps, but we're still exposed, so whoever is on sentry tonight, don't second guess if you see anything moving out there. We'll go to a full stand-to if there's even the smallest of threats."

Sid nodded. "Light and noise discipline – just like back at the armoury."

Jo handed me her empty foil bag and then wiped the tomato sauce off her face with a rag. "I can go on sentry, too," she said with a hint of eagerness in her voice. "I want to help out more. I can do it."

I felt a twinge of pride in the middle of my chest. Jo had been punching above her weight for months now, and she never once complained about it.

Kate smiled warmly. "You're already a huge help, Jo. You're taking care of everyone with water and ammo, not to mention the fact that you don't take up anywhere near as much room as Sid. And you don't smell as bad, either."

As if on cue, the giant Newfie lifted his left leg and let out a loud, vile-sounding fart. "Is there a duck in here or something? I could have sworn I just heard a duck!"

"Gross!" Dawson groaned as she pulled her combat sweater over her nose. "That is so *frigging* gross."

Not to be left out, Jo lifted her leg and let one go as well. "It must be contagious!" she giggled.

I shut off the combat lights and cracked open the firing port beside me. "Whoever said farting was good for morale never spent a day inside an APC with a Newfie. Sid, there is something seriously rotting inside your bowels, dude."

Doug struck a match and then quickly blew it out. "I don't know if this works or not, but at least it'll take the edge off of whatever the hell crawled up Toomey's butt. Listen, we've all eaten so maybe you can all hit the pit. I want to begin my shift – the sooner I'm done, the sooner I can get some sleep."

"Consider it done," Sid said with a yawn. "Toss me my poncho liner, and I'll just zone out right here and now. Oh, and sorry about the fartage, but I've been holding that bugger in all day."

"You can fart to your heart's content *tomorrow*, Sid. We'll be driving hatches up now that we're out of the city."

Dawson fanned the air in front of her face with her right hand.

"That doesn't mean we all expose ourselves – there might be a sniper out there or something. Still, the fresh air will be a blessing."

"Good point, Kate," I said, tossing out poncho liners from a storage shelf. "Okay, troops. Let's get some sleep. First light will be here quicker than you think."

***

I no longer call them nightmares. It used to be that falling asleep meant a blessed reprieve from the day's troubles, but not anymore. Rest was something I now met with displeasure, like an unpleasant task that had to be carried out every single day. Before Day Zero, I'd dream mostly about sex. Afterward, though, my dreams were filled with the living dead.

My dreams follow a pattern, and they almost always deal with my inability to protect Jo. The first night out from the safety of the armoury was no different. I dreamt about physics class at school. I was the only student in attendance – I'm usually alone when the bad dreams hit. Mr. Eldridge, our gangly, six-foot-four science nerd teacher, had his back to me. He was scribbling something about the speed of light on the white board; only the board was filled with crimson-coloured handprints and splashes of blood that dripped down off the shining surface and onto the floor. He spun around quickly, his film-covered eyes staring straight through me, and his jaw dropped open like it was on a hinge, revealing a set of yellow teeth hidden neatly behind thin black lips. The skin on his face was covered with festering sores.

"You'll do well when you join us, David," he croaked. His voice sounded like his throat was filled with liquid. "And you *will* join us. You and your sister … it's only a matter of time."

I bolted upright, hitting my head good and hard on the turret cage. I was bathed in sweat as I gulped for air. Kate dropped down from her seat in the turret with a worried look on her face.

"*Jesus, Dave,*" she choked. "You freaking scared the shit out of me. Oh, God … you're bleeding."

I felt a tiny dribble of blood rolling down the middle of my forehead as I tried to get my bearings.

"Frigging shock dreams," I said as Dawson handed me a clean rag. "Thanks."

"I get them too," she said grimly. "We all do."

"What time is it?"

Dawson glanced at her watch. "About one thirty – you still have forty-five minutes until your shift."

I shook my head as I pushed myself upright. "No point in trying to rack out now. Christ, my head hurts ... anything happening out there?"

"If you mean the coyote I spotted half an hour ago, then yes. Outside of that, it's pretty quiet, thankfully."

"Radio checks coming in from Ark Two every hour?"

She nodded. "Yes ... it's all good. Cruze has everything under control over there. I've been using the other radio to see if I could pick up any other military broadcasts. Doubtful, but I thought I'd give it a try anyway."

I dabbed at my forehead with the rag. "Anything?"

She shrugged hard. "Kind of. I've been getting sporadic words here and there through the static – might be Sanctuary Base, might not. I've been piecing them together, and I think they're getting hammered with a snowstorm or something."

"Better them than us."

"Want to have a listen?" she asked.

"Sure," I said, manoeuvring myself away from the turret cage. Dawson climbed down into the crew commander's compartment as I slid into the cage and slipped on the headset.

I listened carefully, but all I could hear was the faint hiss of the static, so I fiddled with the squelch knob on the radio. I was just about to turn up the volume when I saw a flash of movement through the turret viewing port. I flipped on the infra-red camera inside my periscope and peered inside. The ground, the trees, the low ground; everything was bathed in eerie green light as I scanned the area surrounding us for any signs of life.

Or unlife.

Stumbling through a thicket of diamond willow about thirty meters in front of our carrier was a group of creeps, about twenty of them. They tripped and shuffled through the undergrowth, their hideous faces staring hard at both our carriers.

"Shit," I whispered. "Creeps."

Dawson scrambled underneath the turret cage and poked her

head up. "How many?"

"A couple of dozen."

"They from that group we blew past yesterday?"

I shook my head. "I doubt it – they're too far back. These ones are locals."

The radio hissed in my ears. "Ark Two – you seeing that?" It was Melanie Dixon, with an edge of panic to her voice.

"Ark One, Roger. Stand by," I replied.

"Two dozen isn't a lot of them," said Dawson. "We could pick them off one by one."

I shook my head. What concerned me was where this group had come from – and, more importantly, were there were any more of them out there? It would be easy enough to stand up in the turret and fire off individual shots; but there was still the issue of noise travelling farther at night, and one thing we'd learned in the six months since Day Zero was that creeps always respond to the sound of gunfire.

Our two vehicles were miles from any built-up areas. The closest farm was a few kilometres away, and, unless it had been a survivors' outpost that wound up being overrun, there was no way a group that large could have formed. I pulled my map out of my pocket and shone a red light onto it, running my finger along the contour lines of our ridge and looking for any symbols that would show a likely place for zombies to converge.

I tried not to panic, in spite of the fact that the creeps were no fewer than twenty meters away from the carrier. I gazed at the high feature I'd picked, and the one Cruze had suggested earlier. She'd been right all along, and I should have listened to her. Our carriers had gone to ground about five miles away from the city of Airdrie, and that meant creeps. Thousands and thousands of creeps.

CHAPTER 13

I had made a massive mistake. In the scramble to get out of the city, my hastily assembled route wasn't anywhere near where we should have been, and I cursed the fact that I didn't have the sense to seek out Cruze or Dawson for a second opinion. Surely they would have read the contour lines differently and given me a slap in the back of the head for being so stupid as to plot a course so close to a built-up area.

"Get Cruze on the radio," I said into my mouthpiece.

"Roger that," replied Melanie.

I handed my map to Dawson and pointed to our position. "We're less than five clicks from Airdrie. We've gotta bug out now."

All the colour drained from her face as she stared at the map, and I could have sworn I saw her gulp.

The radio squawked in my headset. "Cruze here … what's going on?"

I pressed the PTT button. "Creeps. At least two dozen and probably a shit pile more. You were right, Cruze. I should have picked another spot."

"Stand by," Cruze replied as I peered out through my periscope. I could see about two hundred meters into the distance, and I spotted another throng of creeps heading up through a dried ravine.

The radio hissed again. "Well, we're in the shit now, so it doesn't matter who was right or wrong. We can take down these creeps, no problem, Dave."

I shook my head. "The sound of our gunfire will bring every monster within earshot, Cruze, we can't stay here. Get your people up, make sure the hatches are locked tight – we're leaving in five minutes."

"Roger that," said Cruze.

"Wake up Sid and Doug," I said to Dawson. "We're getting the hell out of here. There's another few dozen coming up through a dried-out ravine."

"Will do," said Kate. She shook the pair. They were snoring loudly, almost in unison. "Stand to! Stand to! Stand to!"

Sid scrambled for his carbine, elbowing Doug Manybears in the left cheek. "Wha – what?" he said dreamily.

Doug pushed himself upright and wiped the sleep from his eyes. "Is it my shift again ... no, wait, I already did a sentry."

"We've got company. Check the hatches, get your shit in gear and get this carrier going," Dawson said firmly. "We're leaving in five."

"What's going on?" Doug yawned, as he rubbed the sleep from his puffy eyes.

I climbed down from the turret. "Creeps. A couple of dozen bearing down on us from Airdrie."

Sid slipped his left foot into his combat boot. "*Airdrie?* We might as well have the words free food painted on the sides of the carriers!"

"Yeah, well, I did a shitty three-point resection when I picked this spot," I said angrily. "Cruze called it right, and I should have freaking listened."

"God damn it, I gotta take a dump," Sid grumbled as he climbed into the turret. "Let's get clear of here – my piss bottle is full and I don't have another one. Fuck ... I was looking forward to a nice peaceful crap at first light. This blows on an epic scale!"

Doug Manybears scrambled into the driver's hatch as I checked on Jo. She was huddled in the rear corner of the APC, sound asleep. I didn't have the heart to wake her up, so I tucked her poncho liner around her shoulders and then crawled over to the crew commander's hatch. I cursed under my breath at my bonehead move. I probably should have cut myself some slack, given that the only map and compass work I'd ever done was a few patrols on exercise in Wainwright or Suffield, but I wasn't about to allow myself that luxury. It didn't matter that I had less than a year of service under my belt, or that I might have been the most organized person in Sergeant Green's section; we were miles away from safety, a throng of creeps was bearing down on us fast, and if I was responsible for getting us into this situation, it was up to me to get us out of it.

I peered through my crew commander's periscope while Doug primed the engine. The creeps were less than ten meters away, and I could easily make out their gaping mouths in spite of the darkness. I grabbed my headset and slipped it over my head, then flipped on my radio set. A blast of white noise shot through my ears as I slammed my left hand on the volume knob to turn it down.

"Ark one, you there?" said Cruze through a haze of static.

"Go ahead."

"We're just warming up and can leave in two. I'd offer to plot a new course, but I can't leave the carrier to do it."

Fuck.

Cruze should have been placed in charge of our escape, and her last statement simply proved the fact that our team should have chosen her.

The presence of metal can screw up a compass big time. I was hatches down in our APC when I did the resection and any infantry soldier worth his salt would have stepped onto the ground and walked a few feet away from ten thousand pounds of steel and iron. It was an amateur mistake that could wind up costing our team dearly. I couldn't shoot a bearing this time, so I followed the contour lines on the map from our existing position and spotted the dried-out ravine where I'd seen that second group of creeps. It headed northwest of Airdrie and according to the map, it looked relatively free of obstacles, so I ran my finger up to a point that looked to be about five kilometres from our existing position and made a note of the easting and northing for a good spot to rendezvous with Cruze.

"Dammit!" shouted Doug Manybears in a voice that was probably loud enough for the creeps now clawing against our hull to hear.

I slipped my headset off one ear and leaned over his seat. "What's going on, Doug?"

He primed the choke three more times as he pressed the start button, and the lights inside our carrier dimmed for a short moment. "This piece of shit won't start!" he snarled. "Fuck!"

"But how? We kept our power use to a bare minimum all night. Are the batteries dead?"

"They're nearly dead," he said, pointing to the gauges above his head. "We need a slave, ASAP."

I could feel the creeps hammering against the hull, and I

glanced over my shoulder to see Kate Dawson peering out of her viewing port, carbine in hand. Jo, who was now wide awake, was sitting with her knees against her chest in the rear corner of the APC, her hands covering her ears.

"They're all around us!" shouted Sid. "At least three or four deep! There's a swarm of them coming in from the east. Why aren't we leaving yet?"

"We need a boost!" I shouted. "Hang tight and keep an eye on them."

I grabbed the PTT button and pressed. "Ark Two ... we're dead in the water here. We need a slave to get this pig going!"

"Are you fucking kidding me?" answered Cruze, my headset filling with more and more static. It wouldn't be long until my radio drained the last life out of the carrier's batteries. "We can start shooting, Dave, just give us the word."

"No. We need another diversion – something that will draw every one of these pricks away from us. I need you to get someone on the hull of your carrier. "

"Okay, that's freaking nuts!" Cruze snapped.

I ground my teeth together. We were up shit creek unless the lure of fresh meat could get those creeps away long enough for Doug to slip a slave cable into the receptacle on the carrier's side. "It's bait, Cruze. Either you or Mel needs to stand up in the rear hatch. Your carrier has to lead the creeps as far away as you can, then double back. By the time you return, we'll have the slave cable hooked up for a boost."

The radio hissed for a few moments and there was dead air. Cruze was probably breaking the news to her team. I was certain that she was cursing the day I was born. "Mel volunteered," Cruze finally replied. "Make sure Sid has an eye for the creeps because I don't know how long it will take us to get them away, or even if using Mel as a lure will work. When this is over, you and me are going to have a little chat."

I grimaced as pressed the handset. "Fine ... look, the creeps that don't follow, we'll take care of," I said. My voice was flat and hard. "It's about the best idea I can think of. Get moving, Cruze."

The radio squawked. "You fucking owe me, Dave. Ark Two, out."

I slipped off my headset and bellowed, "All eyes on me!"

Sid dropped down from the turret as Kate and Jo scrambled to the edge of the rear compartment.

"What's the plan?" asked Sid.

"We're going to get out of this – got it? We need a boost. Cruze is going to buy us some time by getting Mel to go hatches up as a lure, and Cruze will get the creeps following her carrier the hell away from us."

"Jesus," Doug said. "That's pretty ballsy."

"Yeah, well, if anyone has a better idea that doesn't involve wasting a day's worth of bullets and alerting every creep between here and Beiseker to our position, I'm all ears."

Dawson blinked. "W-Who's going to plug in our slave cable?"

"I will," I said. "And that means that I need Sid and you, Kate, to provide covering fire with your personal weapons. Single shots and only if necessary. When Cruze's carrier returns, we'll have less than no time to dick around. Doug, as soon as the engine is going, I want you to get everyone the hell away from here. I'll ride the hull and pull the slave cable back on board."

Jo gave me a painful glance, and I didn't have time to console her. She understood I was going to be putting myself at risk, but it was my fault we'd gotten into a tight spot, and I was determined to be the one to get us out of it.

"Jo," I said, taking the edge out of my voice. "You stay down below the hatch and keep your eyes on all the viewing ports. If you see anything coming, you be sure to let Kate and Sid know about it. Cool?"

She nodded. "A-Alright. Are you going to be okay?"

I shrugged. "We're a team here in this boat, kiddo. And we're only as fast as our slowest person. I'll be okay if everyone does their jobs, got it?"

She nodded again as I gave everyone the thumbs up. "All right, everyone, my life is in your hands. Sid, you let me know when it's safe to hop out and plug in the slave cable."

He placed a hand on my shoulder. "We got your back, Dave. Try not to worry about it."

I chuckled. "A dead battery. An army of creeps three deep pounding at the hull of our APC. Melanie Dixon is going to be the

Pied Piper. What's the worst that can happen?"

CHAPTER 14

Sid Toomey gave me a running play-by-play of Ark Two's actions. God love Melanie Dixon: she'd armed herself with a baseball bat and was clubbing to death every monster that dared attempt to claw its way up her hull. I made a mental note to worship the ground she walked on if we got through this intact because what she was doing took a huge amount of guts. What I was about to do, on the other hand, would require less in the way of guts and more in the way of dumb luck.

I'd hauled the 20-foot, rubber-coated slave cable out from underneath a floor panel, and cleaned the dirt out of each receptacle. Dawson helped me coil the 50lb monster onto my crew commander seat, and then I nervously gripped the hatch handle, waiting for word from Sid that it was clear to make my move. My throat was dry, and my heart was hammering the inside of my chest like a battering ram. I checked the battery gauge on the wall panel. We had barely enough juice left for another radio signal, so I ordered that Sid assemble a mobile radio and hail Cruze's APC.

"Vehicle radio is dead – I've got Cruze on the man-pack!" Sid shouted, in a voice that sounded like he'd just won the lottery.

"Thank fuck! Are there any creeps around our hull?"

"None that I can see," he said.

I gripped the handle tighter. "Are you sure?"

"For fuck sake, Dave, I don't know! It's pitch black out there, and I don't have any infra-red, so my field of view is maybe a hundred feet or so."

"Everyone listen up!" I bellowed. "I'll go hatches up first. If the coast is clear, I'll hammer on the hull of the carrier. Kate and Sid … get your asses topside and provide cover as soon as you hear me!"

"Don't worry – we've got your back!" answered Dawson.

I took a deep breath and said a little prayer as I exhaled heavily and gave the hatch lever a sharp turn to the right. It opened with a loud screech, and I poked my head up to make sure everything was clear.

The first thing that hit me was the sharp stench of diesel in the air. I did a quick look to my left and right, pushed the hatch door wide open and lifted myself topside. In the distance, I could make out Cruze's panel markers, showing the rear of her carrier. She was climbing a sharp incline, and there were dozens of creeps hot on her tail. I hammered on the hull with the heel of my boot, and in seconds, both Sid and Kate Dawson were standing in their respective hatches, carbines in hand.

"Cover me!" I shouted as I hauled up the slave cable. In the distance, I could hear the sound of branches being snapped to pieces as Cruze's carrier lured the monsters away from us.

I hauled the slave cable to the nose of the carrier, dropped down onto my belly and shone my flashlight on the side of the hull. The red beam offered little illumination, but I spotted the slave receptacle just above the front right tire. I reached down and wrapped my hand around the receptacle cover, giving it a sharp twist to unlock it.

I managed to get the cover free, pulled the male end of the slave cable over the receptacle and plugged it in. A bead of sweat rolled down the center of my back as I gulped another breath of air. We were ready for a boost. All we needed was for Cruze to make it back to our vehicle, and it would be a simple job to plug them into the front of our carrier. Doug would get the juice to turn over our engine, and we could get the hell away from Airdrie.

I was close to feeling we might actually make it out of our predicament when I caught a flash of movement coming from a copse of bushes no more than thirty feet away. The air filled with the sound of broken branches, and a surge of panic shot straight into my bowels. It was another group of creeps. I scrambled to my feet as I spotted the front panel markers on Cruze's carrier, heading down the incline eight hundred meters away.

"We've got company!" I barked.

"Both sides, Dave!" shouted Dawson. "Where the hell did *they* come from?"

Sid climbed out of the turret, carbine in hand and helped me to my feet. He cocked his weapon as I scrambled back to my hatch and grabbed my carbine from its rack above the radios.

"Everything okay?" asked Doug.

"Just freaking great! Stand by and stay down. Keep an eye on

Jo!"

He gave me a thumbs-up, and I pulled my torso out of the hatch. I climbed to the highest point of the carrier and stood back to back with Sid while Kate pulled her carbine to her shoulder and took aim.

"This is going to get freaking ugly!" she shouted.

We watched the group of creeps emerge from the bush line, their arms stretched out toward us. The creatures, smelling fresh meat, immediately quickened their pace as they headed to the carrier.

I cocked my weapon and lined my sights up with the closest monster, a woman dressed in a torn nightgown, still wearing bedroom slippers. Her dead eyes met mine as I took a deep breath and flipped the safety off my carbine with my right thumb.

"Single shots," I said, trying to control the bile rising in my throat. "One at a time."

"Roger that," said Sid. I could feel him shaking against my back.

"Watch and shoot," I said, as I began to squeeze the trigger.

My carbine kicked in my right shoulder as the bullet tore out of the barrel and into the top of the monster's head. The creep dropped like a stone. Three more stumbled out from the bushes, and I fired off three quick rounds, each bullet thumping into cold, dead flesh.

"That's four," I said, lowering my weapon a few inches and scanning the horizon line for Cruze's carrier. The air filled with loud pops as both Dawson and Sid fired their weapons. Another creep lumbered through the bush line, a small child who was probably Jo's age when she'd been bitten. She was stick thin, and there was a huge chunk of flesh missing from the right side of her neck, exposing the muscle, sinew and bone beneath. I fought the urge to throw up as I squeezed off another round, hitting the monster in the right side of its head and sending it flying back a good three or four feet.

"We're going to have to get out of here fast, Dave!" shouted Dawson. "The sound of our weapons is going to send every freaking creep in Airdrie our way!"

"Tell me something I don't know!" I growled as I fired a round at a creep clad only in a pair of torn boxer shorts. It landed on top of the body of the little girl. "How are you doing for ammo?"

"Half a mag left," said Sid. "I've got three full mags in my pocket."

"About the same for me," said Dawson, squeezing off a round.

I could hear the roar of Ark Two's engine as it approached from the east and lowered my weapon again. I spotted the APC's panel lights filtering through the bushes no more than 100m away, so I shouldered my weapon, scrambled down to the nose of the carrier and grabbed the other end of the slave cable. I'd just picked it up when I spotted movement in the bush line.

"Shit!" I snarled, as I hauled the cable back up to the turret. "There's more coming out way … this is going to be tight!"

"When isn't it a tight spot?" Dawson groaned, firing off another shot.

A cloud of dust filled the air as Cruze's APC barrelled through the bushes, smashing into creeps and grinding them underneath the front wheels. I grabbed my flashlight and flicked it on, waving my arm in a circular motion as I directed the APC to the right side of our carrier. Kenny Howard was the best driver in the King's Own. He deftly manoeuvred his APC with the ease of a NASCAR driver and pulled up mere inches from the engine compartment of Ark One. I glanced at Melanie Dixon and noticed the business end of her aluminum baseball bat was smeared with blood and brain matter. She pulled a rag out from her back pocket and wiped the gore off her bat, then slipped it under the camouflage net attached to the turret.

"Next time you can be the bait – let's get this boat of yours rolling! There's a small army of the pricks behind us, and they'll be here in minutes!"

I craned my neck over my shoulder to see that both Sid and Dawson had their weapons trained on the bushes. Pam Cruze popped out of her crew commander's hatch. She had a shotgun slung across her shoulder and a determined look in her eyes.

"Nice to see you again, Dave. Let's get you plugged in."

"Cover me!" I raced across the front of her carrier, slave cable in hand. I knelt down and reached over to unlock the receptacle cap, then slid the slave cable into the slot and gave it a sharp twist.

"We're plugged in! Gun your RPM'S!"

Cruze poked her head in and reappeared five seconds later as Ark Two's engine raced. I felt a wave of heat rising off the grill as I got back to my feet. Leaping across the hull, I jumped into my own hatch.

"Start her up, Doug!" I shouted. He pressed the start button. The lights inside our carrier flickered weakly as the engine turned over.

"Come on you piece of shit!" Doug roared. He fiddled with the neutral start switch for a second, and then pulled the choke out. I glanced at the electrical gauge and saw that it was drawing a full charge from Cruze's carrier. We had enough juice. Doug pressed the start button again, and the engine started turning over. He kept it pressed this time for more than twenty seconds. "Get Cruze to race her engine – we're not getting enough power!"

"Are you sure?" I asked. "The gauges tell a different story."

"I'm the fucking driver, Dave, you're not! *Just do it!"* Doug snapped.

I didn't have to be told twice. I popped my head out of my hatch and bellowed to Cruze. "Race your engine as high as you can, we're not getting enough power!"

She gave me a thumbs-up. That's when I spotted the first wave of creeps no more than 25m away. "Shit!" I barked. "Get this pig going, Doug. We're about to be swarmed!"

He pressed the start button as I climbed out of my hatch and readied my weapon.

"They're coming from all directions!" Cruze bellowed in a voice filled with panic and adrenaline.

A huge cloud of blue smoke poured out of our carrier's exhaust port and floated around both vehicles, obscuring our vision of the creeps bearing down on us.

"Fuck!" I shrieked as the engine continued turning over, pouring more and more smoke out of our vehicle. The air filled with the sound of weapons firing, dropping monsters on the ground one after the other.

There was a loud *whoosh* from the direction Cruze's APC, followed shortly by a *pop* that split the air. Seconds later, we were bathed in yellow light as a parachute flare lit up the darkness.

It would have been better if we were still in the dark because the haunting phosphorescent light revealed a wall of monsters at least ten deep, tripping and stumbling through the bramble. Their unblinking eyes fixed on our two vehicles as dozens upon dozens of creeps lumbered through the acrid smoke towards us.

"Doug ... get this boat started or we're all dead!" I thundered, as I fired off shot after shot. The engine continued turning over and then, miraculously, it coughed, sending a plume of black smoke out of the exhaust port. That was followed by a slow and steady rumble.

"We're good!" shouted Doug. "Get the slave and let's get out of here!"

"No freaking time!" I glanced back at Kate and Sid who stood on either side of the turret, firing into the smoke. "Screw the slave cable, Cruze, get your people the hell out of here!"

"Ya think?" she barked. "Catch up to us!"

The monsters pounded at the hull. I clubbed one that was crawling up the carrier's nose with the butt of my rifle. It slid down across the trim vane and onto the ground. "Everyone inside and hatches down!" I shouted, diving into my hatch.

I heard two loud clangs confirm that both Sid and Kate were secure as I dropped down on my crew commander seat and closed the hatch. *"Go! Go! Go!"* I roared.

The carrier snapped into gear and pushed forward into the swarm of creeps, ploughing them underneath the hull. My heart was racing wildly as I peered into my periscope. There was enough smoke outside that I could only see a few feet in front of us, so I couldn't make out any reference points to aim the carrier. We were driving blindly now – we could hit a rut or roll the carrier.

"Keep us below ten kilometres an hour until we're clear of the creeps," I shouted.

Doug nodded as we pushed on, hitting bumps every two or three seconds. "Maybe another fifty yards until we're out of the smoke!' shouted Doug.

"Keep it steady then," I replied, patting him on the shoulder. "We just need to clear this area, and we'll be good to go."

I slipped on my headset just in time to hear the radio squawk followed by Sid's voice. "I can see over the smoke. Make a hard right and then straighten your wheels, Doug. We'll be out of this in no time."

I pressed the PTT button. "Thanks, Sid. You navigate until we're clear."

"Will do," he replied as I slid off my headset and turned in my seat to face the rear of the carrier. My shirt was dripping with sweat, and my throat was as dry as sandpaper, but I was alive. All of us were, though from the look on Dawson's face, it had been too close a call for her liking. I glanced at Jo, who mouthed the words "are you okay?", so I motioned for her to come up to the front of the APC. She crawled across the jump seats and stood in front of me, her left hand gripping the turret cage to stay upright.

"I'm okay, Jo – are you okay?" I asked, wiping the sweat away from my eyes with the sleeve of my combat shirt.

"You're bleeding," she said, her face awash in concern. "Did they ... did they bite you? Is that why you're bleeding?"

I shook my head. "No – that's what happens when you bump your head after having a lousy dream. Nobody got bitten, Jo. We're all together, and we're going to make it out of here, okay?"

She let out a huge sigh of relief and then threw her arms around me. She buried her face in my chest and started sobbing. I pulled her close and whispered gently in her ear.

"I know that it was insane here for a few minutes, Jo. It was scary for all of us."

She sniffled loudly and gazed up at me. "I thought you got bitten ... I thought you were going to turn into a creeper. I don't want you to die. Mom died and ..."

I kissed the top of her head and squeezed her hard. "Jo, I promised you I would never leave you, and I meant it. I'll fight an entire battalion of those monsters to protect you, and so will everybody else. We all love you, and I'm not going anywhere, got it?"

She sniffed again and said, "I got it. I'm okay now – just real scared about everything. There's no place to hide out here."

"There's an entire world of places to hide," I said, correcting her. "And where we're going, there won't be any need to hide from the creeps because there won't be any creeps."

"A-Are we going to make it there?"

I nodded. "Jo – we are definitely going to make it there. We don't have any other choice. Now I want you to go back to your spot and try to get some rest, okay?"

"Okay," she said, giving me another hug. "I'm sorry I got upset."

"You have nothing to be sorry for, Jo. Go get some kip."

She scrambled back over the jump seat and slipped the helmet onto her head as I spun around and gazed out through my periscope. We'd made it out alive – this time. But I had no idea how many more "this times" we'd have until the monsters would finally succeed. As the nose of our carrier cleared the cloud of diesel exhaust, I saw miles of rolling farmland ahead, and Cruze's panel markers in the distance. I exhaled heavily as I felt my throat tighten. My hands were shaking, and my eyes began to blur through a stinging film of tears.

"I gotta stay focused," I whispered to myself, biting my lip so hard that it started bleeding. "I can't … I *won't* fall apart."

CHAPTER 15

Doug told me that our radio was the reason for the drained battery. A damned freaking ancient vehicle radio set that dated back to the early 1960's. Something inside its pre-transistor era circuitry had sucked the juice on our carrier's battery set dry, and it was a miracle that Ark Two's batteries hadn't been sucked dry as well. As long as the carriers were moving, the engine generated enough power to recharge the batteries but not when they were shut down. We decided to use man packs for communication from now on whenever we went to ground.

We kept on driving for another 90 minutes. Our APC's rolled across acre upon acre of farmland and, every few miles, fording streams of ice-cold water flowing in from the mountains 200 km away. We'd gone hatches up at first light, each of us armed with a carbine and a new determination to make sure we'd never have another close call like the one we'd just lived through.

Every military history book I'd ever read said that soldiers have always dealt with the aftermath of a battle in their own private way. Some write letters home to family, while others immerse themselves in cleaning their weapons or sharpening their bayonets, preparing for the next inevitable skirmish. But the only thing going through a soldier's mind during these relatively silent periods is a gambler's game, wondering what the odds are of making it out of the next battle alive. It's probably how the human mind is hard-wired. Nobody has time for post-traumatic stress disorder anymore – we're all too busy trying not to get torn to pieces.

For our team of survivors, there was vehicle maintenance to perform as soon as we reached a safe place to stop.

I manoeuvred my hatch door in front of me to act as a wind screen as I gazed over at Ark Two. Pam Cruze was standing tall and proud, her face a mask of determination as her carrier bounded over the uneven ground. I felt a small nudge of envy as she glanced my way, sending me a short nod that told me everything was okay with her team. Even though Cruze was the same age as me, she possessed qualities that I didn't. She always kept a sharp, business-like approach to those of us left alive, and it didn't matter if she was doing something as insignificant as drawing up a sentry list or assigning tasks for her team. There was purposefulness to Pam Cruze that I lacked, and I secretly wished that I could be even one tenth as brave as she was.

I'd have been happy if Pam was leading our group, and I'd even pushed for her to take command, but she told me to get my head out of my ass.

We kept a healthy distance from the small farmhouses that dotted the landscape. Dead livestock lay rotting in the fields, fallen victim to either starvation or disease. Most were ripped open, their ribcages exposed to the dry, dusty air, and we couldn't tell whether they'd been eaten by creeps or coyotes. We could have gone scrounging, but after our run-in on the outskirts of Airdrie, I think every one of us wanted to put as much distance as possible between our APC's and built-up areas. I pulled my map out and oriented it to the rolling farmland. By my estimation, we'd pushed on a further 30km from where we'd gone to ground. We were probably somewhere between the tiny village of Cremona and the town of Carstairs. I folded up the map and stuffed it back in my pocket as I hailed Cruze on the radio.

"Ark Two, how's your levels?" I asked.

Cruze ducked down into her hatch and reappeared a few seconds later, her eyes fixed firmly on the way ahead. "We're about three-quarters full. My boat is running a little hot, though."

"Roger," I replied. "We're closer to Cremona than we are to Carstairs – it's probably a good idea for us to stop and check fluid levels."

"Sounds good to me," she answered. I raised everyone in our carrier on the intercom.

"Bring her to a stop, Doug. Listen up, everyone … we're going to do some quick carrier maintenance before we press on. Get out the oil, the coolant, and the tool kit. Sid, you'll help Doug while Dawson and I keep watch. Be ready to move out on a minute's notice." The air brakes hissed as the carrier pulled to a stop, and Doug lowered his driver's seat and removed the engine panel. I climbed up top along with Dawson, our weapons at the ready. We'd stopped in the middle of a field that probably had gone fallow the year before; the ground was chalk-coloured and the chill morning breeze kicked up small plumes of topsoil that drifted across the front of our carrier. An old barn, grey and weathered after decades of unrelenting prairie wind, stood about 500m to our right. The closest farmhouse had burned to the ground, and the only sign that human beings had ever lived there was the crumbling foundation poking up out of the scorched grass.

There were also charred human remains.

"They've been there a hell of a long time," said Dawson. "Probably died in the first month or so – just like pretty much everyone else. I wonder how fast it spread out here, in the rural parts of the province."

Jo called out to me. "Is it safe for me to come up top? I don't want to be stuck inside anymore. I feel like a sardine."

I scanned the area for any signs of creeps or survivors, and reached down into the rear of the carrier to pull her topside. Jo crawled over to the turret and took a seat on the hatch cover. "You wanted to be a help," I said cautiously. "So here's your job: sit tight on the turret and keep a lookout for Doug and Sid. If you see anything that looks like a creep you start shouting, okay?"

She blinked. "Okay … but what if I see something else – someone like us?"

"One second," I said. I dropped back into the carrier, reappearing a moment later with a pair of binoculars. I knelt down in front of Jo. "Good thing you mentioned that, kiddo. See, I always knew you were way smarter than me. All right, here's my binos – you know how to use them. If you see anything, creep or otherwise, you let us know. And then you high-tail it back down into the carrier."

She nodded firmly as Sid Toomey jumped down from the side of the carrier, a cotton duck tool bag in one hand, and a flashlight in the other. He did a quick walk around the hull to look for any visible signs of damage and then crawled underneath.

"The hull looks okay," he called out. "No damage to the prop-shafts."

"Good!" shouted Doug Manybears. "Now get back in the boat and find me some oil – we're down about two quarts. And some water, we need to top off these batteries."

Cruze's carrier was parked about 200m to our left, and I could see Melanie Dixon and Kenny checking the trim vane while Cruze stood lookout. I did likewise, keeping a watchful eye for movement from a copse of poplar trees on the horizon. "Please tell me we won't need a slave again, Doug, because our cable is somewhere on the outskirts of Airdrie," I said as I pulled out a dipstick that was as long as my leg.

Doug's head popped up through the crew commander's hatch. He had a smear of grease across his forehead and a large aluminum funnel in his hand. "That's why I packed a spare," he said with a wink. "It's under the secondary floor panel in the rear."

"You are a wise man, brother. Did anyone ever tell you that?"

Sid Toomey climbed up the side of the carrier and tossed his flashlight into the turret. "Geez, do you two guys need a room or something? I'm gonna gag here."

"He's not my type – not enough Sarcee in him," said Doug. "Also, he's the wrong sex."

"Mmmmm sex," Sid purred. "I'd forgotten what that looked like."

Dawson tossed a shell casing at Sid, hitting him in the side of the head. "Yeah – maybe can the potty talk when we're around you-know-who?"

Sid's face flushed red, and he quickly climbed into the turret. "Sorry about that – didn't see the midget there. I'll do a disappearing act."

I glanced at my watch. "How much longer until we can get rolling, Doug?"

I heard a few clangs from the engine compartment, followed quickly by a string of angry sounding words in the unmistakable dialect of a First Nations person with a huge knot in his face. "Assuming this piece of crap starts up properly, maybe five minutes. Don't get your hopes up, though – I've been wrong before."

"We *can* get it going, though, right, Doug?" said Dawson, her eyes fixed firmly on the old barn.

His head popped up through the driver's hatch this time, wrench in hand. "If I have anything to say about it, we will," he replied. "Toomey is just topping off the batteries with water. Once he's done, I'll try."

I glanced over at Cruze's carrier, and she threw me a wave. I nodded back, then gestured that I was going to hail her on the radio. "Jo ... we're going to leave in a few. Want to hop back inside and get me the man pack? Oh ... and maybe a granola bar or something, my stomach is growling."

"You bet," she said, dropping back in the rear hatch. I heard the sound of gear being moved around down below, and in seconds, Jo stood up and heaved the radio onto the top of the hull. "Here you go – I'll come back in a minute with a granola bar for everyone."

"Thanks, kiddo," I said, grabbing the handset. "You're like our nanny. I always wanted one of those."

"I'm not a nanny," she said with a slight edge to her voice. "I'm part of this team so don't talk to me like I'm just a kid, okay?"

I grimaced and felt my face beginning to redden. "Um ... I guess you told me. Sorry, Jo."

"Uh-huh," she said as she started shifting kit around the back of the carrier.

I knelt down to fiddle with the squelch for a moment and then hailed Cruze through the handset. "Ark Two, we're going to move out in five if you guys are ready."

The radio hissed. "All our levels are good, no damage to the carrier. We can leave as soon as you give the word. Where do we want to RV?"

I pulled out my map again. "Stand by, Cruze," I answered. "I need to shoot a bearing, and Doug needs to start up the rig. If we're dead in the water again, we'll need a boost."

"Roger that," she said through a haze of static.

I unfolded the map and chewed my lip for a moment, studying possible access routes that would keep us clear of built-up areas. The closest military detachment that wasn't in a city was Alsask on the border between Alberta and Saskatchewan. That would be our first destination, and I hoped like hell there would be some remnants of what used to be the Canadian army for us to link up with. The best thing would be to avoid even the smallest towns and head on a north-east bearing – that meant a combination of cross-country driving and using cattle-and-grain-farm back roads from Carstairs to the border. And, at some point, we'd have to cross over Highway Two. There would likely be roamers because of the inevitable car pile-ups. I decided that we'd drive up until we were a few hundred meters from Highway Two, and do a little reconnaissance.

I poked my head into the driver's hatch and said, "Doug – you ready to roll?"

He nodded as he replaced the engine panel. "Yep – everyone good to go?"

I glanced back over my shoulder to see Jo waving at me and Dawson's legs standing on the jump seat. Sid was seated comfortably in the turret, so I gave Doug a thumbs up and told him to start the carrier.

He leaned over to disengage the neutral start switch and then pressed the start button. To everyone's surprise, Ark One started up without even a groan of protest. I patted Doug on the shoulder and grabbed my handset for the intercom.

"Sid and Dawson – cover me. I'm jumping off to shoot a bearing."

I lifted myself topside and scampered down the nose of the carrier, onto the hard dusty ground. I pulled out my Silva compass and looked out on the horizon line for the tallest object I could find. In seconds, I'd spotted it; an electrical tower about 5km away. I pulled out my map, oriented it to the ground and then scanned it for a symbol showing where there might be power lines in the area. As luck would have it, the map didn't show me a damned thing, so I quickly shot three bearings and did a three-point resection to confirm my place on the map, just as I had learned from Sergeant Green. We were precisely 8km from Carstairs – the power line would have to suffice as a reference point. I'd shoot another bearing when we arrived, and then another one after that; I wasn't going to take any chances after my colossal cock-up the night before.

I folded the map and stuffed it in my pocket. According to the resection, the highway should be a few kilometres past the electrical tower. There was some high ground near a junction with grid road 83, so it seemed as good a spot as any to survey the main Edmonton highway for any possible threats.

In minutes, I was back in the crew commander's hatch. I slipped on my headset and raised Cruze on the radio. "Ark Two –

confirm this location for me, over."

The radio hissed. "Ark Two, send, over."

I squeezed the handset. "Grid 923 561. Verify, over."

A gust of wind blew a cloud of dust a few feet away from the nose of the carrier, and I crossed my fingers this time, hoping Cruze would confirm the grid reference.

"Ark One, it checks out," said Cruze.

I heaved a sigh of relief and said, "Thanks, Cruze. We'll RV at the electrical tower on the horizon. Once we get there, we'll have a quick scan of Highway Two – we need to get safely across."

"Good plan, Dave," she answered. "We'll steer clear of Red Deer. Where's our final destination today, do you figure?"

I pressed the handset, and the radio crackled. "A place called Dinsmore. Highway 582 runs through it, and the map shows we should be pretty much alone the entire way. It's around 120 clicks from here. Your fuel topped up?"

"Yeah, we're good," Cruze answered, glancing down at her map too. "Looks like a decent route to take for now. Let's hope we don't run into any unwanted company along the way."

"Roger that," I said, feeling a nudge of comfort that Cruze agreed with my plan. "Let's roll."

"Let's roll," she answered, her radio hissing loudly.

CHAPTER 16

We ate on the fly.

Individual Meal Packs, or IMP's, taste pretty lousy even when they've been heated. Eating them cold does little to kill the nasty flavour of the damned things. The aluminum pouches are often half-filled with liquid, so depending on what your meal is, it might be dripping wet. Naturally, I got another ham omelette which looked more like an over-stretched hockey puck – assuming hockey pucks are yellow disks with flecks of mystery meat inside. I washed it down with a cup of instant coffee - again, cold. We'd decided early on that we'd have our hot meal after we secured a safe zone in Dinsmore. Usually, a hot meal would be something to look forward to, but IMP's leave little to the imagination, so you need to pretend you're eating something else entirely or you'll go nuts. Still, I think everyone in my carrier was thankful for being together as a group, and for having survived another day.

It took us a good 20 minutes to arrive at the electrical tower. The steel and iron skeleton stood five storeys high, and if you followed the power lines, you'd see another electrical tower every 1000m or so. The ground was flat and relatively free of obstacles, though we had to cross over a number of grid roads. I fought the urge to use them, even though it meant everyone in our two APC's bounced around like they were ping pong balls. We didn't want to raise massive plumes of dust that would attract creeps or survivalist nut jobs.

Cruze's APC pulled up next to mine, and together we surveyed the ground. We were perched atop a small ridge, a dusty breeze blowing through the steel girders of the electrical tower. Cruze kept her eyes fixed on Highway Two. The good news was there weren't any pileups, but that didn't mean there wouldn't be dangers to face, once we found a suitable spot to cross.

"What do you think?" I asked as I lowered my binoculars.

"It looks clear enough," she said as she climbed onto our carrier. "Mind you, we're up on high ground, so it's hard to know for sure. How far do you figure we have to go to cross? I'm thinking about five or six clicks anyway."

"That's what I figured," I replied. "There's probably going to be cattle-fencing on both sides of the highway. We'll have to cut the wire if we're going to get both carriers through. I'll do it."

Cruze snorted. "I thought the rule was, never volunteer for anything."

I shrugged as I gazed out through my binoculars. "Someone's gotta do it. Might as well be me. Listen, about what happened this morning … I fucked up royally."

She cocked an eyebrow and said, "I know. And everyone else knows, too. You can't afford another screw-up either. This team is looking to you to get us to Sanctuary Base alive, so at least when it comes to navigating, double check with Dawson or me. I don't think anyone is going to question you on tactics if we wind up knee-deep in the shit again. You proved yourself as a good tactical leader with the nut jobs that attacked us."

I nodded, and I felt my face begin to flush. At least Cruze was still backing me. It was the only positive aspect of our near miss a few hours earlier.

"I didn't want to be in charge, Cruze," I said quietly, deliberately avoiding her gaze. "Christ, why the hell would anyone want to be in charge? I'm a freaking military strategy book worm. I read tactical manuals and military history stuff."

She shrugged. "You're the guy who helped Sergeant Green come up with Plan Z in the first place. You were his 2IC – he picked you to back him up."

"And I picked you to back me up," I replied.

"Which I am doing to the best of my ability. But for fuck sake, Dave, if you have doubts about our next move, talk to me. Talk to Dawson if you have to. You can't bear all this shit on your shoulders, got it?"

I heaved a weary sigh and said, "Got it. So we need to cut that wire then."

"You'll also need some help to pull back that barbed wire and ground-guide the carriers through. I'll give you a hand."

"Thanks, Cruze. For everything."

"Yep."

"How's your fuel?"

Cruze gave me an uneasy look. "We've about a quarter of a

tank right now. I've got four jerry cans left – this pig burns diesel like it's nobody's business. How about you?"

I glanced back at the jerry cans strapped to the side of the carrier. "About the same. At this rate, we'll be hoofing it by this time tomorrow – we're going to have to do some major-league scrounging. Your people up for that?"

Cruze exhaled heavily and then gulped back a mouthful of water from her water bottle. "Yes and no. I think we'd all like to get out and stretch our legs, but everyone is scared shitless about the chances of another close encounter after nearly getting our asses chewed off this morning."

"Yeah … we'll have to provide covering fire from the carriers in case we get into trouble. I'm thinking that we'll go in with my carrier while you do perimeter security. I'd like you to take Jo with you while we're out there … can you do that?"

Cruze cocked an eyebrow. "Don't you think Jo should be asked about how she feels? She's a pretty damned good shot, Dave. It might be good for her to –"

I cut her off. "If our carrier runs into trouble, you'll be able to scoot the hell out of there – if she stays with us and something happens to me, then I can't be there to protect her. Just do this for me, okay?"

She threw me a sympathetic smile and slipped on a pair of combat gloves. "It's cool, Dave. I'll grab some wire cutters out of the tool-bag and fill everyone in on the plan. Ready to move in five minutes?"

"Yeah," I said, with a note of relief in my voice. "Thanks, Pam – I'll go break the news to Jo, and let my team know about our next move."

***

Jo didn't kick up a fuss about moving into Ark Two, but I had to promise to let her act as lookout when we crossed over the highway. Dawson took the news that I'd volunteered our team for scrounging with grudging acceptance. She knew we'd eventually have to get more fuel for the carriers – she just hadn't counted on our running out of diesel so quickly, but she held me to my promise about finding something for her to read. Sid, on the other hand, was a breath away from doing the happy dance. Of everyone left alive after Day Zero, Sid Toomey was the one person who actually seemed to enjoy fighting the monsters. He'd even fashioned a close-quarter combat tool: an aluminum baseball bat with a four-inch spike that he'd welded smack-dab onto the sweet spot. He gave it a name – *the eradicator*. I'd seen him take down five creeps in less than ten seconds with that thing, swinging it with the precision of a major-league home run champion. A murderous fire burned in his eyes whenever the opportunity for close-quarter combat arose, and it was as if Sid had a sixth sense for a creep's next move – he always seemed to know where a monster was hiding or when it was about to lunge at him from the shadows.

Sid was also a natural born scrounger. Every military unit has one. A scrounger is the guy who can get anything for anyone, more often than not, for a price. Before Day Zero, I'd seen him scrounge up everything from fresh rations to a brand new Jeep. If anyone was going to find us diesel, it was Sid.

I was grateful for having him on my team. We all were, even if he drove Kate Dawson nuts nine times out of ten. If I wasn't a guy and completely oblivious to the way the female mind works, I'd say that Kate was carrying a torch for the big goon – or maybe a book of matches.

Naturally, he made a big show of pulling *the eradicator* out of his rucksack, and Dawson made an equally big show of rolling her eyes. I decided he'd be team leader for the scrounging party. Dawson and I would follow his every command – the fact that Sid Toomey had his bat in his hand made our chances of surviving a run-in with the creeps that much stronger.

I crawled back into my crew commander's seat and confirmed that Ark Two was ready to go, then tapped Doug Manybears on the head and pointed to our destination. He slipped the carrier into first gear, and we coasted down the forward slope of the hill, the engine retarder brake shrieking like a banshee the entire time. Cruze kept her APC no more than a few feet away to my left as I kept an eye out for boulders or anything else that could damage our suspension. The sky grew darker the further east we pushed on, and I felt a few drops of rain tapping against the top of my head. I glanced back at the turret to see Sid puffing away on a cigarette. He threw me a wild-eyed grin and stubbed the butt on the surface of the hull, tossing it as we bounded over the uneven ground. 20 minutes later, we were about 100m from Highway Two, our carriers parked on an embankment that dropped a good 15 feet to the shoulder of the roadway.

Every one of us scanned the area for any signs of recent activity. There was an upturned Winnebago about a hundred yards from where we'd intended to cross, and a dozen cars and pickup trucks on both sides of the highway. But all were a safe distance away from where we'd cut through the cattle fence, and the area appeared to pose little threat.

But the abandoned vehicles weren't what grabbed our attention. The rotting remains of two people lashed to the fencepost a few hundred meters in front of us was what got everyone on edge. I grabbed my binoculars and peered out at the scene. The bodies didn't show any signs of having fallen victim to the creeps. They'd been bound to the fencepost with yellow vinyl rope. Each was gagged, and they looked to have had their throats cut. A home-made plywood sign had been fastened to the barbed wire between the two bodies. The words *"Welcome to Eden. Stay the Fuck Out"* were emblazoned on the weathered surface in red paint.

"What in the bat shit crazy hell is *that?*" Sid choked through a haze of static on the intercom.

"A warning," I said gloomily.

My radio hissed as Cruze's voice filled my headset. "You seeing what I'm seeing?"

"Roger that," I answered, unable to take my eyes off the bodies. "We've edged up onto someone's territory, though I don't see any signs of movement out there."

"I could skirt up the edge of the highway and see if there's any other place to cross," said Cruze.

"Maybe," I replied. "But that would waste our fuel something awful. We need to conserve every drop."

"Well, we can't sit here all day, and we're going to have to cross at some point. If we go north, we'll be cutting it painfully close to Red Deer, and there'll be creeps on the roadway. If we go south, we're back on the outskirts of Airdrie again, and we'll lose whatever frigging distance we've gained."

"Roger," I said. "Get your carrier next to mine. We need to plot a course of action, and we need to do it fast. It's just past two in the afternoon, and we've got a little over four hours of daylight left."

The radio squawked. "Stand by."

I peered out over the edge of my carrier to see Cruze's APC turn hard left. In moments, she was parked inches away. I ordered everyone topside.

There was a fine mist of drizzle coming down now, not enough to get you soaking wet but more than enough to remind us all to dig out our rain ponchos. Doug Manybears bummed a cigarette off Sid and took a deep haul as he whispered something in Sarcee.

"What's that?" I asked.

Doug exhaled a plume of smoke. "Prayer for the dead," he said with an edge to his voice. "Whoever did that shit to them … they're some kind of evil pricks for sure."

Sid cocked his carbine. "Well, let's find the bastards and end them," he said, a little too gleefully for anyone's liking.

Cruze hopped onto the hull of my carrier, shotgun in hand. "Nobody is ending anyone, Sid. Our goal is to get to the Alsask detachment, preferably with everyone here still alive."

"Is it okay for me to come up top?" asked Jo, poking her head through the rear of Ark Two.

Damn. I didn't want her to see the bodies, but she was within earshot of our discussion, so she knew something bad must have happened. She'd also made it clear for hours that she'd like to do more to earn her keep, so I spun around on my heels and gestured for her to climb topside.

"You can come up, Jo. There's some bad stuff up ahead, but you're part of our team – you deserve to know. I've got a job for you."

Melanie Dixon lifted Jo onto the hull of the carrier. She scurried up to the front of the turret and stared wide-eyed at the two bodies lashed to the fence.

"No way any creepers did that, Mel," she said in a surprisingly matter-of-fact tone as she gazed out at the dead bodies. "People did that … people like us."

Mel put a hand on her shoulder. "They're not people like us,

Jo," she said softly. "Not even close."

"All right!" I interrupted. "Everyone keep an eye on your arcs of fire while we figure out our next move. This isn't a freaking social call – we have a decision to make."

The team adopted their firing positions atop the carrier, each covering the left and right sides of the APC. I handed Jo a spare carbine and pointed to my eyes and then to the rear of the carrier. She didn't even flinch as she quickly cocked the weapon and headed to the back. I studied the map alongside Cruze, and then I looked out on the horizon for anything that might resemble potential ambush sites, but aside from the occasional silo and barn, there was nothing that would give anyone a commanding view for miles.

"Whoever did this – they've got our attention," I said, glancing at the bodies.

Cruze fished a granola bar out of her breast pocket and began nibbling on a corner of it. "What are you thinking?"

I pointed to the fence line. "I guess they're trespassers. Two survivors who unwittingly wandered into the tribe's claim and were killed for making that mistake."

"Hell of a mistake to make," she said, taking a big bite out of her granola bar. "Look … it doesn't matter if that pair wandered into Eden or were killed by their own people, we need to cross this highway, and we're going to be encroaching on claimed territory. We're going to come into contact with them. It's not a matter of if, but when."

I glanced back at Sid Toomey, who was puffing on another cigarette and scanning the horizon for any signs of life. "Toomey wants to get into a fight, but I don't. I wish we knew the boundaries of this Eden – we could just skirt around it."

Cruze folded the map and handed it to me. "As I see it, we're in the shit whether we head north and try to flank Eden's territory or whether we trespass on it. I say we cut the wire and push on. We'll just have to be extra stealthy and try like hell to avoid whoever these assholes are."

I stuffed the map into my pants pocket. "That's what I'm thinking, too, Cruze. We still have to do some scrounging. If we run out of fuel, we're going to be hooped, though."

She nodded and placed a hand on my shoulder. "Dave, we've been hooped since day freaking zero, if you hadn't noticed. But from where I stand, we're still armed to the teeth. If these jerks take a shot at us, we'll blow them off the freaking map."

It was going to be a huge risk, but every day since the siege had been a game of managing the risks and hoping you'd pull through. And who was to say we'd encounter anyone at all? For all we know, the Eden tribe might just be a small band of survivors like us. Still, there was a predatory quality to the way in which they'd painted those words of warning.

I decided that in the end, it didn't matter. I crawled back into my hatch and pursed my lips tightly as I fixed my eyes on the fuel gauge. We had slightly less than a quarter of a tank of diesel left, and that meant we had about a day's worth of fuel in the jerry cans. Cruze and I ordered that we top up our vehicles – there was no way of conserving it. We'd cross over, and we'd do some scrounging. We'd find some diesel, today.

And probably wind up in a fire fight.

CHAPTER 17

Everyone recognized that the risks of veering north into the vicinity of Red Deer outweighed the risk of running into whoever the hell had murdered those two people. Sid was spoiling for a fight. Maybe that was his own ingrained sense of justice, or it might have been the fact that he was getting restless, sitting in a turret with twin machine guns and nobody to shoot at.

We fuelled up both carriers with the remaining diesel and cut through the wire on both sides of the highway. All hands were hatches up and keeping a watchful eye for signs of life as the carriers bounced across empty farmland. The drizzle had ended, but the temperature was dropping, and I could see my breath every time I exhaled. It was probably going to snow; not an uncommon occurrence in November when you live on the Canadian prairie.

I slipped off my combat jacket and pulled a sweater over my head. I really hoped it wouldn't snow. Whoever these Eden survivalists might be, they could easily follow our tracks and come up on us from behind. Then again, there's only so much stealth you can use when you're bombing up the back forty in an armoured personnel carrier. The constant rumble from our engines could be heard from miles away, so I decided that whoever was out there, they had to know we were coming.

They just didn't know *what* was coming.

It's one thing to whack a pair of survivors who might have made the tragic mistake of trespassing on your land claim. It's another thing entirely when the trespassers are carrying automatic weapons, mortars, high explosive charges and light anti-tank weapons on board. From a purely tactical perspective, the Eden tribe would be out-gunned. Save for a RCMP station, the closest establishment carrying a stockpile of conventional military armaments was in Camp Wainwright, a good six-hundred kilometres to the north-east.

Surely their land claim didn't stretch that far. I popped back up in the hatch and glanced at my watch. It was just past four in the afternoon, and we'd been driving for more than an hour since we crossed Highway Two. The first place we came to where people might once have lived wasn't even a village. On the map, it was called Neapolis, but it was nothing more than a few barns, a tourist information shack and a couple of rundown bungalows. We skirted along the sides of grid road 3-12 so that we wouldn't kick up any gravel dust – that could be seen for miles by anyone in a sentry post. It was the best I could come up with in the way of stealth. I glanced down at my map. Dinsmore wasn't more than a few kilometres to the east, so I hailed Ark Two on the radio.

"We've still got a ways to go before we hit Dinsmore. Bring your carrier up alongside mine."

"On it," Cruze replied, as we edged up to an enormous red barn.

"We'll stop here, Doug," I said through the intercom. Our carrier came to a gentle stop. Within seconds, Ark Two had pulled up beside us, and I looked around for any signs of life.

The radio hissed. "One road into town and one road out," said Cruze. "If they've got it blocked off, we could be in trouble."

"Agreed. Get on my tail once I cross onto the main drag. We'll creep forward until we see anything that might offer some decent scrounging."

"Well, there's a barn, Dave," she replied. "There might be a tractor or something inside."

"Good point. Give us some cover while we go inside and investigate. How's Jo doing?"

Cruze answered in a haze of static. "Jo's good. She's having a big nap in the back. Mel's doing her level best to let her sleep."

"Cool … let her sleep some more." I answered back.

I hit the intercom. "Listen up! Cruze is going to provide cover for us. Dawson, toss down a couple of Jerry cans and Sid, grab the siphoning tube from the tool kit. Grab your personal weapons, and we'll check out that barn."

I slipped off my headset and grabbed a pair of fully-loaded magazines for my carbine. I climbed up out of my crew commander's hatch and hopped down off the nose of the carrier. Dawson rushed up beside me with a pair of Jerry cans in hand, her carbine slung over her shoulder while Sid tripped off the front of the APC, nearly doing a face-plant in the process.

"You're one graceful SOB," I said, as I watched him get back to his feet and brush himself off.

He shrugged and said, "Whavevs ... I want a small extended line with Dawson in the middle. Keep your weapons at the ready – we don't have a clue what we might be walking into."

I stood up and scurried over to Dawson's left, keeping my left finger along the trigger guard of my carbine and flipping off the safety with my thumb. Dawson tossed an empty can to Sid and pointed the barrel of her weapon toward the barn.

"I'm ready," she said firmly. "Let's get in and get out."

"You good, Sid?" I asked.

He nodded. "Dude, I'm always good. Let's go steal us some diesel."

We crept up to the barn, listening carefully. The chill breeze blew through the waist-high crab grass, and I kept an eye for trip wires and booby traps as we approached the barn door. The wind whistled as it blew through the gaps in the wood. The main door opened and closed, making a clunking sound every few seconds as a length of hemp rope waved back and forth like a pendulum. We got our backs up against the exterior wall and slunk up to the entrance as Sid pulled out his flashlight.

"You guys cover my ass," he whispered, readying himself to shine the light inside. Dawson and I nodded as he aimed his barrel through the gap and flashed the light into the darkness. After quickly scanning the barn, he slowly opened the door with the toe of his boot and stepped inside. Dawson and I followed with our weapons at the ready.

I scanned the drive bay and saw an old Massey Ferguson tractor that was literally buried in bird droppings, at least a few inches thick. If there was any diesel in its tanks, it would have long ago lost whatever octane it once possessed – the tractor looked as if it been parked in the barn for decades. I stepped through the entry, my weapon at the ready, and shone my flashlight across the hay-covered floor. A pair of field mice skirted underneath the tractor's small front tires, and I was startled by a pigeon that took off through a hole in the roof.

"It freaking stinks in here," said Sid, as he eyed a ladder leading up to a hay loft.

"That's the natural smell of decay," said Dawson. "This isn't so bad when you consider the alternative."

"Sounds romantic," he snorted.

"Pfft ... what do you know about romance?" said Dawson.

"Okay ... shut up and keep your heads in the game, guys," I said as I shone my light around the back of the tractor, picking out a wall of hay bales stretching up to the bottom of the loft. As if she'd read my mind, Dawson scrambled over to the door and poked the barrel of her carbine inside. It opened with a screech and Dawson shone a light through the doorway.

"Clear," she said firmly.

I dropped to one knee and gazed up at the hay loft. "I think this barn is a dud, Sid."

"There's a loft, I'll have a quick look, and if there's nothing worth scooping up, we'll head out."

In seconds, he was climbing up a rickety wooden ladder. I gazed around the barn and decided that if it had once been part of a functional farm, then it was probably before I was born. I felt a nudge of disappointment that we hadn't found anything worth scrounging, but there were likely to be hundreds of barns between now and the time our fuel tanks ran dry. I was never a betting person, but there was still a chance we'd find something that ran on diesel; I didn't care if it was a pickup truck.

"Oh shit," Sid called out. "Dave ... you need to see this."

I glanced at Dawson and pointed to my eyes and then the doorway. She nodded as I walked over to the ladder and began climbing up. He pulled me up with one hand, and I steadied myself on the uneven floor. I glanced down and decided that a fall from this height would probably break something important, so I kept a healthy distance from the edge of the loft, following Sid over to a small wall of hay bales. What I saw told me that someone had been in this barn before us. Somebody downright evil.

In front of me was the bodies of a man, a woman and two little girls lying face down. The four were holding hands with one another. Each had a portion of their heads missing, and I spotted four small-calibre shell casings on the floor of the loft not more than three feet from where I stood. The word "Eden" was painted on the wall above them in white.

"These people are a family," I whispered, trying to contain the horror in my voice. "A *family*, Sid."

He nodded, his jaw tightening. I could almost feel the rage bubbling up inside him. "They were fucking executed, Dave. They'd probably come into the barn to take refuge, or to bed down for the night. And these Eden pricks frigging shot them."

"These are fresh kills – otherwise, we would have smelled them the moment we walked in the barn. Maybe they'd arrived in a car or something. Came up the main road and alerted a sentry."

Sid shook his head. "That or a security patrol – to cover this much land, they've gotta be using vehicles, and if that's the case, then they have access to fuel."

I nodded, barely able to take my eyes off the grisly scene. "There's nothing we can do for these four. Let's get back to the carriers and push on to Dinsmore."

He blinked. "You itching for some payback, Dave?"

"I'm not itching, Sid. But Dinsmore is a few miles up the road, and if it's occupied by breathers, then the odds are they're Eden people. And I have to tell you: if they decide to start shooting at us, they're going to pay dearly for it."

Sid slapped me on the shoulder. "That's the smartest thing you've said all day, buddy. Let's head out."

Six people dead. Each of them murdered simply for being in the wrong place at the wrong time. A small knot of anger began burning inside my chest as I gazed down at the two little girls. They couldn't have been much older than Jo when they were killed – put to death because their parents made the mistake of trespassing into Eden. I clenched my fists together so tightly that my fingernails dug into my skin and immediately thought of Jo back in the other carrier. I wanted her with me at all times. Nobody was going to get my kid sister. Ever.

We climbed back down the ladder. Dawson gazed up at me as I slung my carbine over my shoulder.

"We're heading back to the carrier, Kate," I said with a sharp edge to my voice. "Grab those Jerry cans and bomb up."

Dawson didn't have to be asked twice. She dashed to the entrance, grabbing both fuel cans without even stopping.

It was starting to look like Sid was going to wind up in a scrap after all.

And God help the Eden tribe if they decided to start shooting at us.

CHAPTER 18

Sergeant Green always told me that no soldier in their right mind goes looking for trouble. If anything, they like to avoid conflict as much as possible. Killing fellow human beings isn't something that comes naturally to even the best-trained infantryman. All my tactical manuals taught me that the role of the infantry is to close with and destroy the enemy, but they didn't say squat about the end of the freaking world. Conventional rules of engagement ended on Day Zero, and all that I could think about were the two little girls, killed by some twisted individuals who'd decided to mete out their own kind of justice. A harsh, bloody set of laws that mirrored the harsh and bloody new world that we all were living in. I didn't know who the hell the Eden tribe might be or what their fighting strength consisted of, but I did know one thing: those two little girls and their parents were murdered in cold blood.

I stormed through the entrance to the barn and doubled back to the carriers with Sid Toomey in tow. Cruze and Mel Dixon were standing atop their APC keeping a watchful eye on our surroundings.

"Prep for battle!" I barked, as I climbed up the side of my APC.

Cruze threw me a firm nod and then gestured for Melanie to climb into the turret as she slid into her crew commander hatch.

I slipped on my headset, ignoring the rumbling from our engine. Doug Manybears gave me a worried look as he glanced at me over his shoulder.

I spun around in my seat to see Sid drop down into the turret. He cocked both machine guns as Dawson pulled out a case of M69 fragmentation grenades. She gently removed four of them from their containers and flipped off the safety clips. I reached over, and she handed me two grenades which I dropped into the waist pockets of my combat jacket. I took a deep breath as I adjusted the squelch on my radio and then I stood up in my hatch.

"Ark Two stand by for orders," I said amid a haze of static.

I glanced down at the map. Dinsmore was no more than 7km

away from our current location. The gravel road heading in and out of town was wide enough to accommodate two APC's abreast, but I didn't want to present too obvious a target as we approached the village's outskirts. *Infantry Section and Platoon in Battle* said that for mechanized small party raids, the proper thing to do would be to use one carrier to draw the enemy's fire while the other carrier provided supporting fire from the flank. According to the contour lines on my map, there were no natural high features from which Cruze or I could act as supporting fire, so the best option would be to do a combat run right through the center of the village, drawing their fire and identifying their strengths before doing a full-blown assault.

I gave my head a hard shake as the anger in the pit of my stomach bubbled away like an unwatched pot of boiling water. I needed to stay focused; our goal had originally been to scrounge for diesel and supplies. We hadn't counted on running into a stronghold of road warrior wannabes, and we'd already seen that the Eden tribe weren't the kind of people who'd be prepared to sit down and negotiate. I wasn't crazy about getting into a firefight, but six people had been murdered, and I'd be damned if I was going to lose one of our team to those assholes.

I squeezed my handset and said, "Okay listen up. Ark One will proceed to Dinsmore with Ark Two staying three vehicle lengths to the rear. We'll be hatches down on my command, over!"

The radio hissed loudly. "Ark Two, Roger, over."

"If you're wondering why we've gone full-blown tactical, it's because a family of four were shot dead inside that barn. They were put to death just like the pair lashed to the cattle fence back at Highway Two. It doesn't take a rocket scientist to figure out the kind of people we're dealing with. I don't want to get into a fight with anyone, but we're here, and we've all been trained. We'll head into town with the goal of keeping ourselves protected. We will not fire the first shot – I say again, we will draw their fire. Over."

"Copy that," Cruze replied.

I exhaled heavily. "We've all stared death in the face many times over but we're dealing with some seriously fucked up people. I don't know what their strength is, but I do know one thing: this Eden clan is going to rue the day the King's Own rolled into town."

Static sprayed out of the speakers on the radio. "Ark Two, Roger. We knew this would eventually happen … my team is ready. We'll make sure that Jo stays hatches down."

"No," I answered back. "I want her in my carrier. Send her over now."

"Ark Two, Roger that," said Cruze.

I intended for my carrier to take the lead into Dinsmore and that meant a slightly greater risk for Jo than if she were to stay inside Ark Two, but after seeing that dead family, it was the only way I could actually feel right about what we're going to do. If anything happened to Jo in Cruze's carrier, I would never forgive myself for not being there to save her.

Dawson flipped off the combat locks and opened the right rear door of our carrier. Jo hopped inside and threw me a worried look as I motioned for her to come up to the crew commander's seat. She flung her arms around me and gave me a hug. "Everyone is scared, David," she said, her voice filled with the vibration of the carrier's engine. "There's going to be more shooting, right?"

I nodded as I lifted her onto my lap. "Yes, Jo. There's going to be more shooting, but that's the world we live in now. Nearly every day since we started hiding out at the armoury has had some shooting. You know it, and I know it. But this time it's different."

She tilted her head to the right. "Different? How come?"

I pursed my lips tightly. Jo had seen other children die during the handful of times that Mewata Armoury was breached by the creeps. She'd had her own close call with a trio that broke through the old rusted window frame in our sleeping quarters. She'd shot one of them before Sid bashed them all to pulp with his baseball bat of doom.

I decided a little honesty couldn't be a bad thing. I owed Jo that much.

"It's different because we're not going to be shooting at creeps," I said firmly. "It's going to be like those people that were trying to kill us when we were escaping from the city, only these ones are way worse. Do you know what we found inside the barn?"

She nodded. "Four people were murdered – a couple of them were kids. A family."

"And we're a family," I replied. "The bad guys are going to want our carriers, weapons and supplies. They'll gun down every last one of us, Jo. We have to be ready for anything, and if that means we kill them, then that's what we're going to do."

Her eyes narrowed sharply and Jo said, "I'll wear my helmet and make sure that Sid and Kate get bullets for the guns. I'll do my job – you don't have to worry about me, okay?"

God love my baby sister. Sometimes her awesomeness completely overwhelms me. I ran my hand through Jo's stringy hair and then kissed the top of her forehead. "You're braver than me, kiddo. Okay – get back there and get ready, it's going to get crazy here any moment."

She scurried to the back of the carrier and slipped on her helmet as I stood up in my hatch and took a mouthful of air. "Ark Two, we're good to go. Let's move out."

And with that, Doug slipped the carrier into gear, pulling hard left around the barn and onto the main road heading out of Neapolis. I could hear the turret gear engaging behind me as Sid positioned the twin machine guns on his prescribed arc of fire. I peered over the left edge of my hatch and looked back to see Cruze's carrier take up its position on the rear, the turret guns covering the right side of the APC, and I leaned down behind the hatch door and pulled out my binoculars. I was going to look out for any potential ambush sites or areas where we'd likely come under hostile fire.

We cruised down the grid road for about fifteen minutes, the wheels kicking up a massive cloud of dust. I'd have felt sorry for Cruze's team having to take a dirt bath in our wake if I wasn't scared shitless about what we were potentially driving into. Doug maintained a decent clip – I was surprised at how good the condition of the road was. There were hardly any ruts, and the last time we'd seen an abandoned vehicle was back at Highway Two.

I gazed out through my binoculars to see a grain elevator on the horizon, the word *Dinsmore* emblazoned across its weathered wooden siding. I told Doug to slow down our approach, not that it would make a lot of difference: if there were Eden people in the village, they would have heard our carriers approaching. A *Quick Gas & Lube* sign nestled to the rear of the elevator told me there was a strong possibility we'd run into someone, because if there was any fuel left in the underground storage tanks, the Eden clan would be guarding it with their lives.

Ahead was a wall of smashed-up, battered cars, at least three high, spread across the grid road coming into town. The words "Eden Land" had been spray-painted all along the doors and fenders in large block letters. A makeshift barbed wire fence stretched from either side of the smashed vehicles for a good fifty yards. I ordered Doug to bring the carrier into the ditch to our right; I didn't want to offer anyone the chance to take a pot shot at us before we could scope out any likely areas of ambush. The suspension groaned as we crawled into the low ground, and I glanced out to my left to see Cruze's carrier taking up a similar position down in the ditch opposite.

I pressed the intercom. "What are you seeing, Sid?"

"We've got movement up by the elevator ... wait ... hand me your binos!"

I crawled underneath the turret cage and reached up to pass my binoculars to Sid. He grabbed them without looking down, and I threw Jo a shaky thumbs-up.

Sid's voice filled my ears through the headset. "Smart buggers, these Eden types," he said, sounding slightly impressed. "They've been watching us come at them for a while now. There's a cut away near the top of the grain elevator – hell of a good observation post."

"Or a sniper's nest," I said, nearly in a panic. I squeezed the PTT button for the radio. "Everyone, hatches down *now*!"

I raced up to my crew commander's hatch and pulled hard on the hatch door. It slammed shut with a deafening clang. I slipped on the combat lock and peered out through my periscope. Doug's head dropped down as he lowered the seat, and I watched as his hatch door closed amid a small cloud of dust.

I spun my periscope to the right to see if I could spot another access point into the village. Our carriers might have been 10000lb apiece, but they weren't even close to being on a par with actual tanks – we couldn't smash through the wall of cars. I'd just spotted a worn-down trail about 200m to our right when Sid's voice called out through the intercom.

"Contact!" he shouted. "Stand by!"

Suddenly, the hull of the carrier sounded like it was getting pelted by hailstones as we began taking on enemy small arms fire.

"What are you seeing, Sid?"

The turret spun sharply to the right and then back to the left. The whirring of the turret gear filled the inside of our carrier. "We've got a muzzle flash from a sniper in the grain elevator and about five others taking pot shots at us from behind the wall of cars. I'm ready to engage."

"Line 'em up in your sights, Sid," I answered back. "Ark Two, what are you seeing?"

The sound of static filled my ears and then Cruze answered in a sharp voice. "There's a big-ass cloud of dust from behind the barricade. I can't tell what it is, Dave, but from the looks of it, we're talking heavy equipment of some kind."

"Roger," I said as my heart started pounding. "Well ... they started shooting first. Ark Two, engage the barricade with your turret guns. Sid – fire a short burst into that sniper's nest!"

The turret spun a quarter turn as I finally spotted the cloud of dust. It was big enough to suggest that whatever they had pulled out was likely a piece of altered farm equipment – possibly a tractor or a large front-end loader. I spotted the light trail of a tracer round fly into the top of the grain elevator as the general purpose machine gun spat a small burst of rounds over my head.

"Stay in the ditch and push forward with both carriers!" I shouted into the radio. "As long as we're in the low ground, they've only got our turrets to fire on."

"Copy that!" Cruze replied. Doug slipped the carrier into gear and we started crawling forward, the engine rumbling steadily. I gazed out through the periscope to see round after round hitting the hull, bouncing off in a spray of paint chips and sparks. The cloud of dust to the left of the elevator was mixed with thick white smoke, a sure sign that whatever the Eden clan had pulled from behind the barricade was diesel-fuelled. That was a positive development – we'd have something to siphon off if we were successful in taking the village. I could see Ark Two's turret to my left as we edged forward, still taking on small arms fire.

Another burst of rounds echoed through the carrier as the stench of burning gun oil and propellant gases filled my nostrils.

"Got him!" shouted Sid.

I looked up at the grain elevator just in time to see a man's body slumped in the makeshift window near the top. The rifle over his left shoulder slipped off his body and fell to the ground.

"Holy shit!" Cruze's voice roared through my headset.

"What are you seeing?"

"Twelve o'clock and coming up from behind the barricade. That is one big-ass bucket … oh shit!"

Small explosions of dirt kicked up off the surface of the road, one after the other. "Smoke! Smoke! Smoke!" Cruze bellowed.

I couldn't see what Cruze was seeing, but I sure as hell knew from the trajectory of the dirt spraying off the roadway that the Eden survivors had a machine gun.

"I'm hit!" she bellowed.

A tremor of fear seized me as Doug slipped the carrier into reverse. "How bad?" I answered.

There was a moment of heavy static and then Cruze answered. "Mel's bleeding … got clipped in the shoulder with some hull shrapnel."

"Stand by!" I answered. "Smoke away, Sid!"

I could hear the distinctive thunk of our smoke dischargers firing off the left side of the turret. I peered out through my periscope to see the air fill with a billowing cloud of white smoke.

"They've got a heavy machine gun!" I shouted into my radio. "Did anyone see what calibre?"

"It's a .50!" Sid answered in a panicked voice. "I can see it … they've mounted it in the bucket of that loader. Holy shit, where the hell did they get that?"

"Don't know and don't care!" I barked. "Ark Two, how's Mel?"

The radio hissed. "I've got a field dressing on Mel's shoulder," said Cruze. "It's not too bad – I can't find the projectile anywhere but thank God it was shrapnel she got nailed with."

"Pull back now, Cruze! They've got a .50 calibre and if that thing hits either of us, we're screwed!"

"Roger," Cruze replied.

A .50 calibre machine gun is a deadly weapon to face in any battle. Our lightly armoured carriers were no match even for non-armour piercing rounds. The muzzle velocity from the gun alone would give the bullets enough power to blast through our hull like it was a paper target. We had to do something fast – once the smoke cleared we'd be shot to pieces, even if we were better armed than they were.

I looked back over my shoulder. "Dawson ... pull out the 60 mm mortar, I'm coming back, and we're going to take that gun down now!"

She gave me a thumbs-up as she unstrapped the mortar tube from the hull and screwed on the base plate.

I scrambled to the rear of the carrier and pulled a long metal box out from underneath the tarp on the floor. Ripping off the safety wire, I flipped open the lid to see a dozen long black tubes with the words HE FRAG painted on the sides in yellow. I quickly started tearing off the tape holding the ends of the tubes together and gave each a sharp twist. Inside each one was a 60 mm mortar round with charge increments attached just above the tail fins. Dawson threw open the rear door and hopped out of the carrier, keeping low for cover. I shifted my legs out the back and hauled the case containing the twelve rounds onto the crew seat.

I gave Jo a stern look and pointed to her jump seat. "Stay inside, and when I start hammering on the door, Jo, you make freaking sure you look to see that it's me and Dawson before you let anyone in, got it?"

She nodded, the helmet bouncing up and down over her eyes. "Okay ... just be careful," she said, her voice trailing off.

I lifted the case of ammo onto the ground and shut the door, my carbine slung over my shoulder. I quickly scanned the area surrounding us for a firing position with decent cover, deciding on the shoulder of the road a few feet away from the carrier's left side.

"Over there," I said. "Push the base plate in good and hard and I want a fixed firing pin – no lever firing, I want these rounds away as quickly as possible."

Dawson nodded as she scrambled to a spot on the shoulder. I

crouched over, pulled the ammo crate up beside her and then took a quick look up the road. The entire area in front of the barricade was obscured by our smokescreen, but that didn't mean we weren't taking on enemy fire. Small arms rounds ricocheted off the hull of my carrier and whizzed up into the air, the defenders of Dinsmore firing blindly into the field of white smoke. The good news was that I didn't hear the distinctive *pop, pop, pop* of the machine gun, but that would last only as long as our smokescreen did.

I could still make out the entire grain elevator, along with the sign for the Fast Gas station. In a few moments, we'd be raining down a lethal mixture of high explosives and sharp metal fragments on the Eden tribe and I didn't want them to come anywhere near that fuel station.

There is a sight line painted up the side of a mortar for the team to align the gun, but what's really happening is that you're eyeballing it when you aim. You have to estimate the distance to the target, and you have to adjust the propellant increments on the tail fins of each bomb to match your estimate, or the rounds will overshoot the enemy.

I guessed that the barricade was about 500m away, and the machine gun in the front-end loader bucket about 100m further behind. I decided to remove four of the five propellant increments and use the first round as a gauge. "You ready?" I said to Dawson. "We're talking five hundred meters ... you lined up?"

Dawson adjusted the angle of the tube and pushed hard into the dirt. "The first one will decide the rest of the shots. I'm ready to go."

I pulled off the safety wire on each round and laid them out in a row beside me. Then I took one last look up the middle of the road and carefully inserted the tail fin assembly into the tube.

"Here goes nothing," I said shakily as I let go of the round, the tail fins disappearing into the tube.

The mortar kicked, and emitted a loud, hollow *thunk*, the round shooting out of the tube faster than the eye could follow. Seconds later, there was a flash of light, followed quickly by an explosion as the round hit. A mixture of dirt and black smoke drifted high into the air, followed shortly after by bloodcurdling screaming.

"Good aiming, Dawson," I said as I pulled the safety wire off a second round.

She shuddered. "We're firing blindly, Dave. We need to take out that gun."

No sooner had the words left her lips when I saw the bucket lift slowly higher into the air, above our rapidly dissipating smoke screen. Its gun started firing in a series of loud pops, the rounds hitting the road in front of us and ricocheting high.

"We need to take that him out now!" I roared. Dawson tilted the tube forward no more than an inch, and I slid the tail fin assembly into the nose of the tube and released it.

There was another hollow-sounding *thunk* followed seconds later by an explosion, and this time, I could see that we'd landed a round behind the barricade. The Eden tribe's machine gun started firing full auto now in an attempt hit us; the rounds kept ricocheting off the road about 30 feet to our front.

"That got 'em," Dawson shouted. *"Fire for effect!"*

I pulled the safety wires and propellant increments off the remaining ten mortar rounds and started dropping them into the tube one after the other. Round after round of high explosive, high fragmentation bomblets rained down on the Eden tribe's barricade, filling the air with a deadly mixture of metal fragments and explosive force, but that .50 calibre machine gun kept on firing at a murderous rate.

We quickly ran out of mortar rounds. I had another case inside the back of the carrier, but I didn't want to waste them firing blindly at that barricade. Judging from the wails of the Eden tribe's wounded, they'd taken on serious casualties – now the only thing left to do was to silence their machine gun. I raised my carbine to my shoulder and took aim through my scope. Two men, who looked to be about middle-aged, were seated firmly inside the enormous bucket I was just about to squeeze off a pair of rounds when a sharp burst of automatic fire shot out from the turret of Ark One, tearing into the men and sending a splatter of gore into the shining steel bucket. I lowered my weapon and motioned for Dawson to get the mortar back into the carrier.

She picked up the tube and raced back to the carrier, banging on the door with the base plate. It swung open seconds later, and

Dawson climbed safely back inside. My heart pounded like a jackhammer as I pulled my weapon back to my shoulder and gazed down the road at the carnage we'd caused. Through a thin haze of smoke, I could see a number of cars in the barricade were on fire. Voices called out from behind the barricade, laced with pain and anguish.

Regret burned through me, even as I tried to remind myself that they'd shot at us first. We were simply defending ourselves against the people who'd killed that family in the barn, a few miles back. It was suicide for outgunned amateurs to engage a pair of fully armed APC's in combat, but clearly the Eden tribe hadn't figured that one out in time. I lowered my weapon as I spotted a strip of white cloth dotted with a smattering of blood fixed firmly to the barrel of a hunting rifle.

Dinsmore had decided to surrender, and I whispered a small prayer of thanks. Without Cruze's quick thinking in calling for a smokescreen, we would have been ripped to shreds by that heavy machine gun. I shouldered my rifle and plodded back to the carrier, where Jo handed me a bottle of water. I slugged it back in a series of shaky gulps, then wiped my mouth with the sleeve of my coat and handed the bottle back to Jo.

"Good shooting, Sid!" I shouted.

"Yeah ... you see that flag?"

I crawled into the back and pulled the door closed. "I saw it. How bad are they?"

The turret spun quickly to the left and then to the right. "I can't see any bodies, but I do see a chick running around back there with a first aid kit."

I climbed back into my crew commander's hatch and flipped open the door. I slipped on my headset and looked over across the road at Cruze, who was peering at the carnage through a pair of binoculars.

"Ark Two," I said into the radio, my voice still shaking. "Weapons hold ... move up and secure the area. We can't offer a lot, but we'll do what we can for their wounded. Keep your guard up."

The radio hissed. "Will do. Are we expecting a counter attack?" asked Cruze.

I sighed heavily. "Beats the hell out of me, Cruze. We're six months past the end of the freaking world – why should we expect anything less?"

CHAPTER 19

We pulled into Dinsmore and parked both carriers in front of the now smashed barricade. Tiny shards of glass, mixed with countless strips of torn metal and barbed wire lay scattered about in all directions, and the air smelled of smoke and cordite. A thin stream of blood trickled from underneath the shattered wall of cars, collecting into a pool inside a tire track. They'd probably used the front-end loader to build their barricade.

We found a young female, who didn't look much older than any of us. She had matted blonde hair that was filled with dirt, and her face was dotted with small flecks of blood. She was dressed in a pair of torn jeans and a grease-stained sweatshirt featuring a faded image of a RUSH album cover and her hands and forearms were covered with blood as she applied pressure to a middle-aged man's neck wound. A human leg lay against a battered automobile door, its former owner lying on his back. His lifeless eyes stared up at the chalk-coloured sky – his Remington hunting rifle was twisted around his arm by its sling.

The man with the neck wound looked to be in his mid-forties. His breathing was shallow, and he struggled to say something to the woman, but all he could manage was a gurgle.

When someone dies, it's as if the body becomes deflated somehow. Your muscles relax, and your chest falls as your lungs empty out that last breath of air. Your eyes sink back into your eye sockets, and your face becomes loose, almost flaccid.

That's what I saw the very moment that man died. Beside him was the body of a teenage boy, probably no older than Sid or me. His midsection was torn open – his intestines spilled out across his lap like they'd been dumped out of a bucket. A few feet away, draped across the hood of one of the cars, lay the body of a man whose jeans were coated in arterial blood. A gash about six inches long had been torn into his left thigh. Even in death, the man held his rifle, the shining black barrel aimed straight down the middle of the grid road leading into town.

The lone survivor of our attack cursed violently as the man she'd been tending to died with her hands pressed hard against his neck. She lunged toward us, her eyes blazing with hatred. Sid whipped his carbine across his chest in a sharp, almost fluid movement. He landed a hard butt stroke to her forehead, and she dropped like a stone.

We caused this.

The survivors of Dinsmore might have fired the first shot, but we ended it in a haze of smoke, high explosives, and burning metal. I would have felt pity for those who'd died, but as I gazed at the grim scene, all I could think about was that family of four, murdered in cold blood back at the barn, and that if we didn't protect Jo, if *I* couldn't protect her, then she'd wind up just like them.

Sid pulled out a couple of nylon cable ties from the pocket of his combat pants. He knelt down in front of the girl and flipped her onto her stomach as she moaned loudly. He pressed his knee on the center of her back and bound her wrists together, giving the end a sharp tug. She wasn't going anywhere anytime soon.

He grunted. "Does this mean she's a prisoner?"

"Of what?" I said flatly. "We're not at war, Sid."

The giant Newfoundlander stood up and gazed out at the carnage. He motioned to the closest dead body. "You sure about that, Dave?"

"Get her back to the carrier," I said, ignoring his comment. "We'll question her once we move past the barricade. She'll have probably come to by then."

Sid nodded as he bent over and picked the girl up. She moaned a couple of times as he slung her over his shoulder like she was a sack of flour. I walked over to the three dead bodies and collected their weapons. They wouldn't be in need of them again, but we might.

The rumble of our engines filled the air, and I was just about to head through a gap in the barbed wire fence to scope out the area, when at the last second I decided against it. Dinsmore might have been a tiny village and we'd just killed five of its residents, but that didn't mean there wasn't a sniper willing to take pot shots at me. We still had about an hour to scrounge before nightfall, and I had no desire to stay longer than that – the sound of the mortar explosions would have echoed for miles. That meant the Eden tribe might come running from any number of small towns and villages between our position in front of the barricades and the Alberta-Saskatchewan border.

Not to mention creeps.

And where *were* the creeps? How in the hell could a group of six survivors keep a tiny hamlet clear from the wandering hordes of monsters? We'd already had our own run-in with the creatures a couple of hours down the road – it didn't add up.

I doubled back to the carriers and scurried behind Ark Two so that I could check on Melanie Dixon. I noticed a series of four oblong dents in the armour just behind the crew commander's hatch. Each ding was about an inch and a half long, and the armour looked like it had been folded back – that's how powerful their gun was. Below the dents was the actual hole where the .50 calibre round had penetrated.

We lucked out, pure and simple. If another round or two had managed to make its way inside, it could have hit the fuel tanks and brewed up the ten thousand pound machine, burning everyone inside alive.

Our prisoner was huddled in the corner next to the engine panel. She had an angry-looking red welt on her forehead, and her stringy blonde hair dangled limply onto her shoulders. She glared at me through narrow green eyes, and she stuck her jaw out defiantly and started kicking at the tarp underneath her feet.

"You killed them all!" she shrieked. *"You're murderers – every last one of you!"*

"Just like your people killed a family of four in a barn less than ten clicks from here!" Cruze barked as she cocked her carbine and placed the barrel against the woman's right temple. "Another freaking word out of you, and I'll make sure you join them."

"Cruze, put your freaking weapon away!" I snapped. "She's no good to us with a bullet in her head."

She ground her teeth together and slowly pulled her carbine away from the girl's head. "All right ... fine. But we're going to have to do something with her. She's a liability."

I glanced over at Melanie Dixon. She'd taken off her combat shirt, and there was a field dressing bound tightly onto her left shoulder. "You okay, Mel?" I asked.

She glanced down at her shoulder and her eyes panned over to the prisoner. "I'd like to know where the hell they got a .50 cal from."

"No shit," said Sid, as he lit a cigarette. "That's serious hardware."

I hopped into the carrier and flashed a menacing glare at our prisoner. "We need to fuel these pigs up, and you have diesel, lady. That front-end loader doesn't run on unleaded. How much is in the tanks at the gas station?"

Her eyes blazed furiously, and then she spat in my face. "Fuck you! Fuck all of you!"

I took a deep breath and wiped my forehead with a rag. Then I glanced over at Cruze and said, "Organize the team. Get the Jerry cans and prepped. I want everyone ready to move out with five minutes notice. In the meantime, we need to figure out where they got that gun."

Cruze nodded and lifted herself out of the hatch as Melanie Dixon twisted her legs over the edge of the rear door and jumped out onto the gravel. In seconds, I could hear Cruze barking orders to my section while Mel kept a close eye on the prisoner, her carbine in one hand.

"Do you have a name?" I asked.

The girl's lips arched up into a thin maniacal grin, and she mouthed the words *fuck you*. Any other time, I would have admired her defiance, but not this time. We needed answers so I decided to take a less antagonistic approach. I reached under the tarp and pulled out a foil envelope containing sliced peaches in syrup. I tore it open with my teeth and then fished out a large slice with my Buck knife. I edged forward and held the dripping slice of fruit a few inches away from the woman's mouth.

"We're not the enemy," I said, jiggling the peach slice like a worm on a hook. "Your people shot at us first. What do you call this place now – is this Eden?"

Her eyes panned from the peach slice on my end of my knife, over to the pouch. I could have sworn I heard her stomach rumble, so I pulled the slice away and slipped it into my mouth.

"We're what are left of the King's Own," said Mel. "We busted out of Calgary yesterday morning, and – "

"You're from Calgary?" she said, sounding astonished. "You actually made it out of there?"

"Barely. We had more than fifty people when Day Zero happened. We're heading north – going as far the hell away from built-up areas as we can get."

"You won't make it," she said, still eyeballing the foil pouch.

I said nothing, choosing instead to let the effect of the foil pouch sink in. There was silence for about a minute when she narrowed her eyes and gave me a cold, hard once over. She glanced around the inside of the carrier and then finally said, "Day Zero, huh? That's what you're calling the first day of the outbreak?"

"Yeah ... what do you call it?" I answered.

She snorted, "This is the part where you try to get all chummy with me and spout off about the dead being the bad guys followed by a lovely talk about how we all have to work together to fight a common enemy. I've heard it before so save your breath."

I shrugged and then gently placed the envelope of fruit on her lap. "You can have those if you want. But I need you to answer some questions."

She cocked an eyebrow. "Why should I tell you anything? You're going to shoot me anyway – you might as well get it over with."

I shook my head. "We aren't murderers. If we could have slipped through undetected, we would have done it in a heartbeat. Your people started shooting at us, and we had to defend ourselves. Where did you get that machine gun from and what exactly is this Eden?"

"Okay, first off," she said, sliding her back up against the engine panel. "You're riding around in armoured cars with guns pointing at us. We thought you'd come to wipe us out. You could have hoisted a flag or something to show us that you had peaceful intentions."

Mel snorted. "Peaceful intentions? You guys have a .50-calibre heavy machine gun. That isn't exactly a peaceful farm implement."

"And these are our fucking farms!" she snapped. "The land you've been driving on has been claimed by survivors of all the farms in the region. While the world burns, we're trying to rebuild – it's not utopia, but it's something."

"No, it's the new Garden of Eden," said Melanie with an uncharacteristic smugness to her voice. "It's just going to be heaven on earth, isn't it? Never mind that you assholes work hand-in-hand shooting at anyone who is an outsider."

"It's a fucking start," she spat at Mel. "This territory has been named Eden because those of us still alive have been given a chance for a new beginning. Anyone who wanders onto our land is a risk to every last one of us still alive. Ever since the end came, Eden survivors have cleansed our farms and villages of the monsters, and we have lost people in the process."

"So have we!" Melanie shot back. "Christ, Dave – just get the information we need so we can get out of here!"

I motioned for Mel to calm down and then drew my attention back to the prisoner. "I'd be more inclined to believe your noble purpose if we hadn't found a family murdered in a barn a few miles back. Oh … and the way you just string up innocent people on a cattle fence at Highway Two? Classy."

She clenched her jaw tightly and said, "They probably got caught by one of the security patrols. The same thing with the two up at the highway – nobody from Dinsmore was involved."

I gave her a small shove. "You say that like it suddenly makes everything okay. Two little girls were murdered – two freaking kids!"

"Bullshit! None of our people would ever do such a thing. Fuck this … I don't even know why I'm arguing with you morons. There's no freaking chance you're going to make it off Eden land alive. The patrols are the *law* here, and while I don't agree with their methods, they don't shoot trespassers … *only* looters. We have to protect what's ours if we're going to survive. Nobody has the right to steal from us and you know something? You'd do the exact same thing if you were in our position."

She wasn't entirely wrong about protecting vital food and ammunition but shooting looters? We'd all agreed that we had to protect our provisions with our very lives. There wasn't a giant leap between protecting your provisions and dispatching a harsh form of justice. Even I wasn't naive enough to believe that. Then again, who made them or anyone the judge, jury and executioner? If Eden was an attempt to start over, you'd think the survivors have come up with something better than roving patrols making arbitrary life or death judgements on some poor unfortunate that made the mistake of showing up on their radar.

Sid Toomey appeared at the rear doors, Jerry cans in hand. "We're all good to go, Dave. How's the prisoner?"

"She's just about to tell us where to find some diesel because she knows that we're going to disappear as soon as we fill our cans. Take Kenny and Cruze and scrounge whatever fuel you can find – I'd start with that front-end loader. Oh ... and take the bolt out of that .50 cal – we can always use the spare parts. Take the barrel too."

"Will do," he said as he trudged off.

I glanced at the box of rations poking out from underneath the tarp, and I chewed my lip. I'd planned on releasing her as soon as we'd fuelled up our carriers – she was a security risk for everyone on the team, not to mention another mouth to feed. At the same time, we knew nothing about these security patrols save for the fact they were armed and would be a tactical threat: if they'd somehow managed to scrounge a fifty calibre heavy machine gun together, then it was entirely likely the survivalists were in possession of other dangerous weapon systems and ordinance.

Then it hit me.

These people had run into the Army before, or maybe a former military unit had defected to the Eden tribe, bringing all their weapons with them. That was the only explanation I could think of. If some military elements had defected after Day Zero then we'd be riding into any number of ambush sites or worse, properly defended positions.

She had to come with us.

Not as a hostage, but as a guide. The prisoner was our only source of information about Eden, their defences and their weapons. If we were going to make it through the land they'd claimed as their own, she was our only hope.

"I can tell by the look on your face that you're starting to understand just what you're up against," she said in a surprisingly calm voice. "Don't you just hate it when the cold hard truth comes up and gives you a swift kick in the nads?"

"Shut the hell up!" Mel snapped.

I fought back the urge to tell our prisoner precisely where to go and instead, focused on trying to gather as much information as I could before I broke the news to her that she was coming with us.

"Do you have a name?" I asked again. "Mine's David. The person standing outside the rear doors with her carbine aimed straight at the center of your visible mass is Melanie. I strongly recommend against pissing her off."

Her eyes panned over to Melanie who stroked the butt of her carbine for effect. "Dawn-Marie," she said after a short moment of silence. "Are you going to cut these handcuffs so that I can eat the peaches?"

I reached into my web belt and pulled out my KFS set. I removed the fork and the knife and slipped them back into the frog on my web belt, and then I dropped the spoon into the pouch of sliced peaches. I glanced back at Mel and said, "Cover her. If she does anything stupid, you know what to do."

"Not a problem," said Mel as she pulled the carbine into her shoulder.

I took the bag of peaches and placed them a few feet away on the tarp as I took out my Buck knife. She twisted her body over to the right, exposing her hands, and I slipped the blade between the two cable ties and cut them. Dawn-Marie exhaled heavily as she slowly raised her hands above her head. I eased myself back out of arm's reach and pointed to the peaches with my knife.

"There you go – eat," I said firmly.

Dawn-Marie reached over and snatched the peaches off the tarp. She dug into the pouch with my spoon and started stuffing herself with mouthful after mouthful, the syrup dribbling down her chin.

"These are better than what we've been eating," she said, as she gulped down another spoonful of fruit. "I haven't had sliced peaches in months. We've been surviving on a shit pile of canned stuff – mostly beans, pasta and canned meat."

"We aim to please," I said. "Now I want you to answer some questions."

She lifted the envelope to her mouth and drank down the

remaining syrup. "Such as?" she said as she wiped her mouth with her sleeve.

"How old are you?" I asked.

"Seventeen. How old are you?"

"I'm sixteen. Mel over there is fifteen. The oldest person in our group is the same age as you – that's Sid. He's the guy who smoked you in the head with his carbine."

"Just a bunch of orphans ... sort of like me after the monsters killed my family. The only family I had left are dead thanks to you people."

Melanie snorted. "You assholes started it!"

"And your little military unit ended it, didn't you?" she said venomously. "But you won't last. Those patrols will hunt you down and kill all of you!"

I snorted. "Then we're just going to have to do our level best to avoid your so-called patrols. That machine gun ... you've got some military people with you."

She made an enormous effort of rolling her eyes. "No shit, Sherlock. Machine guns don't exactly grow on trees and neither does ammunition."

I nodded. "What are these patrols using to get around? Do they have armoured personnel carriers like us?"

She shook her head. "Not that I've ever seen – huge waste of fuel. Some are on horseback and others are using ATV's and light vehicles."

"How many are in a patrol?"

She threw me smug look. "What? Do you think I'm going to tell you everything? The hell with that! Your little band of weekend warriors will find out soon enough."

Mel climbed into the back of the carrier, her weapon trained on Dawn-Marie. "She's playing you, Dave. Don't fall for her BS – she's trying to mess with your head."

I studied the girl's face and noticed that the defiant glare was still burning, as furious as ever. "Do you have cable ties in your kit, Mel?"

She reached into her rucksack, pulled out a pair of red cable ties and tossed them to me. I swiped them off the tarp and showed them off to our prisoner.

"Give me your hand," I ordered.

She huffed and stuck out her right hand. I slipped a cable tie around her wrist and pulled it tight. I slipped the other one underneath and then fastened her wrist to a welded tie down beside the engine panel.

"Here's the thing about your patrols," I said doing my best imitation of the voice of doom. "If they start shooting at us, you're going to be inside a carrier with our crew. If we come into contact with any of your patrols then you're going to be stuck inside a big-ass lightly armoured rolling target. That means if they hit this carrier and it brews up, you'll burn alive. Have you ever seen an armoured vehicle brew up, Dawn-Marie? It's not a pretty picture."

She tensed up as the entire colour drained out of her face. "So I'm a hostage then?"

I shook my head. "Taking hostages would imply there's someone out there to negotiate with, and you've made it pretty clear that your people don't negotiate."

"And if I refuse to cooperate?" she asked.

I leaned in until I was no more than an inch from her face. "Then we'll make a decision about what to do with you, but don't worry. You said we were all going to die out there once your patrols find us, so put two and two together."

She didn't even hesitate in responding to my veiled threat. "The closest patrol outpost is ten miles away."

"And I bet they heard the shooting," said Mel. "We need to head out, Dave."

I crawled to the rear doors and hopped out of the carrier. Mel kept a close eye on Dawn-Marie as I gazed over to the barricade to see Sid Toomey and Kenny Howard carrying what looked like two full Jerry cans of diesel each. Pam covered them both from a gap in the wire as they plodded around the smashed cars and over to the nose of Ark One.

"It would appear that our scrounging efforts have yielded us some diesel," I said, shifting my gaze back onto Dawn-Marie, who now looked like all the fight had been taken out of her. Cold hard truth tends to have that effect on people. "We'll top off the carriers and move out in fifteen minutes. Oh ... and Mel?"

"Yeah?"

"Be kind to our guest," I said. "But not too kind."

CHAPTER 20

Sid told me there was enough fuel in the front-end loader to top up the carriers as well as our Jerry cans. It would be dark soon, and I wanted to put as much distance as possible between us and Dinsmore. After a quick consultation with Cruze, we decided we'd keep going for another hour or so. Our destination was a thick stand of trees about 20 km to the northwest. We'd be hatches down for a second night – not entirely desirable, given that every one of us was dead dog tired of being crammed inside the APC's, but necessary, given the threat of armed patrols.

So we pushed on, bouncing across farmers' fields and traversing at least half a dozen grid roads. The temperature had plummeted – small flecks of snow began falling, landing on the hull and then melting from the heat of the engine. We'd covered nearly five hundred kilometres since we broke out of the city. I wanted to take comfort in our success, but what about Eden? My gut, which was rumbling almost as loudly as our engines, told me that for a huge group of survivors to band together so quickly – well, it just didn't make a whole hell of a lot of sense. Every instinct a survivor possesses is to protect what they've got. Why would farm families create a makeshift society when so many would slit your throat for a freaking can of beans? The Eden tribe possessed military hardware, they'd laid claim to land stretching for miles in every direction, they'd cobbled together roving security patrols. There had to be a central figure that was pulling the strings. But no leader, however skilled in the art of diplomacy or how inspiring he or she might be, could rebuild so quickly after the last one disintegrated unless they had expert help that could only come from one source: the army.

I needed more information from Dawn-Marie.

We pulled into a hide deep inside a thick stand of poplars that stretched for about three kilometres across a ridge overlooking dry, frost covered farmer's fields. When I crawled into Ark Two, it was shortly past nine o'clock. Melanie Dixon was fast asleep against the rear door and Kenny Howard was perched up in the turret, keeping a watch on things with the infra-red.

"Everyone been fed?" I asked, as Cruze made me a cup of hot chocolate from a small pot on her mountain stove.

She handed me the steaming tin mug, and I blew on it before taking a sip. "Yeah, everyone's had some chow – even our honoured guest."

I glanced over at Dawn-Marie, still fastened by one arm to the hull tie-down. She looked like she'd been crying, and I wondered if the tears were genuine or if she was trying to play Cruze's team. She stared blankly at the rear doors through puffy red eyes as I gestured for her to take a sip of my hot chocolate. She shook her head and sniffled.

"You're smart, Dawn-Marie," I said quietly. "By now you must realize we didn't want to get into a fight with your people."

"That explains why you bombed the shit out of us then, doesn't it?" she shot back.

She was still as defiant as ever. I nodded to show that I meant her no harm, so I kept my tone as non-threatening as before. "What happened to your parents? Your brothers and sisters?"

"Dead – what are you, stupid or something? Nearly everyone died in the days after the outbreak."

"I'm sorry for your loss," I replied.

"No you're not!" she snapped. "Empty words at the end of the world – that's all you're good for."

I took a deep, patient breath and said, "My mother took her own life. We were hiding out in Mewata Armoury. We were hunkered down there for six months. She couldn't take it. I guess lots of people made the same choice as she did."

Cruze nodded slowly. "My family died on the second day. They were torn apart in front of me."

The girl shifted her gaze toward Cruze. Her features softened a little. "Everyone has a story of loss, don't they? Christ, what kind of world is this now? People are animals – sometimes they're just as bad as the stiffs. What are you going to do with me?"

I blinked. "What do you want us to do with you?"

She shrugged and her eyes slid over to my carbine. "I don't know … does it matter at this point? We're all going to be dead soon."

Cruze shifted herself across the jump seat and leaned in. "That's a pretty bold statement, Dawn-Marie."

She rolled her eyes. "Are you people freaking dense? They're going to find you. They find everyone who isn't part of Eden. They'll kill all of us including me."

I gave her a surprised look. "Why would your security people kill you?"

"Because I'm not dead back at that barricade," she said flatly.

Wow. I didn't see *that* coming.

It didn't make any sense at all – Dawn-Marie was supposed to be a part of the Eden tribe. If we'd left her at the barricade, she could have provided the patrols with valuable information about our vehicles, weapons and what kind of threat we posed to whoever was in charge. I took another sip of my hot chocolate. At least she was opening up to us.

"What can you tell us about how Eden came to be?" said Cruze as she handed the girl a mug of hot chocolate.

Dawn-Marie blew on the rim of the cup for a moment and took a small sip. "Our farm was about five miles outside of Dinsmore," she began. "Just Mom, Dad and me and my brother, Darcy. He'd turned eighteen the week before everything went to hell. We first heard about the outbreaks on the dish … you know, the satellite TV?"

I nodded. "Go on."

She took another drink and resumed her gazing at the rear doors. "My father decided it was time to take steps to protect ourselves – when the Internet died. TV and radio had stopped broadcasting for a couple of days by then, but we still had power from a backup generator as well as an Internet connection. It's weird how the Internet was the last thing to break down. We followed the outbreak through social media – Twitter offered minute-by-minute updates from people who were trapped in cities and towns worldwide. Mom got infected when she and Dad went into Dinsmore to get provisions. The village was alive with the creatures – Dad said she was attacked inside the truck. He got her home but she bled to death on the way. My brother tried to stop Dad from shooting her, but she turned right in front of us. The thing she became … it was savage. It was like her memory had been wiped and her mind had been replaced with some kind of feral madness … but you know what I'm talking about. You've seen it. Dad shot her in the head, and we burned her body. That was almost six months ago."

I gulped back the last mouthful of hot chocolate from my tin cup, and wiped it out with a rag. Dawn-Marie looked like all of us – dishevelled and carrying a thousand yard stare from walking on egg shells the better part of a year. I'd seen that look before, in pictures of soldiers at the front during the Second World War and in some of the men from the King's Own who'd returned from Afghanistan.

She had a scar over her left eyebrow that looked to be still healing and I noticed the stitches she'd been received were a hell of a mess – like someone had closed the wound with a sewing needle and thread.

Dawn-Marie had given us her personal story of surviving those first terrifying days, but I was no closer to learning about Eden, who ran it and what kind of threat that it posed. And we didn't have time to take a trip down memory lane either. I wanted to find out as much as possible as quickly as possible and get our carriers the hell off Eden land, so I decided to take the direct approach.

"How soon after Day Zero did Eden start to take shape?" I asked, hoping she wouldn't tell me to go to Hell again.

She avoided my gaze for a short moment and that's when I realized she was ready to tell me what I needed to hear. "Eden was an idea that made sense when everything was insane, okay? After Mom died, we fought daily battles against the monsters. We'd drive around in Dad's pickup and shoot the creeps as soon as we saw them – we eventually ran out of ammunition for Dad's hunting rifles, and we had to rely on smashing their heads in. Dad was killed two months ago clearing a farmhouse. Darcy got infected and had to be put down. I was on my own for a week when Sunray's people found me. After that, everything changed."

Sunray?

Cruze and I quickly looked at each other. We knew what Sunray meant because it's a term no civilian would ever use. It means a formation commander, or leader, and Dawn-Marie's use of the term immediately confirmed my suspicions that a military element was probably behind the creation of Eden. Now we just had to figure out precisely who Sunray was.

But we weren't prepared to let her know that we understood what Sunray meant, so Cruze decided to play it cool. She tore into the wrapper on a granola bar and offered the first bite to Dawn-Marie. She shook her head. "Sunray ... is that a person, or is it code for a group in charge of things?" asked Cruze.

"We were told it was a person," said Dawn-Marie. "From the base up in Wainwright. All of Sunray's people are from there."

"How many?" I asked, hoping like hell that we weren't up against a battalion-sized unit. "Maybe a hundred, maybe a thousand ... nobody knows really," she said, her voice trailing off. "They weren't bad at first. They offered hot meals, communication between farms and medical help, a sense of order. I think that's why so many people joined them – everyone was terrified to even breathe. We didn't know where to turn. They promised to protect us, but we'd have to submit to their rules."

Kenny Howard shifted in his perch inside the turret. "All's clear as far as I can tell," he said quietly. "Not that I'm trying to eavesdrop, but I remember hearing they moved troops out of Wainwright to provide reinforcements for the Brigade in Edmonton. They even mobilized the recruits. So whoever this Sunray dude is, maybe he's not infantry. Maybe he's a bean counter or something."

"Assuming it's a he," said Cruze. "Hell, assuming it's just one person – it might be a pseudonym for a command structure of some kind."

I shook my head. "I doubt it. The end of the world presents a hell of an opportunity for your run-of-the-mill megalomaniac. Dawn-Marie, you said that you had to submit to a bunch of rules. What kinds of rules?"

"Stuff about keeping order and security," she said quietly.

"And Sunray's security patrols – two or three man groups. Women and girls would have to watch their backs or they'd take what was referred to as *certain liberties*. I'll let your imaginations fill in the blanks as to what those liberties were. I found out about it the hard way, but whatever."

"Are you fucking serious?" Cruze said with a sharp edge to her voice. Dawn-Marie simply nodded and from the look in her eyes, I

didn't have to ask what she meant.

"They fucking *raped* you?" said Kenny as he peeked down from the turret. "Bastards! If that's the kind of shit this Sunray dude allows then I'll be happy to put a fucking bullet in that asshole's head."

There was dead silence in the carrier for a few moments. Dawn-Marie's revelation confirmed to me that she wasn't one of the bad guys. If anything, she was a victim, and it sounded like everyone living in Eden faced danger not only from the creeps, but also from Sunray, whoever the hell he was.

She glanced at her wrist. "I'd appreciate it if you guys would cut me loose. I can't feel my hand any more."

I reached for my Buck knife and was about to cut the cable ties when Cruze grabbed my arm. "Wait. How can we know to trust her? She might decide to go postal all of a sudden."

I glanced at Dawn-Marie. She looked me square in the eye. "Where the hell would I go? You guys outnumber me, and I've been pretty open about what got me stuck in this tank with a bunch of wannabe soldiers from Cowtown. It's like I said before: I'm dead if they find me because I should have died defending the town."

"I believe her," I said to Cruze as I pulled out the knife. "We're all she's got for now. Dawn-Marie knows that if she does something stupid, she's as good as dead."

Cruze threw me a reluctant nod, so I reached over and cut the tie. Dawn-Marie's arm dropped down onto her lap like a lead weight.

"Thanks," she said, as she massaged her wrist. "Listen ... I'm living on borrowed time. We all are. If Sunray doesn't find us, we'll wind up getting our asses chewed off by the creeps."

"We're in the business of surviving," said Cruze with a note of determination in her voice. "We have a plan – to get as far the hell away from civilization as we can get. We're going north. There's an outpost of some kind up there."

She snorted. "You're talking about Sanctuary Base, right? We've heard about it on the shortwave radio. It's a hell of a trip from here, assuming the place still exists and hasn't been overrun with the dead."

"You had shortwave?" I asked. "Back at the farm?"

"That's right," she said. "All I know about Sanctuary Base is that they're made up of army reservists and First Nations militia – real badass types. My dad was trying to figure out a way for us to get up there and join them – they sounded like they had it all figured out."

"Does this Sunray know about them?" Cruze cut in.

Dawn-Marie shook her head. "If we do then it stands to reason everyone knows. We didn't tell a soul outside of our immediate family. I didn't even tell the two gunners Sunray left in Dinsmore to keep us on our toes."

I cocked an eyebrow. "The two guys in that front-end loader – they were Sunray's people?"

"Yeah. They brought that gun with them two days before your people showed up."

"And that's how they're keeping everyone in order, right?" asked Cruze. "You're all forced into service."

Dawn-Marie tapped her nose. "Bingo. The rules are that the rules change on a moment's notice. Sunray's people took stock of all the vital resources on every farm – from the grain in the bins, to livestock, to fuel. A few farms resisted. They were taken care of."

"That's why you started shooting at us," Cruze said grimly. "If you hadn't, those guys on that machine gun would shoot whoever refused."

She drew her knees up to her chest. "That's right. They were enforcers. Most farms have an enforcer or two in place to keep everyone in check. The security patrols happen when there's a shift change. Two new enforcers arrive to replace old ones – when they leave, they do a roving security patrol on their way to the next farm or small village. They're switched out so the enforcers don't get too cozy with the locals. Two weeks on duty and two weeks later a new couple of enforcers come to town."

"Jesus," I whispered. "He doesn't even trust his own people."

Cruze looked unconvinced. "If all this is true, then why didn't you guys fight back? If people wanted to opt out of Eden then why not whack the enforcers and be done with it?"

"They did radio checks to Sunray every twelve hours," said Dawn-Marie. "If one of the enforcers wasn't on the radio to give a situation report, Sunray would know what happened. An example would be made of them … it might be what happened to those two people you found strung up on the wire. Who knows?"

Holy shit.

Eden wasn't the Promised Land for Day Zero survivors. It was a tightly run prison, whose guards worked two-week shifts. I had to admit, it was a brilliantly simple method of establishing and maintaining control over the population. You either cooperated or faced swift punishment, usually involving a bullet to the back of the head. Maybe that family we found in the barn back at Neapolis were people who had tried to opt out of Eden.

A tiny knot of fear wound itself tightly in center of my chest. Not only did we have creeps to contend with, but we'd somehow stupidly managed to break *into* a prison. Only this one didn't have physical walls, just the threat of summary execution if you didn't play the game.

Sunray.

A military commander who used roving security patrols to keep everyone in line. If his patrols were always on the move then it was entirely possible that Sunray wasn't operating out of a static location – he was probably mobile.

And very likely an infantry officer with a million times more tactical experience than me.

Fuck.

CHAPTER 21

I escorted Dawn-Marie over to my carrier. She was as good as her word and didn't try anything stupid, but I didn't entirely trust her. Not because I thought that she might be loyal to the Eden tribe – her story about being kept in an open prison under the watchful eye of Sunray's people made perfect sense. She just wasn't one of us. She hadn't fought for her life alongside my team for the past six months. She was an outsider, and nobody trusts an outsider that easily.

I spotted Sid walking back from an area of dead wood a few meters behind out carrier. In one hand was a shovel and in the other was a roll of toilet paper. I was just about to rag on him for taking a dump without someone providing cover when he flashed an angry look my way.

"She's riding with us, huh?" he said, more as a statement than a question. Dawn-Marie climbed into the carrier, and the armoured door closed with a dull *thunk*.

"She's got information on what we're up against here, Sid. That .50 Cal back in Dinsmore? There's a military unit running Eden. The commander uses the term Sunray."

I briefed Sid on everything there was to know about Sunray and how Eden had come to be, but from the look on his face, I could tell that he was quite prepared to drop Dawn-Marie off in the first creep-infested community we could find.

He slipped the shovel underneath a tie-down on the side of the carrier and then lit a cigarette, cupping the burning end with his hands as he took a deep haul.

"I voted for you to lead this thing, Dave. But I'm not backing you on that chick. She needs to go … at first light. When we pull out of here, just drop her off on the side of the road. We can't trust her, man. She's not one of us."

The last thing I needed was to get into an argument with Sid Toomey. While I sympathized with Dawn-Marie's story of being trapped in Eden, we needed her about as much as she needed us and what we needed more than anything was information. Dawn-Marie could give us an edge.

"Look … Sid, it's complicated, but the reasons for keeping her with us are tactically sound at this point. I need you to back me up on this, okay?"

He took another haul on his cigarette and said, "I don't like it. You sure you're not slipping because you sure as fuck screwed up getting us swarmed by the creeps back in Airdrie. I didn't say anything about it then."

I clenched my fists tightly and stuffed them in the pockets of my combat jacket.

"Yeah, Sid … I made a mistake," I whispered but you could hear the anger in my voice. "It won't happen again."

He cocked an eyebrow. "Bringing along that chick is a mistake from where I'm standing and want to know something?"

"What?"

He stubbed his cigarette on the hull of the carrier and said, "If I feel that way, there will be others who feel the same."

I sighed heavily as I tapped the rear door with the butt of my carbine. Dawson opened it up, and I climbed inside with Sid in tow.

Sid might have been right about Dawn-Marie, and I scanned the faces of my team to gauge their reaction to her presence in the carrier. Everyone carried a blank expression and had I been playing poker with them, I would have been in a world of hurt.

I briefed Dawson and Doug Manybears in the crew commander's hatch so that we were out of earshot from Dawn-Marie. Doug was practical – he recognized Dawn-Marie's strategic value. She was a farm girl, while the rest of us were city-dwellers. Sure, we each possessed some field craft abilities, but none of us knew the first thing about where to scrounge for supplies on a farm, and, as he pointed out, we didn't even know what kinds of farm equipment operated on diesel versus gasoline. Dawn-Marie could show us what to look for, she was familiar with the area and, the most important factor was that she had knowledge of Sunray's assets. She knew what we were up against.

Kate took the middle ground – probably so Sid wouldn't feel his opinion was being ignored. The giant Newfoundlander had always adopted an act first, think later mindset, and Kate Dawson was the only person who could reel him in.

I finished my briefing, and Sid took the first sentry shift in the turret. I was about to crawl across the floor of the crew commander's hatch to catch some shut-eye when Jo tapped me on the shoulder.

"Hey, kiddo, you should be sleeping. What's up?"

Jo's eyes narrowed sharply as she hopped onto the crew seat. "I stayed awake because I want to talk about something that's important."

I blinked. "Um ... okay. You have my undivided attention."

Jo squared her shoulders and took a deep breath. "I'm part of this team, David, and I want be more like everyone else. I've been a helper since we left the city but I can do other stuff, too."

I cocked an eyebrow. "Yeah? Like what?"

She pointed to my binoculars hanging against the hull. "Well, I'm a good lookout. I can spot creepers from a mile away, plus I'm a good listener. I hear every word you guys say about what we're up against. And I heard everything about Dawn-Marie. I've been keeping an eye on her, you know."

I leaned forward. "We all have to keep an eye on her. Do you think we can trust her?"

Jo shook her head. "I don't think she's one of the bad guys, but that's cuz we don't know her yet so nobody trusts her. And you want to know something?"

"What's that?"

She dug a finger into my chest. "You don't trust me either, David. You think it's all about protecting me, but we protect each other, and I can help ... I want to help. I'm a good shot, I'm small and fast, plus a bunch of other stuff that you're too busy to even notice. You need to let me do more – I don't want to be the little kid anymore."

I took Jo's hands in mine and said, "But, Jo ... you are a little kid. You're just eight years old."

She pulled away and then fired me an angry glare. "I'm nine in a couple of months, and I can shoot better than Kenny or Doug. I've shot creepers, lots of them. I've seen just as much scary stuff as you, and I can do more to help us get to where we're going. So are you going to give me more to do or are you going to treat me like a baby forever?"

I wasn't expecting to get an earful from my kid sister, but she was dead serious about wanting to be a part of the team. It took guts on her part to talk to me about it, but all I could see as I listened to Jo plead her case was the bodies of that family back in Neapolis. If I agreed to let Jo become a full-fledged team member then it meant that I couldn't protect her. I studied her face as I considered the reality of our situation. We'd been attacked, twice. Our carrier could have been destroyed, and we could all wind up dead if I screwed up again. Jo was on the receiving end of that .50 calibre machine gun just like the rest of us. If we brewed up, she'd burn to death and there would be nothing I could do about it. And the entire world was still filled with monsters that would rip her tiny body to shreds if she wound up getting swarmed – if we couldn't escape them.

I sighed heavily and gave Jo a slight nod. "You make a good case, kiddo. I promise to let you help out more, but there's still a ton of stuff you need to learn about field craft and fighting."

She snorted. "There's a ton of stuff you need to learn too. Okay … well at least you're listening to me. I'm going to get some sleep. Maybe tomorrow night I can go on sentry?"

I threw her a half-smile. "Yeah, Jo … maybe tomorrow night. I'll talk to Cruze about it, okay?"

Jo gave me a massive hug and said, "Okay then. Goodnight, David."

***

It was shortly past one in the morning when Cruze appeared at the rear of my APC, carrying a rubber groundsheet in one hand and her carbine in the other. I climbed out, along with Dawn-Marie. It was time to figure out our next move. I closed the carrier door, and then knelt down on the ground. Tiny flecks of snow were falling and the grass was covered with frost. Cruze threw her groundsheet over us to block out the light as we prepared to study the map.

"We're far enough off the grid road that we won't leave any tire tracks," Cruze said, pointing to our location. "When these patrols show up, they're sticking to the roads – they're not driving cross country, are they?"

Dawn-Marie nodded. "That's right. They've got the area

covered pretty well, and they know what kinds of things are going to attract scroungers – mostly food and fuel."

I made a note of our position and then ran my finger along a grid line running due east. "Do you have any idea how much territory Sunray has claimed?"

She shook her head, her eyes fixed firmly on the map. "Not a clue. We'd asked our handlers, but they were tight-lipped about it."

"We have a couple of options here, Dave," Cruze whispered. "We can keep pushing on due east to Morrin, but I'm not crazy about fording the Red Deer River – it's pretty deep. We'd also use a ton of fuel while we're in the water depending on how strong the current is. The other option is to head northwest, but that presents problems too."

I noted the location of Morrin on the map and followed the Red Deer River to the northwest. Cruze was right; it was a huge natural obstacle, and it would offer a defender any number of ambush positions.

It looks like a thick green strip on the map, but the Tolman Badlands natural area is pristine forest, complete with bears, wolves and of course the badlands itself. Full of dry sedimentary rocks and eroded clay-rich soil, the ground resembles volcanic rock in many places – there are coulees and hoodoos, too. Once upon a time, tourists flocked to the fossil-rich town of Drumheller, away to the south – Drumheller was home to the Royal Tyrell Museum of Palaeontology, and every person in Alberta under the age of forty had done a school field trip to visit.

The badlands just sort of appear out of nowhere. You're driving across flat fertile farmland and then suddenly you're heading down a massive hill, and the landscape is instantly transformed like you've taken a trip in a time machine. It's as if God stuck a blunt knife into the land and carved out a jagged strip about two hundred miles long, just to see what it would look like.

It's pretty much impossible to drive cross country through the badlands: you have to stick to roads that cling to the coulee walls, and, if your brakes ever fail, you're as good as dead. Any reasonably intelligent tactician would set up a defensive position on either side of those walls. There are no escape routes on the roadway – it's either up or down. If you drive a vehicle on the shoulder, you'll wind up rolling into the ravine below.

My first instinct was to figure out an alternate route, but there were only two roads that crossed through the badlands; Highway 585, outside of Trochu to our north, and Highway 27, that drove straight east into Morrin.

"We have like … zero options here, Cruze," I said. "We don't have enough fuel to go bombing around from town to town looking for a fill."

"There are farms along the way," Dawn-Marie said. "They would likely be secured by military elements. The ones that were abandoned will have probably been stripped clean by now."

It was time to make a decision. What would be the lesser of two evils – moving straight east along Highway 27 or cutting northeast through Trochu? If Sunray's people had somehow managed to clean the village of creeps, they'd hear our vehicles coming from miles away.

I folded up the map and handed it to Cruze. "Screw it … we're going to continue heading east," I said, trying to sound decisive. "We'll cross the river along highway 27 and go the Morrin route. How much fuel do you have left?"

"The tank is full and we've got two Jerry cans in reserve. That'll buy us about another couple of hundred kilometres before we have to refuel."

I nodded. "I'm about the same. Highway 27 is paved – we could bring the carriers up to 90 km/hr and make up some time. If we don't run into any opposition, we could pull into Hanna by lunchtime, and maybe make the border by nightfall."

"That's optimistic," said Cruze, as she turned her attention back to Dawn-Marie. "Do you know how to fire a weapon?"

She gave Cruze a sour look. "What do you think I've been doing for the last six months, sitting on my ass? Of course I know how to fire a weapon."

Cruze nodded. "Good … because if we get into a fire fight, it'll be a lot like the last one."

"Unless you drive into Sunray's people in some kind of formation or something."

"What Cruze wants to know is whether or not you realize

you're going to be shooting your own people," I said, matching Cruze's tone. "Actually, scratch that – if we give you a weapon, there'll be a full scale mutiny on our hands because everyone here trusts you about as far as they can throw you. For the time being, you'll help out in my carrier."

Cruze cocked an eyebrow. "Are you sure, Dave? It's just Melanie in the back of Ark Two, we've got the room."

I shook my head. "I'm going to send Jo over your way again. She's been stuck inside these rolling sardine cans for more than two days now, and she gave me an earful about being treated like a baby. She wants to help out more, so here's her chance to prove herself. We'll go hatches up at first light, and you can use her as a lookout. Make sure Mel keeps an eye on her."

"We'll all keep an eye on her," said Cruze, shining the red light onto her watch. "It's one thirty – let's get some kip because it's going to be a long day."

***

When everyone in my carrier woke up, I was as blunt as possible; I wanted my team focused on the threat facing us. We were dealing with remnants of an infantry unit, and only vigilance would give us any kind of edge.

Jo was excited about her temporary transfer over to Cruze's team. She'd asked for more responsibility, and this was her chance to prove to everyone that she could contribute something beyond taking care of bullets and beans. She scurried over to Ark Two just as the early morning light was beginning to filter through the dense poplar and diamond willow inside our hide.

After 15 minutes of vehicle maintenance, Doug Manybears started up the carrier and the engine roared to life on the very first try. I did a quick radio check and ordered Ark Two onto another frequency, deciding we'd change radio frequencies every six hours in case Sunray had a command post somewhere that might be listening in. Gulping back a steaming hot cup of instant coffee, I climbed into my crew commander's hatch. My stomach groaned a couple of times to remind me that I needed to eat something, but my nerves were on edge, giving me a slight feeling of nausea. I did manage to eat a granola bar and keep it down. That had to count for something.

We pulled out of the hide at three minutes past six. It had snowed since my meeting with Cruze and Dawn-Marie, not enough to get us stuck in a drift, but more than enough to leave tire tracks all over the place. But we were going to be on the highway in a few minutes, and that meant we'd have a smooth ride for the first time in three days.

We kept a watchful eye on the west side of Highway 27 as it cut a path across the seemingly unending flat land, stretching as far as the eye could see. In the distance, we spotted thin black smudges of smoke on the horizon – probably coming from what used to be the city of Red Deer. I wondered for a moment how many other refugees had left their hiding places, and were now making their own journeys to unknown destinations. Winter was officially five weeks away, but anyone who lives on the prairie knows that we're lucky if we make it to the end of November before the biting cold arrives like an unwanted guest. The wind chill can freeze your exposed skin in less than five minutes, and that's after the cold has stolen the breath from your lungs as you bundle up and try like hell not to freeze to death.

But then again, winter coming meant that the creeps would freeze solid, and I shivered as I considered the possibilities of facing a fully armed military unit. The last thing I wanted was for us to face off against Sunray. We needed to remain vigilant and use our heads if we were going to stay under his radar, but for that we needed more information. Unfortunately, Dawn-Marie wasn't going to be of use there. Her knowledge was limited to Dinsmore and a few scattered farms on land gone fallow. No, what we needed was good, old-fashioned intelligence, and that meant only one thing: patrolling. Stealth, the cover of darkness and boots on the ground were the best way for our group to learn about what we were up against.

Our carrier crawled into a deep gully alongside the highway, and then edged up the shoulder until the nose was level with the pavement. Sid's guns were in the rear position, and he quickly moved his turret into his arc of fire as I watched Cruze's carrier follow our tracks on the snow-covered pavement. A sharp wind blew in from the south, creating miniature snow drifts no more than a few centimetres deep. Our tires ploughed through them, kicking up a blinding cloud of powder to our rear which I'm sure pissed off Kenny Howard no end. I watched as he increased his distance between us to three vehicle lengths and gave Cruze a thumbs-up.

Kate Dawson had covered her head and face with a combat scarf – she looked like was wearing a Niqab. She scanned the area north of us for movement. Ahead lay at least 30 km of highway before the flat dry prairie disappeared into a deep coulee. I hoped the bridge over the river was still there.

Sunray wouldn't destroy a bridge, would he?

I hailed Cruze on the radio. "Ark Two, how's your team?"

"We're good," she answered. "The thermometer on my watch says that it's about minus five outside."

"Feels more like minus fifteen with the wind," I replied. "We're going to have to alter our plans before we head into our destination."

"Say again?"

"I'll fill you in when we get closer – I don't want to talk about this over the radio."

"Roger that," said Cruze.

We pressed on, the APC's rumbling across the snow-covered highway. Dawn-Marie stood opposite Kate Dawson, using the turret as a wind break. She was shrouded in Jo's poncho liner, but I could have sworn that her lips were turning blue. It wasn't even seriously that cold yet.

I hailed Dawson on the intercom. "Your partner-in-crime looks to be freezing to death. Have her go hatches down if she needs to warm up."

"There's lots of good heat blowing back from the engine cover," she answered back. "I might have to throw on a bikini or something."

Doug Manybears voice filled my headset. "Are bikinis allowed after the end of the world? I need to keep my mind on something else – where we are right now feels like a desert. But that's got me thinking about sand, which got me thinking about the beach and bikinis again. Now I'm thinking about naked ladies. Thanks, Dawson. I'm now thinking about smut at the end of the world."

"You think too much," Sid cut in. His voice was as hard as

granite. "Think less, drive more."

I could see Doug's helmet-covered head shaking back and forth in the driver's hatch so I leaned across the hull and shouted in his ear.

"I think about bikinis every single day when I'm not thinking about getting eaten alive! If your brain is coming up with visions of half-naked ladies, that's a healthy sign."

"All Sid thinks about is bashing creeps with the eradicator!" he shouted back. "Half the time I wonder if he even likes girls. He sure as hell doesn't like the new chick."

I patted Doug on the shoulder and glanced back. Dawn-Marie had moved to the other side of the carrier and was now enjoying the warmth from the engine blowing onto her face. She threw me a small wave, and for the first time since Dinsmore, she looked more relaxed.

I would have waved back, but I could feel Sid glaring at me. Instead, I just offered a small nod, and then turned my attention back to the road ahead. We pushed on for another forty minutes, and I was struck by how little the land changed. It was as if we were in a cartoon where the animators keep using the same backgrounds, over and over again. Not a house or a barn to be seen in any direction, though we did pass a number of oil pumps, dotting the land like giant metallic insects.

In better times, they'd have been pumping raw crude out of the ground to be shipped to the refinery at Bowden. That was the extent of my knowledge about the oil industry, though I did wonder whether Sunray had seized the refinery when he moved in from Wainwright. There would be plenty of oil in its giant storage tanks.

I was dead tired, and hadn't slept more than two hours in the last day. The cold wind numbed my skin, to the point where I thought my entire head had been filled with novocaine. I was actually daydreaming – when I realized that I'd dropped my guard, I gave my face a good hard slap. It rattled me back into the present just in time to see a small rise on the horizon in front of us. I tapped Doug on the shoulder and motioned for him to slow the carrier down to a crawl, and then I dropped back into my hatch and grabbed my binoculars.

I stood up high in my crew commander's hatch as the APC dropped to a walking speed, and peered out at the tiny ridge. I could make out the tops of poplar trees on either side of the highway and a few thin tendrils of smoke rising into the flat, grey sky.

"Ark Two, contact ... wait out," I said, trying to contain the knot of fear that had been growing ever since we crossed over into Eden. I pulled out my map and followed the contour lines showing the ridge to where I thought our position was on the highway. We were no more than 5km away, and if there were any of Sunray's assets in that ridge, they'd have seen us coming for miles. I quickly glanced to both sides of the road for a place we could conceal our carriers if they decided to start shooting. Outside of the cattle fencing that had been following us ever since we left our hide, there were no man-made structures. What's worse, there was no low ground either. We were positioned on a stretch of road in an endless sea of flat, open country. It was an armoured commander's dream for a battle run with tanks going full throttle, but it was a nightmare waiting to happen for a pair of APC's manned by people who weren't even of legal drinking age.

I tapped Doug on the shoulder and pointed to the ditch on the side of the road, and we crawled down off the snow-covered pavement. Glancing over the rear of the hull, I saw Cruze's carrier following closely behind, then looked up at Sid in the turret and pointed to my eyes. He nodded once, understanding I wanted him to keep his guns aimed at wherever the smoke was coming from. I dropped down into the back of the carrier and crawled over to the rear doors. Kate Dawson gave me a worried look.

"Is everything okay?" she asked.

"Probably not," I replied, as I flipped the combat lock and then tugged on Dawn-Marie's pant leg. "Scan the area for any vehicles or people out there."

"Roger that," she said, as she stood up in her hatch, her carbine resting against her shoulder.

Dawn-Marie dropped back down inside the carrier as I opened one of the rear doors. "What is it?" she asked. "How come we're stopping?"

I gestured for her to come to the rear of the carrier as Cruze jumped off the nose of Ark Two, landing a few feet away.

"Did you see the smoke up ahead?" I asked.

Cruze nodded. "Yeah ... I spotted it just after you gave your contact report on the radio."

"What do you think?"

Cruze pulled out her map and unfolded it across the jump seat. She pointed to the ridge and then to where she guessed our position to be. "I think we're about three clicks from the ridge. Out of range for pretty much all small arms ammunition or even an eighty-four millimetre round."

"But not too far away for a TOW missile," I said grimly.

"If they had a TOW, they'd have used it by now. We're well within the 4000m range."

Dawn-Marie blinked. "Um ... what's a TOW missile?"

"Tube launched, optically-tracked, wire-guided missile system," said Cruze and I said in unison.

Her jaw dropped. "*Seriously?* They might have missiles?"

I shrugged. "I don't see why not. If Sunray came from Wainwright, he'd have access to anti-armour weapons systems. Whether or not any of his people could hit the broad side of a barn with one is another story. But it's possible that he could have them."

"Jesus."

"Have you been down this highway before?" asked Cruze.

"Yeah, lots of times," Dawn-Marie replied. "That ridge ahead is the starting point for a big freaking hill that curves down into the coulee. The bridge over the Red Deer River is maybe 3km down from the top of the hill. It's all badlands down there – you have to stay on the road, because the ground eats anything with wheels."

I moved to the left side of the carrier and peered out with my binoculars again. "Two fires are burning in there somewhere ... I can't tell if it's on the forward side of the river or the opposite bank. It all looks the same from here."

I handed the binoculars to Dawn-Marie and gazed out on the horizon. Through the corner of my eye, I could see Sid Toomey glaring at me from the turret.

""Fuck, Dave, you're freaking whipped and you haven't even seen her boobs up close yet!'

I ground my teeth and was just about to climb back into the carrier when Dawson hopped up on the hull and drove her boot into Sid's shoulder.

"Shut the hell up and keep your head in the game, Sid!" she barked.

"She's a liability, Kate!" he snapped. "Who the hell does this chick think she is, helping Dave and Cruze figure out what's best for the rest of us?"

Dawson leaned into the turret and grabbed Sid by the collar.

"We live or fucking die as a team, asshole!" she barked, shaking the giant Newfoundlander with no shortage of effort. *"Now do your job and – "*

A whip-cracking sound filled the air, and I looked up in time to see the top of Kate Dawson's head explode in a mist of blood and brain matter. The force of the sniper's round sent her tumbling over the right side of the carrier, to land in the snow with a hard thump.

"NO!" I screamed as I raced around the rear door, but I knew she was dead before she hit the ground. I dropped to my knees and started pounding the earth with my fists. *"NO! NO! NO! NO!"*

Through a stinging film of tears, I gazed down at Kate's eyes, staring up at the cold empty sky as the snow underneath her head turned from white to crimson.

Kate was gone.

THE NORTH

CHAPTER 22

Somewhere between our carriers and the ridge, a sniper lay in wait. Another bullet whizzed over my head, and I dove into the snow beside Kate's body.

Jo. She was hatches up in Cruze's APC. I quickly looked over my right shoulder and spotted her alongside Mel Dixon, staring in wide-eyed horror at Dawson's body. I stuck out my right arm and motioned for them both to drop back down inside their carrier. Jo threw me a jittery nod and together they disappeared beneath the hull.

"Did anyone see a muzzle flash?" I roared. *"He'll pick us off one by one if we can't find him!"*

"Negative! Dawn-Marie and I are crouched behind Ark One," Cruze called out. "Are you okay?"

I wasn't okay. Someone had just blown away my second-in-command. A mix if rage and ice cold terror gripped me as I hugged the ground. I was furious with Sid Toomey, whose outburst had forced Kate to silhouette herself on the top of our carrier.

"Ask Sid if he can see anything!" I bellowed. Slowly, I turned my head and lifted it slightly, so that I could peer over Dawson's body at the ridge ahead.

Snipers can render themselves invisible to the naked eye just by using what's available to them – leaves, grass, tree branches, a ground sheet, a shadow inside of a blown-out building.

And this sniper was *very* good. He could have picked off Sid, but the giant Newfoundlander would have died in his turret. Dawson had fallen off the carrier when she was hit. The sniper knew it would draw someone stupid – like me – over to her body.

Hello target number two.

One shot, one kill. That's what happened to Dawson, and that's what was going to happen to me – whoever was out there had me pinned down.

"He can't see anything!" Cruze shouted. "We need to draw his fire, Dave! It's the only way we'll be able to see the muzzle flash. Even that's going to be tough if this guy is good."

162

I shouted back. "Options?"

"We could set out a smoke screen and give you a chance to hustle back to the carrier?"

"No – it's windy enough that the breeze will just blow the smoke back in our faces."

Another crack whizzed over my head, and this time, I heard the distinctive thump of the round hitting the ground behind me. It was time for me to use my limited field craft if I was going to have a hope of getting back to the safety of the APC.

"Are you okay, Dave?" Dawn-Marie shouted.

"What the fuck do you think?" I snapped. "Get inside the carrier until this is over! Cruze, did you hear that shot – any idea where it came from?"

"Not a clue!" she answered back. "What are you thinking?"

"I'm thinking that my second-in-command has been shot dead, and I don't want to join her," I answered. "Tell that asshole Sid to use his sights and keep scanning the area for any movement. I need to draw this guy's fire! Stay put ... got it?"

"Got it, Dave. Don't worry, Sid will spot him!"

Given that Sid had been on me for more than twelve hours about getting rid of Dawn Marie, I wouldn't have expected him to lose any sleep if I became the next person from our team to wind up dead. Where the hell was that sniper? I shut my eyes tight and visualized the pages from *Infantry Section and Platoon in Battle.*

"Target indication ... target indication ... fuck! What did it say?"

Another whip snapping crack split the air over my head followed by a thump, and then it hit me: A crack and then a thump – that was the answer! The tactics manual had a partial section on using the crack and thump of a bullet to determine likely firing positions.

This is the idea: the gap between the sound of the bullet passing by faster than the speed of sound – the crack, and the report from a rifle a fraction of a second later – the thump - will tell you the distance. If the crack and thump are close together the sniper is 300m away or less. If there is a slight delay, the sniper is from 300m to 600m away. If there is a noticeable delay, the sniper is out past 600m.

I decided the sniper had to be directly in front of us somewhere, because I'd be dead already if he was to our right flank. He was probably staring straight through a high-resolution scope, his crosshairs trained on Dawson's body. If I moved my head up even an inch, he'd remove it for me, no questions asked. I needed a distraction that would divert the shooter's attention – something that would buy me enough time to get back to the carrier.

"Cruze!" I shouted. "Get a frag grenade out, pull the pin and lob it across the road to your left."

"Stand by, Dave!" she answered, her voice was strained.

I lowered my head and tried desperately to control my breathing. My heart was racing a mile a minute. If my plan didn't work, I was as good as dead.

"Got it primed and ready, Dave!" Cruze called out.

"Do it!" I shouted.

I could hear Cruze's boots crunching around in the snow to the left side of the carrier. There was silence for a second or two, and then a loud explosion thundered across the barren land. With a jolt of adrenaline, I immediately pushed myself up and dashed back to the safety of the carrier's rear. A shot rang out, and I heard the thump – there was a noticeable delay. The sniper was out past 600m.

Cruze threw her arms around me the moment I reappeared at the rear door. She gave me a quick bear hug, and then let me go as I slid down the back of the carrier into a squatting position. My heart was still pounding at the walls of my chest like a jackhammer, but least I was alive. I only wished I could say the same for Dawson. I exhaled heavily a few times to catch my breath and then Cruze helped me back to my feet.

"What do you want to do, Dave? – He's still out there." Her voice was shaking.

"Fuck knows – the shooter could be anywhere."

I could have sworn I saw Cruze's face flush for a moment. It was rare for her to panic, but seeing Dawson get her head blown off, combined with the prospect of my getting killed, had rattled her nerves.

"Sorry, Dave," she said, her voice still shaking. "Kate and I were … *close*."

"I had no idea, Cruze. Listen … we can mourn later. Right now, we have to take down that sniper because we're sitting ducks."

"I have an idea," she said quickly. "We can do a combat run. We'll go hatches down and leave Ark Two here. That sniper might have a spotter, or they could be one of those security patrols that Dawn-Marie mentioned. If they're mobile, they'll high-tail it back to their vehicle the moment they see us barrelling toward them. And I'm coming with you because I'll expose myself if I go back to Ark Two."

"That sounds good to me," I replied. "Let's go."

I gave Cruze a quick pat on the shoulder as she climbed into the carrier, taking a seat in the spot where, moments earlier, Kate Dawson had been standing. I climbed over Dawn-Marie and onto my seat and then slipped on my headset.

"Ark Two, this is Ark One … orders. Remain static and hatches down. Cruze is coming with me. All eyes on the ridge and report any movement. You will provide supporting fire on my command. Over."

There was silence for a few seconds and then Melanie Dixon answered. "Copy that."

I grabbed the handle for the crew commander hatch door and pulled it down over my head, slipping on the combat lock as the remaining hatches slammed shut in a series of clangs. I peered into my periscope and surveyed the way ahead. Dozens of tiny snow squalls drifted across the highway. I could still see the pair of thin smoke-tendrils in the distance, and wondered if the sniper was acting as a sentry for a larger force, and whether we'd be driving into ambush once we took him down. If he was smart, he'd stay put until our carrier passed his position. If not, then he'd be cut off, then, and still be facing imminent death at the hands of a vengeful Dixon, or worse, Cruze.

If Cruze had it bad for Dawson, she'd kept it a secret. I couldn't even begin to wonder what was going through her head right now. I could only hope she would concentrate long enough for us to locate and capture the sniper. He'd be of no use to us if we killed him.

"Ease this pig onto the highway and floor it, Doug," I shouted into the intercom. "Sid, this is your chance to do something frigging positive for the first time today. You have the best chance of spotting this asshole, so if you see his firing position, don't fill the guy with an entire belt of ammo. I need him still breathing so I can question him."

The intercom hissed, and a very subdued-sounding Sid answered, "Roger that."

The engine groaned as we crawled up the shoulder and back onto the roadway. We quickly levelled off, and I scanned my periscope left and right. There had to be vehicle tracks somewhere that could lead us to the sniper's rig, but my hunch was that he'd done as we'd just done before heading out; moved into a copse of trees and used it as a hide.

But if that were the case, he would have had a long walk to his firing position. He'd probably be wearing white camouflage to cover his olive drab combat fatigues, and he'd likely have strips of white linen wrapped around the fore stock and scope of his weapon.

"We're going sixty," Doug shouted into his intercom. "Do you want me to bury the needle?"

"Keep it steady," I answered. "If we start getting hit, take evasive action into the ditch."

"Will do," he said, leaning into his driver's periscope.

Ahead lay nothing but snow-covered farmland, with empty sloughs scattered here and there. I spotted the bloated bodies of dozens of dead cattle, their legs sticking out straight like the branches on some rotting tree.

A rotting cow carcass would make a hell of a good place to hide when the land is flat and empty and covered with freshly fallen snow. I pressed the PTT button as I swung my periscope hard to the left.

"Doug, slow her down to about twenty," I said into the intercom.

"Copy," he replied. The engine retarder brake screeched like an animal in a snare. The APC slowed right down, pushing my face into the cushion on my periscope as we crawled up the highway. On both sides of the road were cattle corpses – the sniper could be hidden behind any one of them. Then I manoeuvred my periscope hard to the right, and spotted a pair of dead cows about two hundred yards in front of me. Both bodies appeared to have fallen on a small pimple of land jutting out of the flat ground. I ordered the carrier to stop, and gave Sid Toomey a firing mission.

"Two hundred … four fingers right of the center of axis … dead cattle on small rise. One controlled burst … watch and shoot!"

"Roger," said Sid, sounding slightly more determined this time.

The turret whined sharply as Sid lined up his guns with my target indication. I heard a metallic clunk as he cocked both guns, and then Sid's voice filled my headset.

"Do you want a burst from both guns?"

"Just the GPMG – not the .50 calibre," I answered, my eyes fixed firmly on the two dead cows. "A small burst, Sid … maybe five to ten rounds."

"Will do."

The turret whined a final time, and the carrier was filled with the deafening *braaap* of machine gun fire, followed by the clangs of the metal links falling down from the turret and landing on the floor. The first few rounds tore into the carcasses in a straight line, ripping up flesh and sending it spraying back behind them. The remainder flew into the ground, kicking up snow mixed with dirt and grass.

A flash of movement appeared from between two dead animals – a quick blur of white and then darkness as the sniper adjusted his position. I wondered what I'd do if I were in the same boat, and decided I'd probably try to crawl slowly away from the corpses, into anything that even remotely resembled low ground.

"Contact!" I said, nearly spitting the word. "Weapons hold. Doug … get this carrier up and across that Texas gate to our right. I'll ground guide you after that. Sid – did you see him?'

The intercom hissed. "Negative."

"Keep your guns trained on those dead cattle as we move up. Do not fire until you receive word from me."

The carrier pitched to the left. I dug my hands into the handle on my periscope and pressed my head hard against the cushion. We made another sharp right turn over the edge of the highway and onto a thin snow-covered gravel road. In seconds, we were bouncing across the Texas gate – then we drove down a small shoulder and straight into the farmer's field.

"Left!" I shouted, as the carrier narrowly missed ploughing through a dead cow. "Now straight for a hundred meters."

"I got movement!' Sid shouted into the intercom. "There's two of them – they're crawling into an empty slough."

"Copy that," I answered. "How far?"

"No more than two hundred yards, Dave. I can whack them easily from here."

"Take down the spotter," I said venomously. "Leave the shooter alive."

There was a quick burst of fire, and I saw propellant gases drifting across the hull of the carrier.

"Target neutralized," Sid shouted. "The other guy is making a run for it!"

And then I spotted him – a male dressed in white camouflage pants and a thick wool sweater bolted upright, a few yards behind the dead cattle. He threw his rifle onto the ground and sprinted.

"Cut that man off, Doug!" I shouted into the intercom.

The carrier snapped into gear as we barrelled across the field, the engines screaming the entire time. In less than a minute, we'd caught up to the sniper. Doug drove in a wide circle around him as the turret moved to the left, Sid keeping both barrels fixed firmly on him. Cruze threw open her hatch, her carbine at the shoulder, and fired a single shot that hit him in the leg. He toppled over, landing face first in the snow, and then he tried to leopard-crawl away.

"Everyone hatches up!" I shouted as I threw off my headset and dropped back down into the carrier. "We've got our shooter. Dawn-Marie, you'll stay inside the carrier until I send for you."

Doug brought our APC to a screeching halt as the brakes hissed, letting out surplus air through the reservoir underneath the engine. I climbed up to the top of the carrier and then scrambled down the nose, nearly tripping myself up in the process.

A small trail of blood stained the snow as I raced up to the man. I dropped to one knee and lowered my weapon as he continued clawing his way across the snow. Blood from the wound in his right leg had saturated his white camouflage pants, but he kept on going, trying desperately to put some distance between the two of us. I raised my rifle to my shoulder and fired off another pair of rounds.

"The next one is going into the back of your head, asshole!" I shouted. "Don't think that I won't!"

He stopped crawling immediately and then he stuck out his arms in front of his head, holding them inches above the ground.

Cruze raced up from behind me and dashed ahead, her weapon covering him the entire time. I hustled my ass forward until I was standing directly in front of the sniper.

"*Don't* ... just don't shoot!" he stammered. "I give up."

"Cover him, Cruze," I said angrily. I gave him a hard kick to the ribs and then dug the barrel of my carbine into his side, giving it a small shove. He rolled over onto his back, his face a mask of pain. The bullet I'd fired into his leg had landed just above the knee, but he wasn't bleeding out like I'd severed the artery – or he'd have been dead by now. I glanced up at Cruze, who was fishing a field dressing out of the pocket of her combat pants. I shook my head quickly, and she stuffed it back into her pocket.

"You killed my 2IC," I snarled as I dropped to one knee. "How many of you are there up ahead?"

His face twisted itself in knots. I could tell he was fighting the urge to spill the beans.

"Answer him, prick!" Cruze said venomously. "Kate was the best of us, and you killed her."

The sniper rolled his head toward Cruze and then back to me. His eyebrows arched up. "You ... you're freaking *kids*!" he gasped, as if he couldn't believe he'd actually said the words. "I got shot by some fucking *teenagers*!'

"And you shot one of ours, asshole," I growled. "You're about ten seconds away from having your skull splattered across the field unless you tell me what's down in the coulee."

He nodded quickly, his hands still held up over his shoulders. "Okay ... okay, I'll talk. I was just following fucking orders!"

I gave Cruze a quick nod, and she pulled the field dressing out again, ripped open the packaging and removed the large yellow gauze pad. She pressed it hard onto the man's leg. He cried out in pain as she reefed on the strips of gauze to hold it in place.

"You won't die. Yet," she said.

I motioned for my APC to move onto our position. It arrived in less than a minute, leaving a huge cloud of snow in its wake. The rear doors flew open and out jumped Dawn-Marie, who took one look at the sniper and lunged at him, kicking him repeatedly in the leg.

"You son of a bitch!" she roared. "I'll fucking kill you!"

Cruze dove across the sniper and tackled Dawn-Marie, the pair landing hard on the ground a few feet away.

"Looks to me like you two have some history," I said. "Cruze, when you've got Dawn-Marie calmed down, we'll stuff this asshole into the carrier and question him."

"Roger ... *ugh* ... that!" Cruze huffed as she fought to restrain her.

"Good," I answered, my eyes boring into the sniper. "Pal, you'd better get ready to fess up. And you'd better like digging holes in the ground."

He visibly gulped. "H-How come?"

"Because you're going to bury our friend Kate Dawson."

CHAPTER 23

I checked the body of the spotter for Intel and found a cotton-duck-covered field message pad. I tore off the cover and flipped it open. Each page that had been written on was folded in half – a neat way to refer back to earlier orders, but not the smartest of tactical moves – you might wind up getting killed, and anything left in that pad is valuable information for whoever killed you should they check your body.

Clearly, the dead man broke that rule. I scanned the pages looking for anything that would be of use. All I found were map references and timings – ten full pages of them. I quickly pulled out my map and checked to see where the grid references led, but they didn't make any tactical sense: each location was either middle of farmer's field and area of high ground or in the center of thick bush. The timings were interesting, though, and I decided to question the sniper to see what they meant, assuming he was in the mood for sharing.

All soldiers are trained to keep their traps shut – that's why interrogation techniques have become so complex over the years. I wasn't planning on waterboarding the guy, but I was going to make it crystal clear that his life depended on answering questions. I also had an ace up my sleeve. Dawn-Marie recognized him. I made a mental note to have her with me when I started asking questions.

Climbing back into the carrier, I ordered Doug to take us back to Ark Two. I left the navigation up to him, turning my attention to the rear of the carrier. Our prisoner's hands were bound behind his back with cable ties. He stared at the floor while Cruze and Dawn-Marie kept a close eye on him. He wasn't bleeding to death, but a 5.56 millimetre bullet was lodged in his thigh – that would have to come out if the guy had any hope of keeping his leg from becoming infected and eventually turning gangrene. It probably hurt like hell, too.

Good.

A few minutes later, the carrier rolled to a halt alongside Ark Two. Jo did her level best to give me a big smile, only it wasn't working. Her eyes were puffy, and she'd been crying pretty hard.

I climbed inside and lifted her chin with my index finger. "Hey, kiddo – how are you holding up?"

Jo offered the tiniest of shrugs and sniffled loudly. "I'm okay," she said in a whisper of a voice. "I'm just sad because of what happened to Katie."

I drew her close and gave her a warm hug. "I know, Jo. It's not fair that she was killed. Katie was the bravest person I've ever met, but we have to be grateful that she didn't die … badly."

Jo gazed up at me and blinked a few times. "You mean that it's a good thing it wasn't a creeper that got her."

I nodded. "That's the worst way to go."

She sniffled again and said, "Are you mad at Sid?"

"Sid made a big mistake, Jo," I replied. "And I think he knows he let everyone down, especially Kate. That's why it's so important that we've got each other's backs. We can't let our feelings cloud our judgement, because it has an effect on everyone in the team."

Jo's eyes darkened as she lowered her eyebrows, shifting her gaze to the floor of the carrier. "You have the bad guy that shot Katie now, right?"

I nodded. "That's right. I need to question him. We have to find out as much as we can about Sunray and all the people who work with him."

What she said next sent me reeling.

"I want you to kill him, David," she said in a cold, hard voice. "He killed Katie, and I want you to shoot him in the head just like he shot her."

Holy shit.

I might have done a lot of things wrong since Day Zero, but I'd tried my level best to protect Jo from the worst of this dangerous new world. I'd long known that there was no way to shield her from every bad thing that could happen, but if we were going to survive, I was desperate to provide my little sister with that most precious of commodities: hope. But maybe I didn't understand Jo as much as I'd thought. The long months of scraping by, of surviving by inches and facing threat after threat after threat had changed my little sister, in spite of my best efforts. She was a soldier now, just like the rest of us.

A child.

Fucking.

Soldier.

I dropped down onto the jump seat opposite Jo unsure of what to say to her. She gave me a curious look, and for the first time in my life, I didn't have any answers for her. I couldn't look her in the eye and tell her that it was okay to shoot someone who was your prisoner. I just couldn't do it, so I took the coward's way out: I didn't give her a definitive yes or no. Instead, I just answered her question by *not* answering her question.

"We'll figure out what to do with him once we get the information we need," I said, sounding deflated. "In the meantime, you stay hatches down and rest up, Jo. It's going to be a long day and everyone needs to focus."

"Alright, David," she said easily. All the stone cold seriousness had left her voice, and the old Jo had returned.

For how long was anyone's guess.

***

We shrouded Dawson's body in a groundsheet, binding it tight with bungee cord. A few minutes later, we pulled both carriers into an area of low ground about a hundred meters clear of the highway. I booted the sniper out of the back of the carrier and then tossed him a shovel.

"Start digging, prick," I said menacingly. "And don't get any crazy ideas about going ape shit with that shovel on our people because I'll shoot you where you stand."

He nodded quickly and then hobbled a few feet away from the rear doors to begin his task. And surely he was thinking the grave was meant for him. I'm sure everyone on the team would have liked to give Kate a proper burial in a place that wasn't a dried out slough in the middle of a farmer's field. Somewhere peaceful with trees overlooking a valley, but there wasn't any time.

"Dig faster, asshole," said Cruze as she watched the shooter scraping madly at the partially frozen ground. "The sooner we get this done, the sooner we can get the fuck out of this exposed position."

Sid leaned against the back of the carrier and slid down against a rear wheel. He avoided my gaze as the gravity of Kate's death started to sink in. He stared across the snow-covered field as he fished a cigarette out of his pocket.

"Fuck ... I should have kept my mouth shut," he whispered as he ran a sleeve across his eyes. "I caused this, and now Kate's gone and – "

"You're fucking right you caused this, Sid," Cruze interrupted. "And Kate would probably kick you in the balls for wasting time crying over her."

"I'm not crying, okay?" Sid answered.

Kenny climbed out of his carrier and fired a murderous look at the shooter.

"Prick," he hissed. "Please tell me he's digging a grave for himself."

I shook my head. "No – we're going to bury Kate then we're going to get moving. I'll interrogate this asshole later. If he's smart, he'll cooperate."

"And if he doesn't?" said Cruze.

The shooter glanced nervously over his shoulder at me and stared at my carbine.

"He'll talk," I said threateningly.

Jo kept inside the carrier and didn't even bother poking her head out to look at our prisoner. He was dressed in camouflage combat fatigues – the new ones they'd issued to the regular force as opposed to the tattered hand-me-downs the reservists got. He had brown hair that had grown shaggy at the back, and his eyes had that same haunted expression you saw in the eyes of everyone who survived Day Zero. He looked older than us, with crow's feet around his eyes and a thick five o'clock shadow. I'd have pegged him to be in his late twenties to early thirties. On his combat jacket were three chevrons on each sleeve – he was a sergeant. His regimental affiliation was nowhere to be seen – not that it mattered anymore because the army as we knew it was long dead.

The shovel scraped against the partially frozen ground and echoed across the field as the team looked on. I gazed down at Kate's shrouded body and felt my throat beginning to tighten up – we'd survived so much over the past few months. We'd seen other members of the King's Own die in the weeks and months after the siege, but the loss of Kate Dawson hit everyone hard. Doug Manybears crawled out the back of Ark One and began chanting something in his native language, his voice lilting up an octave. A haunting, mournful song poured out from between his lips as he knelt before Kate's body.

He continued singing for another fifteen minutes until the grave was completed. The sniper climbed out and sat down on the dirt covered snow under the watchful eye of Mel Dixon. Doug and Sid gently carried Kate's body to the grave and slid her down the edges. A sharp gust of wind blew across the spoil from Kate's grave, and we all just stood there looking down at the body of our friend. It was as if each of us was waiting for someone to conduct a makeshift service. I'd have said something, but there really wasn't anything to say that would lessen the shock we'd all experienced.

And it was shocking. We'd all seen comrades die, but it was always at the hands of the creeps. This was different. Kate Dawson wasn't being hunted by a monster. She wasn't in the throes of battle – she'd climbed atop the carrier to do her job as my second-in-command, and she wound up shot to death.

"Fuck this," said Mel Dixon as she turned on her heels. "If anyone wants me, I'll be inside Ark Two."

Her feet crunched loudly in the freshly fallen snow as I grabbed the shovel and tossed it to the prisoner. "Fill the hole – you've got five minutes."

"Then what?" he asked with a groan as he got back to his feet.

"You'll know when it happens," I said coldly.

***

We stood around Kate's now filled-in grave as Jo crawled out of the carrier. In her hands, she carried Kate's SPECTRA helmet which she placed in the center as a kind of marker.

"Hang on, Jo," said Sid as he disappeared around the carrier. He returned a few moments later with a large stone about the size of a basketball. He brushed off the snow and tossed Jo a thick felt marker from his breast pocket.

"It's not a proper headstone, but it's better than a helmet."

Jo wrote Kate's name on the flattest side of the stone along with the image of the sun shining in the sky and some birds flying in the distance. Sid carefully placed the stone the head of Kate's grave and wiped his eyes again with the sleeve of his combat jacket.

I put a hand on Jo's shoulder and said, "That was nice, baby sister. Thanks for doing that. Wherever Kate is, she's probably smiling down on..."

"Mother-fucking contact you assholes!" Melanie roared from her turret. *"Get your shit in gear – there's an enemy APC skirting the forward edge of the tree line up ahead!"*

In seconds, we were under fire. Tracer rounds flew over the top of the carrier. We quickly dropped what we were doing and scrambled into the carriers. Once inside, I frantically cable-tied the prisoner to a gun rack and closed the rear doors and hatches.

"What are you seeing, Sid?" I shouted as I crawled into my crew commander's hatch.

"Armoured Recce!" he bellowed. *"Jesus H. Christ, we gotta get out of here, they've got a freaking Cougar!"*

I fumbled with the headset and pulled my hatch lid down over my head as I peered into my periscope to see a cloud of snow behind the rear wheels of a heavily camouflaged Cougar light tank. The Cougar, though it was the exact same vehicle as the one we were driving, possessed a very significant advantage: a turret from a British Scorpion battle tank and a 76 mm main cannon. A well-placed shot from that gun on any part of our APC, and we'd brew up faster than a coffeepot at a truck stop.

"We need to get the hell out of here now!' I shouted into the radio.

Doug Manybears was already taking evasive action, having pulled a wide U-turn in the low ground beside the highway. I peered through my periscope just in time to see the muzzle flash from the cougar's main gun. Less than a second later, our carrier pitched sharply to the left as the high-explosive round hit the pavement to my right.

"Smoke! Smoke! Smoke!" I screamed into my microphone as the turret spun around overhead.

Three loud thunks later, and the smoke canisters were away.

"That round came too freaking close for comfort!" Cruze shouted into the radio. "My smoke is away, we've got good cover!"

"Copy that – both vehicles onto the highway now – bury the freaking needle and keep your guns at the ready!"

Doug gave me a thumbs-up as I fumbled with my map.

Our sniper had been part of a recce element. That explained why we hadn't seen a vehicle anywhere. The spotter and the shooter had likely been conducting a foot patrol when they saw us barrelling up the highway. The smoke we'd seen was probably from a small fire the rest of their team had been using to warm up – it was well below zero outside. I'd driven us straight into a trap. Part of me hoped we'd wind up getting broadsided by an anti-tank round, because ever since the moment we broke out of the armoury, I'd made piss-poor decisions and got us all into firefights at every freaking turn.

I heard the turret spin around quickly from behind as Sid's voice filled my headset. "He's still a good distance back, but he's on our tail!"

I snapped out of it, peering through my periscope for a bit of land we could use for cover.

"Are we out of range of that gun?" I barked.

"Yeah … barely." Sid answered.

"Keep that needle buried, Doug! We need to put more distance between us."

Doug Manybears answered through a haze of static. "It's buried. I don't know how much faster I can make this thing go. We gotta figure out a way to take down that Cougar."

"No shit! Ark Two – get your ass parallel to our carrier. We'll slow down slightly and let you take the lead."

The radio hissed. "Are you nuts, Dave?" shouted Cruze. "He'll have two big fat olive drab targets to fire at!"

I pressed the PTT button as my heart raced. "Only for a couple of seconds. Just do it!"

"FUCK!" she bellowed.

The pitch from our engine dropped only slightly as the APC's engine break kicked in. I could make out the nose of Cruze's carrier in my peripheral vision, so I ordered Doug to let Ark Two take the lead. An enormous cloud of snow filled the air in front of the trim vane as Cruze's APC moved ahead.

"How are we doing for distance now, Sid?" I shouted.

There was a short pause, and then Sid answered. "Jesus – we're within range. He's maybe eight hundred meters back."

"Any smoke left?" I asked.

"Three shots left on the right dischargers. What's the plan?"

"The plan is we get up another screen, and I'm going to jump out of the carrier into the ditch."

The radio squawked. "Don't you freaking do it, Dave. He'll mow you down!"

I clenched my jaw tightly as I glanced back to the jump seat where Dawson used to sit. My idea was a massive risk and entirely suicidal, but it was all I had. I pressed the intercom button. "Sid, get ready to fire off that smoke on my mark. Stand by."

"Roger that," he answered. I quickly unplugged my headset and raced to the back of the APC, climbed onto the left rear jump seat and rolled back the tarp on the floor. Beneath it was a fibreglass case, containing two 84mm high explosive anti-tank rockets. I quickly sliced off the safety wire that sealed the box and flipped it open. Inside were two plastic tubes about as long as my arm. I lifted one out of the box and placed it between my knees, giving it a sharp twist to the right. The packing tube came off, exposing a long black cylinder with a yellow band painted across the shiny surface. I handed the anti-tank round to Dawn-Marie as I spun around and pulled the rigging off the Carl Gustav recoilless rifle stowed just underneath the hatch door. It was clumsy, heavy and usually a two-man-operated weapon, but my second-in-command was dead, and we'd all be joining her if I didn't get the weapon loaded quickly.

I glanced up at the sniper, whose face had turned ashen. He must have known all along there would be a Cougar coming out of the coulee at some point. "Your buddies are hot on our tail. How many are in that Cougar?"

"The driver and crew commander," he said, staring at the weapon.

"And what's down inside that coulee?"

"Unit outpost," he answered.

"How many?"

"A couple of dozen."

"All civilians?"

He shook his head.

I glanced at Dawn-Marie, and she gave me a sharp nod. There was a frightened look in her eyes. I had a hunch that she too knew what was down inside that coulee. It would have been nice if she'd have told me before we'd left the hide.

"Is he lying to me, Dawn-Marie?" I asked as I slid the long projectile into the firing tube.

"No – it's an outpost. At least, that's what our handlers told us. They threatened to send us there if we broke any of Eden's laws."

I looked at the sniper and remembered the coordinates inside the field message pad I'd found on the dead spotter. I wanted to question him about the pad's contents, but there wasn't any time – this was confirmed by Sid's shrill voice blasting down from the turret.

"*Five hundred meters, Dave!*" Sid hollered. "*If you're going to do something, you'd better freaking do it now!*"

"*Who is Sunray?*" I barked, my eyes never leaving the sniper. "*Who is your commander – is he down in the coulee?*"

Kate's killer must have known his number was just about up. His lips arched up into a cruel smile, and he started to chuckle. Dawn-Marie bashed him in the side of the head with our first-aid kit, and his giggling morphed into a fit of laughter.

"*Answer him!*" Dawn-Marie snapped.

The sniper shifted his gaze to the front of the carrier "Freaking kids. You're already dead, and you don't even know it."

I lunged at him, dropping the now fully-loaded recoilless rifle onto the floor of the carrier.

"*Who is Sunray?*" I roared, shaking the man like a rag doll. "*Where is his location?*"

He blinked a couple of times and stared me straight in the eye. "Sunray is Major J.T. Martins. Commander of the battle school. You won't find him, because he's on the move – he's *always* on the move. You might as well all shoot yourselves right now – because when he gets his hands on you, you'll be begging for that bullet."

I'd heard enough. I cut the cable tie on his wrist and then slid over to the right rear door and flipped off the combat lock.

"Sid!" I bellowed. "Get your ass down from the turret, right now!"

Sid's feet dropped down to the bottom of the turret cage. He squatted next to the sniper as I threw open the rear door; a jet of cold air rushed into the carrier, along with a heavy dusting of snow. I glared at the sniper with a look that could melt iron bars. "You killed my second," I shouted over the wind. "You tried to kill me, and your people have been trying to kill us ever since we set foot in Eden. The freaking creeps are the enemy, not breathers! You made your choice. Now I'm making mine."

Sid Toomey drove a size-16 combat boot into the sniper's shoulder. He toppled over the edge of the jump seat and out onto the snow-covered highway, his body barrel-rolling through a snow squall. Sid lifted his carbine and raised it to his shoulder.

"Kill that son of a bitch," I snarled.

A pair of shots rang out. I didn't bother to see if they'd hit their target.

Sid climbed back up into the turret as I plugged my headset into the intercom jack again. "Sid – fire off those remaining three smoke now!" I shouted, heaving the loaded Carl Gustav onto my lap. I swung my legs over the edge of the rear door, ignoring the snow that was blowing into my face.

"Smoke's away!" Sid shouted.

"Doug, slow this pig down to a crawl – I'm getting out!" I bellowed.

I saw him raise his thumb, and seconds later, the engine retarder brake kicked in with a deafening metallic shriek. I looked at Dawn-Marie. "When I jump out, close this freaking door and tell the driver to floor it. He's in charge now – got it?"

She looked at me nervously and gave me a short, quick nod. "Tell the gunner to keep his eyes on the rear of the carrier. If he sees that I've taken down that Cougar, tell them to double back and get me."

"And if you don't?" she asked. Her voice was shaking.

I gazed out the back door to see that the entire highway behind us was covered by a thick blanket of white smoke. The carrier was now moving at a walking pace, so I hopped out the back, hefting the recoilless rifle onto my shoulder.

"Then it won't matter," I said, pushing on the thinly-armoured door. "Now go!"

The door shut with a loud clang and the carrier took off, kicking up another cloud of snow in its wake. I had one shot – one single chance to destroy the light tank. I wasn't going to waste it. Under the cover of our smoke screen, I raced across the highway and into a ditch, and cocked the Carl Gustav. The sound of the Cougar's engine echoed across the empty farmland as it drew closer. I dropped into the prone position and heaved the anti-tank gun onto my shoulder. I could feel the vibration of the Cougar's weight shaking the ground underneath my chest, and I took a deep breath, peering into the telescopic sight on the side of the firing tube.

What happened next would decide whether I lived or died. Whether my team would make it through another day and whether I failed my sister Jo. My heart was hammering as fast as a two-stroke engine, and my throat was sandpaper dry. I gulped back a mouthful of cold air as the Cougar rolled past, temporarily blinding me with a face full of snow. I quickly shot up on one knee and lined up the crosshair with the enemy's rear doors. Exhaling slowly, I watched the crosshairs slowly drop until they were parallel with the base of the hull.

"This is for you, Kate," I whispered as I squeezed the trigger.

A jet of intense heat burst out of the back of the gun as the anti-tank round thundered up the highway. There was a bright yellow-orange flash, followed less than a second later by an explosion that shook the ground beneath me. The Cougar rolled to a screeching halt. I watched the rear doors flying through the air, landing on the pavement about 50 feet away from the burning vehicle.

And then it brewed up. Liquid fire poured out the sides of the turret as a man engulfed in flames scrambled out of his hatch. He screamed in an inhuman voice as he fell over the side of the burning machine, landing face-first on the pavement. He didn't get up. Thick black smoke filled the air as I lowered the gun. I started walking up the highway in a scene better suited to an action movie.

I'd just killed three men in less than five minutes, and I'd done it without an ounce of remorse.

I knew what was down in the coulee, but that knowledge had come at a terrible cost. Kate Dawson was dead, and my little sister's innocence was dying as well.

We weren't going to make it to Sanctuary Base. I knew that now. If we had any hope of surviving and rebuilding our lives, we had to destroy Eden. The only question left was how to find Sunray.

And kill him.

CHAPTER 24

Journal Entry: 17 NOVEMBER 01:30 HRS ZULU

I'm scared to death. We all are. Doug picked me up shortly after I destroyed the Cougar. I left Cruze in charge of both teams while I took a few minutes to get a grip on my nerves. I can't stop shaking. I've had small tremors in my hands ever since our close call outside Airdrie, and the loss of Kate Dawson is fucking killing me. I actually burst out bawling, but I buried my head in my lap so that nobody would see. The engine muffled the sound of my sobbing, but I think Doug knew that I needed a moment – he got on the radio to tell Cruze to find us a new hide on the map.

Sid probably knew about my little case of shell shock, too, but he didn't say anything about it. I wasn't in my right mind. It's possible that I'm still not in my right mind as I write this. I can't sleep – all I can think about is Kate and how she didn't stand a chance against that sniper. Maybe I should have ditched Dawn-Marie – had I done so, Dawson would still be here. I'd have accepted her death a lot easier, if it had come during close-quarter combat with the creeps or in a firefight where we could see the enemy who was shooting at us. But a sniper round to the head was so arbitrary. She deserved a better death than that.

Dawn-Marie just went to sleep. She's been up all night talking to me about what led her to where she is now, stuck inside an APC and clinging to the faint hope that we might somehow live through this. Me, I'm beginning to doubt our chances. We've learned that Sunray is a full-blown infantry major – the commander of the Battle School in Wainwright.

Why didn't he get assigned to a command position with a field unit after Day Zero happened? Most of his troops would have been mustered - so why not him? And what about his current force? I don't know a huge amount about the Battle School, but I do know there were more recruits than trained soldiers. The training cadre was regulars – I wonder how many were left up in Wainwright when the end came.

I feel like I can't compete against someone with that kind of experience. I can shoot, I can patrol, I've dug a few trenches and helped build a full defensive position, but that's pretty much it. I picked up a few tricks from Sergeant Green during the six-month siege at the armoury, though. I know how to wrap an explosive charge and set it off. I know how to read a map – barely. I've learned that reading the ground in front of you comes with experience, and that I'm still a noob.

We're all noobs, and that's probably why I'm suddenly worried about whether we're going to make it. Even if Sunray's people are as inexperienced as my team, at least they have a leader who knows what to do next. Sunray is a senior officer – that means he's been in the regular force for at least ten years. He's probably seen combat, and he knows how to act when he's under fire. I've only had a couple of days to learn how to think on my feet in a combat situation – nothing like Sunray.

Well, I guess I should count creeps in all of this though they only have one tactic – swarming.

Actually, we haven't seen any groups of creeps since Airdrie. They're likely confined to the built-up areas – Dawn-Marie said Sunray's people have been pretty thorough in cleaning up any stragglers that wander into Eden. She knows a hell of a lot about Sunray's people and how he operates. Like, a ton. Still, I wonder whether she's telling us everything we need to know or if it's possible that I'm being played. Then again, she sure as hell knew that sniper and her story of girls getting raped? Maybe that explains her reaction when we captured him ... maybe I should have let her shoot him instead of Sid.

She's useful for now ... I think. Damn, I don't know if she is or isn't. I'm going to put things to a vote as to what we should do with her because something just isn't sitting right with me.

I hope to hell that will satisfy Sid because most of his resentment is aimed squarely at me. He blames me for Kate's death, and maybe in a way, I'm also blaming myself.

It's getting colder outside – I think it's close to minus 20 right now. The Siberian Express must have rolled in. Only on the Canadian prairie can you count on sub-zero temperatures at the end of November.

Cruze picked a really good hide – a copse of trees at least a square kilometre in size, a few clicks from the coulee. Actually, the fact that it's snowing outside is a Godsend at this point, because freshly-fallen snow covers up vehicle tracks. Everyone is breathing a little bit easier because of that. We hauled out the winter camouflage nets covered our vehicles to break up their outlines, so we're well hidden. We're going on a reconnaissance patrol in a few minutes. Me, Melanie Dixon and Kenny Howard. Cruze is going to keep things together back here in the hide, Sid is catching some kip, and Doug is going on sentry.

I'm still shaking. I can't seem to make it stop, and I don't want anyone to know how bad this is getting. That's why I'm going to let Mel navigate when we go out on patrol. Kenny and I will provide security. We're going in light, carrying about 120 rounds of 5.56 millimetre ammo for our carbines and one hand grenade each. We're going to be dressed from head to foot in our winter whites, including mukluks and wind pants. We need to make it into that coulee and try and figure out what kind of outpost is down there – their strength, their weapons, any defensive traps, whether the bridge is wired with explosives. And we need to make it out alive. There aren't many physical obstacles to cross according to the map, and there's cloud cover, so it'll be darker than on a moonlit night. I think I might have forgotten what the moon looks like. I can't remember when the last time was I saw it.

We're leaving in 15 minutes. I'm bombed up, I've got the first-aid kit, and I've actually managed to stomach a hot meal. It wasn't a ham omelette, either. I had Salisbury steak and a mug of instant chicken noodle soup.

***

We did a last check on each other before we headed out. Mel and Kenny had stuck strips of white adhesive tape along their carbines, and still had enough left in the roll that I could do mine properly too. Each of us was dressed in white nylon camouflage shirts and pants that covered our combat fatigues. We all wore white balaclavas as well, so really the three of us looked like snowmen. Each of us jumped and down a few times and listened for anything that made loud noises; all that I heard was the thump, thump, thump, of their water bottles and one magazine pouch each, holding their three other clips of ammunition.

"Okay guys," I whispered. "We're good to go. Are we all ready for   this?"

"Ready," said Mel, as she pulled the balaclava over her face.

"I was born ready," said Kenny, as he slipped a 30=round magazine into his carbine. "You know ... sort of."

I nodded. "Good. We'll zigzag in open country, Mel. I know this is going to add a couple of clicks to the route, but we'll be leaving tracks, and we don't need a straight line back to the hide."

"I know," she whispered back. "I'll set up the ORV once we're in the bush line for the coulee. I've also got an alternate route back – I hope to hell Cruze has the coffee on. It's flipping cold out tonight."

"Freaking right it's cold," I answered. "Kenny, are there fresh batteries in the night sight?"

He held out the night vision scope and said, "Yeah – I just popped in four fresh D-Cells and tested it. I'm good to go."

"Okay ... noise discipline, guys. We've all done patrolling before when we were training, but this time, it's the real deal. There's every reason to expect they'll have set up trip flares or obstacles. We'll move in, spend about 30 minutes scoping the area out, and then haul our asses back to the hide."

The pair nodded in unison as I pulled the balaclava down over my face and exhaled heavily. "All right, let's get on with it."

I wasn't carrying the map this time – that was Mel Dixon's job. I was dead dog tired. By rights, I shouldn't have been going out on a patrol at all, but I was on edge. I needed to see with my own eyes what was down in that coulee. We left the hide at two o'clock in the morning. The snow crunched beneath our feet with every step. If Sunray was half the commander he'd been made out to be, he'd know by now that a military element was in his territory, so he should be expecting reconnaissance. At the same time, we should be expecting a patrol to come take a good hard look at what my team was up to. All I could hope for was that it wouldn't be tonight.

It can be gloomy, going out on a patrol at two o'clock in the morning, but we weren't feeling it. Our first stop was an observation post on the forward edge of the hide. Under normal circumstances, there'd be a slit trench or shell scrape dug into the ground and covered with good camouflage. Because we'd only pulled into the hide a few hours earlier, this OP would simply be a well-camouflaged member of our team – Doug Manybears – lying in a snow drift, armed with his personal weapon and the second of our night vision scopes. We scurried up to the OP and dropped onto our bellies, keeping a watchful eye for any movement in the distance.

"How's it looking, Doug?" I asked as I gazed out into the darkness. Snow was falling with large puffy flakes. In another time and place, a person might have thought they were pretty.

"All's quiet from what I can tell," he whispered. "A lot of deer out there, though. I guess the creeps don't like to eat venison."

"They'll eat anything that breathes," I said. "We're heading out now, and we don't expect to be back until just before first light – probably around seven in the morning. We're relying on you to keep the team safe while we're gone. If any creeps come staggering through here, bash them. No guns."

He lifted the night sight back to his eyes and peered out. "And what if any of the Sunray peeps decide to come at us?"

"Then you listen to Cruze. Got it?"

He nodded. "Yup. You guys better get a move on, be safe and good luck."

"Thanks, man," I said, motioning for Mel to take the lead. She doubled out in front of the OP and pulled out her compass. "Keep warm."

Mel Dixon aimed her Silva Compass out in front of her nose and shot a bearing. In seconds, she'd stuffed the compass underneath her white camouflage shirt and motioned for the two of us to follow. We'd zigzag across open country, presenting as little silhouette as possible. Our first objective was a swamp about 1000m from the hide. The next was a small copse of trees about 1500m before the edge of the coulee. The last leg would take us 800m into the thick woods on its perimeter.

Our objective rendezvous point was about 300m south of the highway, cutting very close to any possible defensive traps. But if the sniper's information was accurate, the action was in the belly of the coulee. I felt confident that Mel would get us to our ORV safely. After that, it was anything can happen time.

We pushed on, carrying a quick pace in the darkness. A few inches of snow had fallen since we established the hide. At least the wind had died down. I kept my eyes focused on the arc of fire to my right. Every few minutes, I'd look over my shoulder to see Kenny Howard about 10 meters behind me. He had the worst job on the patrol; keeping a watchful eye for anything that might come up on us from the rear. That meant he'd have to walk backwards every few minutes, and on more than one occasion, he tripped and landed flat on his back.

We ducked underneath a cattle fence and pressed on, Mel checking her map every few hundred meters or so. After about 30 minutes of trudging over uneven ground, I spotted a slight depression in a farmer's field that stretched for about 200m in either direction. Thick stalks of weeds and bramble jutted up from the snow, so we moved alongside them and dropped to one knee. Mel Dixon doubled back to my position, and we quickly examined the map.

"This is the swamp," she whispered. Her voice was so quiet that I could hardly hear her.

"Good," I said, taking a quick glance at the map underneath a dot of red light. "Let's get moving on the second leg."

She quickly oriented the map to the ground and then shot a bearing. Within seconds, we were back on our feet, hugging the edge of the swamp.

We had 1500m of open ground to cover, and now the wind had picked up. The icy breeze still somehow managed to penetrate my thick wool balaclava. I was warm from the past hour's physical activity, but every now and again, I'd feel a finger of cold stabbing at the back of my neck or blowing up underneath my parka. I didn't bother checking my watch – time seems frozen somehow when you're on a patrol. And your eyes play tricks with you. Shadows appear to be living things that move with the grace of a ghost. Tiny squalls of snow drifting across the open fields came alive with every sharp gust of wind, dancing and twirling like miniature tornadoes, and disappearing when the wind changes direction.

Mel pushed on through a head wind like an ice breaker cutting through pack ice. Her eyes never left her objective on the horizon.

Every few minutes, she'd raise a hand and we'd drop to one knee and listen. All that I could hear was the sound of that icy breeze scraping against the snow and kicking up miniature snowstorms that blew across our feet.

We made it to our second objective intact – Kenny didn't land on his back even once. We skirted around the edge of the copse, careful not to trip on any low growth or deadwood. In the distance, I could see the silhouette of the forested area that formed the coulee's border, and this time, we waited a full fifteen minutes before pressing on.

Something was making a sound inside the small wood. My first hunch was that we'd stumbled into some deer, but they would have bolted into the night. It was a slow, repetitive snapping sound – that's the only way I could describe it. After about two minutes, we found the source of it: a lone creep lying against a tree. Snow had blanketed its legs, and its arms were stretched ready to ensnare the unsuspecting traveller. Only this creep was barely moving; its limbs freezing up as the temperature dropped. We kept our distance and gazed out at the creature. Its film-covered eyes stared straight at us, and if it had been a few degrees warmer, the monster would have been on us by now.

"That freaking thing is near frozen solid," Kenny whispered as he spun his weapon around so the butt was facing the creature. "Want me to put it out of its misery?"

I shook my head. "We'll leave it. Remember … noise discipline. We're close to the objective."

"Then let's get going," Mel said, her tone matching Kenny's. "Only 800m more."

So we pressed on, feeling a little bit edgy about having run into a creep. Still, if there were any others lurking about, they'd be frozen solid, or well on their way to becoming popsicles.

We could see the objective ahead. Mel double-checked her map a final time and gestured for Kenny and me to follow. She quickened her pace, ploughing across the open country with her weapon at the ready. In no time, we'd made it to the perimeter woods. We skirted into the bush line and dropped onto our bellies, locking our feet together in an all-around defence. Mel handed me her map, and I aimed the tiny beam of light onto our location to confirm we'd arrived where we were supposed to. Bless Melanie Dixon and her freaking awesome navigation skills – she was only off by 20m from the line she'd traced on the map. It was time for me to take over. After about five minutes of creeping through the thick wood, I found a boulder the size of a small truck that jutted out of the ground like a headstone.

I made a circular motion with my hand as I pointed at the rock and whispered, "ORV."

Kenny immediately dropped down into the prone position and put his carbine to his shoulder. "I'm good, Dave. Be careful out there," he said grimly.

"Same password as back at the hide," I whispered. "If we're not back within an hour, head for the hide."

He nodded. I patted him on the shoulder and motioned for Mel to follow.

And so we headed into the coulee. I had a sick feeling, all of a sudden. This was as close as we'd ever been to doing something that old-school military officers would have described as "fraught with peril." We were deep inside occupied territory, and we faced a well-armed, probably well-defended enemy somewhere in front of us. If we screwed up, Mel and I would be dead, no questions asked.

So I decided we couldn't screw up. We just couldn't.

CHAPTER 25

The forward slope of the coulee was difficult ground. Every few feet, large rocks threatened to trip us as we crept forward. I made mental notes of prominent natural features inside the wood.

We weren't planning on going down to the bottom – just to find a spot with a clear view for Mel and I to lie down prone and observe. Seeing as how Sunray was mechanized, like we were, I decided he'd be near the bridge over the Red Deer River. He owned this territory, and the road heading east and west crossed that bridge. I didn't have to wait long to find out if I was right. We skirted around a snow-covered hoodoo when we heard the sound of a generator humming away below us. We leopard-crawled forward, brushing the snow away from our faces, until we were hidden neatly behind a clump of frozen dead wood.

The first thing we noticed was the sharp smell of wood smoke. I reached for the night vision scope, pressed the toggle switch and peered out into the darkness. The snow-covered landscape was at once bathed in unnatural green light. To our left was the main highway, snaking down the steep walls of the coulee to an iron bridge that I guessed to be about 800m below our position. Six-foot pickets had been pounded into the ground about ten feet from each other, forming a razor-wire fence that stretched out across the bridge's western edge. They'd fashioned a gate with a roll of double concertina razor wire, and there was a lone sentry pacing across the deck of the bridge.

I panned over to the right, and saw a roadway on the other side of the bridge, skirting the edge of the river. It led to a small parking compound where a pair of Cougars was parked, their guns pointing toward the highway leading in and out of the coulee. I spotted a flickering area of whitish-green light to the right of the tanks; a large bonfire blazed away, making my night vision goggles useless, so I handed them to Mel in exchange for a set of binoculars.

"Keep watch on the bridge," I whispered. "Make a note of everything you see."

Mel nodded as I flipped off the lens covers on my binos and began to scope out the area near the bonfire.

Five men were standing around, smoking cigarettes and warming themselves as the fire blazed furiously in the darkness. To their right was another small parking compound, containing two eight-wheeled Mini-Coyote LARVS –light armoured reconnaissance vehicles, armed with 25mm chain guns and pairs of light machine guns. I shuddered. Between the Coyotes and the Cougars, our two obsolete APC's were massively outgunned.

I continued scanning the eastern edge of the river, following the roadway to a large fenced compound. It stretched north of the riverbank up to the tree line, with three modular tents surrounding it. I decided the tents must be some kind of makeshift staff quarters, but, for the life of me, I couldn't understand why they'd built a compound in the first place.

And then I saw them. A small group of men and women, dressed in civilian clothes. They sat huddled over a small fire inside the compound, while a lone sentry paced the perimeter of the razor wire fence, armed with a shotgun. But that wasn't what sent a chill down my spine. It was the trio of lumbering creeps, each chained by the ankle to a post driven into the ground on the compound's south western corner. Several oil drums filled with wood blazed away on the outside of the fence. I suspected they'd been put there to provide just enough heat to stop the creeps freezing solid as the temperature dropped.

Civilians locked inside a fenced compound – with chained-up creeps?

I adjusted the focus on my binoculars, and stared hard at the creatures as they shuffled and stumbled around the post, occasionally lunging at the group of civilians. To my horror, I saw human remains scattered across the blood-soaked snow within arm's reach of the monsters.

"Jesus!" I gasped, nudging Mel in the ribs and handing her the binoculars. "Look over there."

She gave me the night scope, and peered down the forward edge of the coulee until she saw it.

"That is some seriously disturbed shit," she whispered. "What do you think it means?"

"From the bodies surrounding the creeps, I'd have to say that ..."

"Jesus, Dave ... they're feeding people to the living dead? That's freaking sick."

"I can't think of anything else, Mel," I said grimly. "Maybe Sunray is using this compound as a way to deal with anyone who causes problems for his new utopia. It's like ... it's like a micro death camp. Only they're not gassing people. They're leaving them to the creeps."

"I can spot only one way into the coulee, and one way out," she whispered. "These guys are armed to the teeth."

I nodded. "And we have to save those people," I said angrily, unable to divert my eyes away from the wired compound. "We need to end this – whatever *this* is."

She nodded. "Let's get the hell out of here."

"Agreed," I whispered, slinging the night vision goggles over my shoulder. We retraced our steps, and in minutes, we were back at the ORV.

"Easy," I whispered, as I dropped to one knee.

Kenny had his carbine aimed straight at me. "Viper," he replied. "What did you see?"

"Enough," I said as I checked my watch. "It's four thirty-five – there's still well over an hour and a half of darkness. We'll double back at the high port and then Mel, and I will give everyone a full debrief once we get back.

He grimaced. "That bad?"

I nodded. "That bad, Kenny. Let's go."

***

We made it back to our hide undetected, trudging up to the sentry post at five minutes past six, where Doug Manybears was pleased to see us. I sent Mel and Kenny back to the carriers and told them I'd join them in a few minutes. I needed to talk with Doug. I dropped down onto my belly alongside the gangly Sarcee, and he handed me a granola bar to munch on.

"How's it look out there?" he whispered.

"Ugly – why aren't you back there getting some sleep?" I said quietly as I peeled back the wrapper and took a bite.

"I decided to let Cruze get some extra rest – she's really looking wiped out, man. Sid did his turn and then I'm out here doing Cruze's shift."

I swallowed a mouthful, and stuffed the remainder into my pocket.

"How's Sid's headspace?" I asked. "He's taking Dawson's death pretty hard."

"Sid is Sid," he answered. "He's got major issues with that new chick, but Cruze is keeping him in line."

"And Dawn-Marie? Do you think we can trust her?"

Doug gave a small shrug. "Beats the hell out of me, brother. I stay out of that shit, you know? I mean, if what she's saying is true, that she's as good as dead if this Sunray dude finds her, well, I guess she has to realize her best shot is with us."

"Do *you* trust her, Doug?" I asked, scanning his face.

"Nope ... but I don't *not* trust her, either. I think that if she was going to cause problems it would have happened while we were at half strength – when you guys were out on patrol. And anyway, Jo seems to like her."

That was a positive sign. Jo had an amazing ability to read people. I slapped Doug on the shoulder. "Thanks for that, bud. I don't think I've spent enough time asking you for your opinion ... sorry about that."

Doug nodded, his eyes fixed on the horizon. "We drivers are very spiritual people, Dave. We keep our traps shut and observe. I'll look forward to the debriefing after my shift. Later, man."

"Later, Doug," I said as I turned on my heel and headed to the carriers. When I got back, I was pleased – no – downright floored by the fact that the team had pitched the ten-man tent from the toboggan. It was nestled snugly in a depression, surrounded by thick poplar and blue spruce trees. Everyone's kit was lined up along the front guide lines, and I noticed a faint glow filtering through the fabric. A hollow sounding hiss from the Coleman lantern was all I could hear, outside of Sid's snoring, so I slipped off my web gear and put it in front of the guide line with my weapon. I reached out for the zipper on the front flap and said, "Light."

The Coleman lantern stopped hissing, and the warm ambient glow disappeared. I unzipped the flat and crawled inside.

"Welcome back," said Cruze as I zipped up the flap. She turned on the lantern again, filling the interior of the tent with a soft orange glow. A pot of water was simmering on the stove, and she handed me a steaming mug of hot chocolate.

"Thanks." I gazed around the inside of the tent – it looked like a picture from the winter warfare training manual. The sleeping bags were arranged in a semi-circle around the tent pole, and the ground was covered with pine boughs. Combat glove liners and mukluk booties were hanging from the tent liner to dry, fixed firmly in place by safety pins. A garbage bag was taped to the tent pole – it was half full of empty ration wrapping and napkins. Kenny and Mel were seated on their valises. Each was sipping at a mug of hot chocolate and had stripped off their parkas and mukluks.

"Nice job, Cruze," I said, as I squatted down and took a seat on my valise next to a snoring Jo. "We could have crashed in the carriers – you guys didn't have to do this, and anyway, Sid should have set this up. Doug told me he took your sentry shift."

"He did, and I owe him," said Cruze. "It's been snowing like crazy out there – probably six inches since you guys left."

"And freaking insanely cold," Mel said blowing into her hands. "The winter has decided to come early. It would have been nice to get acclimatized."

"It's the prairie," said Kenny, as he gulped back a mouthful of hot chocolate. "Snow today and maybe 20 degrees tomorrow – you never know."

Cruze took a seat next to the stove and eyed me closely for a moment. "What did you see, Dave?" she asked. "What's down in that coulee?"

I glanced uneasily at Mel, who threw me a quick nod. "We spotted a pair of Cougars and two Coyotes with machine guns. There's a hell of a lot of razor wire surrounding the bridge, and we saw a compound of some kind – like a pen."

Cruze's eyes narrowed. "A compound? What's inside?"

I blew on my mug of hot chocolate to cool it down. "Civilians," I said ominously. "And three creeps chained to a post. I think it's some kind of execution thing … I don't know what the hell to call it. All I know is there were human remains around those creeps and five civvies hunched over a fire."

Cruze kicked at the tent floor with the heel of her mukluk. "I'd like to say we could head north and cross over near Three Hills, but we won't have enough fuel for that."

I shook my head. "Nope, not enough fuel by a long shot. What we saw down in that coulee, it's freaking sick, Cruze. It's like a death camp on a microscopic scale."

"It is a death camp," Mel interrupted. "You don't lock breathers in with chained-up creeps unless you have one intention – to make people think they might wind up there if they don't toe the line."

Cruze gave me a wary look, and I could tell she knew what I was thinking. We had zero options at this point – we needed to push eastward, and the coulee was the only way we could go. And we couldn't just barrel down that highway with all guns blazing, because there were two light tanks that could take us out without the gunner even breaking a sweat.

And it *was* a death camp.

I couldn't imagine what kinds of crimes the five civilians in that pen could have committed, but nobody deserved to be torn apart by creeps. If Sunray truly wanted to make people disappear, he could simply shoot them dead. This was something else entirely. It told me that Major J.T. Martins was a madman and that anyone who willingly followed him didn't deserve to live.

Our plan of making it to Sanctuary Base and starting over was looking more and more like a pipe dream, and I think that Cruze knew it too. What started out as a mission to escape hell on earth had turned into a different kind of hell, where survivors were forced to live in a makeshift police state and the threat of death guaranteed a warped kind of order.

We had to get those people out of that pen, and that meant only one option, although I shuddered when I thought about the risk.

The last of the King's Own would go on a fighting patrol and save those civilians.

CHAPTER 26

Journal Entry: 18 NOVEMBER 0639 HRS ZULU

What should we do with Dawn-Marie? She's only been with us for a couple of days. We'll have to leave her back at the hide along with Jo and Kenny when the patrol leaves the hide.

I'm so freaking tired. I've debriefed Cruze, and I've sworn Mel and Kenny to secrecy about what we found in the coulee until I've had a chance to fill in the entire team. The last thing we need is a lot of speculation about why Sunray had slapped together a makeshift death camp. Look at me, keeping secrets from Sid Toomey. Am I punishing him or have I lost faith in him? I'm going to need him on the patrol. He's a one-man wrecking-crew, and our best machine gunner.

What we're about to do might spell the end of every last one of us. I have no idea what kind of fighters Sunray's people are, but they've had more training than us, and they've spent six months out there battling creeps instead of barricading themselves in like we'd done. But Sanctuary Base isn't going to happen until we get past Sunray. I think everyone on the team kind of knows that by now, although we're all afraid to say it. We could abandon the carriers and start gum sucking it cross country on foot, but it will take us weeks, and we honestly believed we'd have gotten much closer with our carriers by scrounging diesel and pushing on. I guess we didn't realize the sheer totality of this messed-up new world it until we'd broken out of the city. We didn't have a clue that we'd be going through occupied territory, or that we'd be fighting skirmishes against former soldiers – for crying out loud, we thought the enemy would be the creeps!

I'm starting to understand why Mom took her own life. She couldn't cope, and now I'm wondering how I'm going to cope enough to keep giving Jo a light at the end of the tunnel. Maybe she's luckier than the rest of us – she's just a kid, she only has a few years of the old world for a frame of reference. This terrifying world of creeps and sudden death is Jo's new normal – maybe she's better able to adapt to it because she doesn't really remember much else.

I'm going to crash for a few hours. If I don't, I'll probably lapse into a coma. Cruze and Doug and Sid can run the OP for now. This afternoon, we'll have a team meeting and hammer out our next move.

***

I awoke to someone nudging me in the ribs. "Get up – it's near noon," Sid grumbled.

I opened my eyes and looked around the tent. It was empty, and everyone's kit had been cleared out.

"What's the situation?" I said with a yawn.

"The team got up about forty minutes ago – Cruze had me pull the GPMG out of Ark One. Everyone is doing a count on our ammo and supplies. We're going on a fighting patrol, aren't we?"

I pulled myself out of my sleeping bag and slipped on my mukluks. "Yeah, Sid – just after last light."

He handed me a cup of instant coffee. "There's been a lot of movement over the past few hours. Another armoured recce probe – we could hear their Cougar. Cruze and I checked it out."

"What did you see?" I asked, not at all surprised. We had, after all, whacked their sniper crew, not to mention destroyed one of their light tanks.

"Just the one vehicle," he answered. "They must have been looking for their people – you just know they spotted the burned-out hull of that Cougar and the bodies. They know we're coming."

I gulped back the coffee and handed Sid the mug, then rolled up my sleeping bag and began stuffing it into the valise. "Yep – they know we're coming. They just don't know what form it will take. Where's Cruze?"

"She's outside, supervising," he said, eyeballing me closely. "That chick – we need to get rid of her."

I ignored Sid's comment and tossed him my valise. "Here – chuck this outside the tent. Check on the ammo with the rest of the team."

He didn't even try to catch the valise, allowing it instead to bounce off his barrel-sized chest and drop to the floor of the tent. "One man, one kit," he said impatiently. "And you didn't answer my question about the chick."

"She stays with us for now," I said firmly.

I could see his neck beginning to flush and his face twisted itself into a knot. "She isn't one of us," he growled. "She's an outsider – it's her fault that Dawson is dead and ..."

"And you're an ass, Toomey," barked Cruze from the entrance of the tent. She was cradling her carbine, and her eyes bore right through him "You can blame Dawn-Marie all you want, but it was your BS attitude that got Dawson up on the top of the carrier to give you a frigging reality check. You don't call the shots here, and the minute you feel like you're ready to take over, you just make bloody sure you come and see me about it because I Goddamned guarantee that you'll fucking lose that fight."

My heart was pounding so hard that I could feel it in my temples as Sid looked back over his shoulder at Cruze. He took a step back from me and said, "So this is what it's come to, Dave? You're letting the women band together, and now you're their frigging lap dog. You're letting Cruze fight your battles ... fuck you're a loser."

I'd had enough. In a fluid motion, I ducked down and pivoted my body in a wide circle, sweeping my left leg underneath the giant Newfoundlander and sending him falling hard onto the floor of the tent. I jumped on top of Sid's chest and grabbed a handful of his combat jacket.

"We're supposed to be on the same freaking team, Sid!" I barked, shaking him hard with both hands. "Kate Dawson was one of the bravest people I've ever known, and now she's fucking dead. If you'd have done your freaking homework and actually listened to Dawn-Marie, you'd have figured out by now that the civilians in Eden are fighting us because they're under *martial law!"*

Sid grated his teeth together and spat in my face. *"It's your fault we're stuck in this hell hole!"* he thundered. *"We could have picked another route – we could have gone anywhere but here!"*

I pushed my knee into his chest, and Sid let out a foul-smelling gust of air. "Listen, you asshole. In the bottom of that coulee is something too terrible to imagine. Sunray has set up a *death camp, Sid!* He's throwing civvies to the creeps. That's what we're up against! Eden is a prison, and it doesn't matter anymore which way we go because everywhere we turn there's someone or something that wants to kill us!"

He struggled to push me aside, and I leaned into his chest with my knee. Cruze rushed in from the entrance of the tent and placed a calm hand over my clenched fists.

"Easy now, Dave," she said in a near panic. "Step off before your sister sees what's going on. Think about Jo, Dave – we're all doing this for Jo."

I stared hard into Sid's glaring eyes as he fought to catch his breath. "Is that what we're doing now, Dave? You want to have it out because I don't agree with you?"

"Enough!" Cruze shouted as she grabbed me by the collar and hauled me off Sid Toomey. "Get your ass outside the tent, Sid – in a few hours, you're going to have plenty of time for payback."

The walls of the tent were spinning, but I was clear enough to see Sid stomp out of the tent. Cruze turned on her heels and threw me a fiery glare.

"What the hell is wrong with you, Dave!" she snapped. *"We need you to lead and not take a fucking shot at one of our people because you don't feel like answering a question!"*

I slowly got back to my feet and said, "I feel like I'm coming apart – Kate's death, Eden, that Cougar. But what's we saw on patrol, Cruze – it's unreal."

"The whole freaking world is unreal, Dave, now get it together. We have to rely on each other if we're going to survive."

"To what end? Everything is gone now – what's down in that coulee is just a tiny window into how bad things truly are. We didn't have a clue when we decided to pull out of the city. Survivors have been reduced to killing each other off, and for what? A Jerry can of diesel? A case of canned soup? What's the freaking point, Pam?"

Her features hardened, and she dug her finger into my chest. "The point is that we're still alive – *Jo is alive.* Every single person barricaded in a hiding place somewhere on this smouldering planet is still alive. Humanity isn't supposed to go out this way – I refuse to believe it. The creeps? They're dead flesh – they'll eventually rot away. At some point in the future, there won't be any more of them – but human beings will continue to exist. and they need to have a purpose. Maybe our purpose is to save these people in Eden – had you ever thought about that? Just maybe we can still do some good."

I deliberately avoided her gaze, feeling ashamed of myself. Cruze had just given me a glimpse into her own personal light at the end of the tunnel, which was a good thing because I was having trouble finding one of my own.

"I'm an ass," I said after a moment or so of silence.

Cruze nodded and placed her hand on my shoulder. "No ... you're just being an asshole. There's a difference. But you got us out of the city, you got us this far, and you'll get us past Sunray. Got it?"

I gazed at her and forced a weak smile. "You're pretty good at this, Cruze. Anyone ever tell you that?"

She nodded again and gave my shoulder a squeeze. "I'm good at a lot of things, Dave. Let's get our shit in gear."

***

Pam Cruze flipped open her field message pad and began to read.

"We've got 2 Carl G's with 8 more rounds. There are 10 belts of .50 calibre ammo, along with 23 belts of ammo for the light machine gun. There are 2,000 rounds of small arms ammunition for the carbines. We've got a case in each carrier of frag grenades, along with a case of smoke. Um ... 100 rounds of 60 millimetre mortar HE, and that's pretty much all we've got."

I nodded. "Good. All right everyone ... I wouldn't have asked Cruze to do a count on our ammunition if I didn't have a good reason. I think by now that you've all guessed what it is. I'm going to be honest about what we're facing in that coulee."

"Fighting patrol, Dave?" asked Doug. "What did you guys see down there, anyway?"

Mel Dixon was first to answer. "Sunray has got civilians penned up with creeps – we think it's a death camp. It might be just one of many for all we know. It's small enough that he doesn't require a major commitment of troops to man the place. It's protected by a pair of Cougars and a couple of Coyotes with light guns. But there's more."

I glanced at Sid. He clenched his jaw tightly and then dropped his cigarette butt in the snow. He turned his attention to Dawn-Marie. "You knew about this?"

She zipped up the collar on her jacket and rubbed her hands together to warm them up. "People disappeared, and our biggest fear was that we'd wind up being lined up against a wall and shot to death if we didn't follow the rules. It wasn't until about a month and a half ago that we started to hear rumours of the abattoir."

Kenny blinked. "*Abattoir?* What the hell is that?"

"It's French for slaughterhouse," said Cruze, turning her attention to Dawn-Marie. "How did you hear about it?"

"From our handlers. They made a point of telling everyone that if they didn't do as they were instructed, they'd be shipped off to the abattoir. Being from the farm, well, everyone knew what that meant ... but nobody had a clue where it was. I doubted it even existed until people started disappearing from Dinsmore. A couple of families that had been deemed to be shit disturbers – they were rounded up and shipped off. Nobody ever heard from them again."

"And you didn't fight back?" asked Cruze, her voice laced with suspicion. "People were taken away, and you just stood by and watched?"

Dawn-Marie nodded. "Please ... what were we going to do? They could wipe us out in a heartbeat with the amount of military hardware they possess. We just did what we had to do in order to survive, and if that makes us collaborators, then I guess that's what we are. I can't change how you see me."

"Dinsmore had a population of a couple of hundred," I said slowly. "But there were only a handful of people shooting at us when we rolled into town."

"Yeah, everyone else died during the outbreak. There were four hundred people in town –whittled down to less than fifty after two months. Some of the townsfolk left to find another place to start over. I don't know what happened to them."

I kicked at the snow with the toe of my boot. "We don't know how many people are left in Eden. We don't even know how far Eden stretches or how many towns and villages that Sunray has claimed. But we know what the hell is down in that coulee, and we have to stop it."

Doug eyed me closely and made a grunting sound. "What are you proposing we do?"

I looked each person in the eye in turn. "We're going to go in and save those people. We saw human remains – it looked like they're feeding the people to them. Why they don't just execute them using a gun or something, I don't have a clue."

"To save on bullets," Cruze said resolutely. "And maybe to keep his own people in line."

As warped as it sounded, Sunray's abattoir made perfect sense. He could put the fear of death and dismemberment into the civilian population to guarantee order. No wonder the people back at Dinsmore took up arms and shot at us. Death from a gunshot wound or being blown to bits by a mortar round is a hell of a lot more desirable than the prospect of being ripped to pieces and eaten alive.

"We have a choice to make," I said, focusing my attention on Sid Toomey. "We can skirt the coulee cross country and head north to another highway – maybe we'd avoid Sunray, but it's unlikely. Or we can try and do some good – we can save those people."

"And the guards," said Jo in a surprisingly firm voice. "If they're feeding people to the creepers, they should get the same treatment as the guy who shot Katie."

I heaved a weary sigh. "So what does everyone want to do? I say we go in there and bring the freaking wrath of God down on them."

Sid was about to say something, but Mel beat him to it. "We go down there and take those pricks out."

Doug stepped forward. "Yeah – I'm thinking the same thing. We need to do something to help those people – we need to get them out of there."

"I'm with Dave," said Cruze. "There's no guarantee we won't run into Sunray if we leave, and I just couldn't live with myself knowing that we could have done something to save them."

Kenny Howard raised a hand. "It's what Dawson would have wanted," he said quietly. "She'd have been the first person to volunteer."

I looked at Sid. "It's your choice now. It's a team decision.

What do you say?"

He lit another cigarette and said, "I'm not stupid enough to believe that Sunray isn't already out there looking for us, and when he does find us, we're going to be facing off. I'd rather face off on our terms, so yeah, let's fucking do this. What about the chick, though?"

"The name is Dawn-Marie, asshole," she snapped.

I glanced at her. "Not everybody gets to go with us. Someone has to stay back with Jo."

My little sister glared at me. "But I want to go, David! I want to fight."

I dropped to one knee and gave her hand a small squeeze. "I know you want to fight, kiddo – but I'm going to need you back here putting together first-aid stuff. Dawn-Marie will be back here, too."

"Whoa!" Sid barked. "You can't leave the kid alone with her."

I stood up and said, "I'm not. We need a driver to stay back too – we might need the vehicle for anyone who gets wounded. I'm not going to pick someone – it's either Kenny or Doug."

"I'm a way better shot than Kenny, and he's the best driver we've got," said Doug. "You cool with staying back, bud?"

Kenny shrugged. "I guess so. It's going to be a freaking small fighting patrol, though, with just the five of you going. What's your plan?"

I trudged back to Ark One, climbed inside and reappeared moments later with the 60millimetre mortar tube in one hand and a bomb in the other.

"We're going to drop mortars on these bastards," I said coolly. "And they won't see it coming."

CHAPTER 27

Journal Entry: 18 NOVEMBER 17:58 HRS ZULU

We've just completed rehearsals for the patrol, and everyone has been briefed. We made the best representation of the bridge and river that we could, back in the tent – I just hope it'll live up to the real thing.

We can't afford a single mistake. Sid is bringing the receiver group for the GPMG. Mel and Doug will make up fire team one, carrying the 60 mm mortar along with a case of rounds. Cruze is taking the second mortar, and I'll be hauling what's left of the bombs from Ark One – a dozen rounds. I'll also haul the tripod for the machine gun. I've had Kenny scanning frequencies on the radio to see if we might be able to pick up something, but no luck – I imagine they've got their radio communications scrambled. As for us, we'll bring along one radio set.

We're going to hit them from three locations. From the northeast, Doug and Mel will take out the sentry on the bridge, along with the pair of Cougars. They've only got one M72 each, so they'll engage their armour only if their crews mount up. I'll be helping Sid set up a base of fire on the bridge and the modular tent. Cruze and I will cross the bridge and do the same thing on the opposite bank while we wait for Doug and Mel to haul ass over to their secondary position. From there, the plan is to use fire and movement up to the compound – at which time we'll shoot the creeps and free the people inside. I'll fire off a red pen flare to signal that the area is secure and the civilians are free, then we'll take one of Sunray's vehicles and double back to get our two APC's. We'll re-org down in the coulee and decide where to go from there.

I can't imagine how we're going to get through this without taking some casualties. I think we're all trying to push that out of our minds. I have to trust that if I end up getting killed, the survivors will take care of Jo. I was going to have a sit-down with her and explain that I might not come back, but she's not stupid.

She knows the risks – we all do. She's always told me that she loves me and believes in me. I'd like to believe in me, too, but I'm scared to death.

And I think that if we survive what is to come, we have to accept that we're fighting a war with two fronts now: the creeps, and Sunray, or those like him.

I'll close off this journal for now. I don't know if I'll be around for another entry. I don't know if any of us will be.

* * *

We left the hide on a northeast bearing, keeping a good ten paces between each person. Once again, we were relying on Mel to get us there in one piece, and Doug provided rear security as we trudged through ankle-deep snow. The temperature had plummeted once darkness set in – according to Mel's wristwatch thermometer it was below minus 20.

After about 40 minutes of walking, we made it to the snowdrift-covered highway. We crept into the ditch on the western edge, and everyone dropped down onto one knee to have a listen. I doubled up to Mel and peered out over the empty expanse with my night vision scope.

"How far?" I whispered, focusing on the tree line that bordered the edge of the coulee.

"Another 1500m or so," she said. "It'd be faster if we just high-tailed it up the road."

"When has anything been easy since we left the armoury? ... Wait a minute."

"What is it?"

I adjusted the focus on the night scope and panned from my left to my right. I could see a glimmer of white light amid the soft green glow of the landscape. White light meant a concentrated source of light, from either a fire or a man-made source. It disappeared into the tree line.

I stuffed the scope back into its case. "They're either expecting us, or I just spotted a foot sentry, or possibly a patrol."

Mel gulped. "Shit – do you think they saw us?"

I shook my head. "I doubt it – but we're going to have to be extra cautious going in. The route we planned is wide of the highway. They probably have the road covered by an anti-tank gun. If we add another 1000m or so and sweep wide to the right, we can probably get in unnoticed."

"That's going to add time to our patrol," she said grimly. "But I don't see that we have a choice. Let everyone know and give me a minute to reroute."

I patted her on the shoulder. "Will do. Hang in there, Mel."

I scrambled back to my position on the rear, filling each team member in on what I'd seen. In 15 minutes, we were tracking across another open field, crouching low to reduce our silhouette. We'd increased the gap between each person to 20 paces, just in time for the wind to change direction. The elements were conspiring against us – the icy breeze was blowing full into our faces, and every few minutes, we had to brush away the frost as it collected around the eyeholes on our balaclavas. Snow had been falling straight since midday, drifting across the field and blanketing the scattered corpses of frozen cattle. This was a more physically demanding patrol than the last – each of us was weighed down with heavy weapons and ammunition. After more than an hour of trudging across the open landscape, we cut across to the edge of the woods, stopping every few minutes to have a listen. The air was tinged with the smell of smoke, so we knew we were close to our objective.

I took over the patrol just short of the wood line, leading the team through a thicket of diamond willow until we were well into the copse of trees. The uneven ground was filled with ruts and deep trenches that offered excellent concealment. I selected a point between two enormous boulders as our ORV. The team dropped into all round defence, each person keeping a sharp eye on their arcs of fire. The next thing I had to do was to lead each fire team to their positions without being seen.

After a quick moment to orientate our position to the map, we broke into our groups, and I started out down the steep forward slope of the coulee. Behind me was Mel's team, followed by Sid and Cruze, watching our backs. We still couldn't see our objectives at this point, but we were close – the smell of wood smoke was getting stronger. The trees offered a blessed reprieve from the relentless wind, and I think we were all glad to be out of the open land, even if it meant we'd soon be in the middle of a fire fight.

We slowly trudged through ankle-deep snow, each of us being extra careful not to make a sound. We hadn't run into the patrol I'd spotted earlier, but we could see the highway ahead, winding down the face of the coulee. The area for Mel and Kenny to set up their mortar came into view – an opening in the trees, surrounded by waist-high grass that bobbed and swayed with each gust of the cold wind. I dropped to one knee and held up my hand. We ducked into a depression and once more gathered into an all-around defence.

"Okay, Mel – this is your spot," I whispered. "Set up the 60 mm mortar just above us, and, once you hear our rounds land, take out whoever is on the bridge."

She nodded. "What about that foot patrol? They'll be able to spot us from the sound."

"Trust me – they'll come crashing through the bush once the shooting starts. At that point, it won't matter if you open fire on them with your personal weapons – and once Sid starts firing, they'll be looking for the muzzle flash from our machine gun, not you."

"Let them come," Sid rumbled.

I glanced at Sid and almost felt sorry for that patrol if they decided to try and take him out.

"All right," I whispered. "I want rounds in the air within thirty seconds of hearing the first blast from our mortar. You'll cross the bridge only after I send up a green flare."

"And if you don't make it?" said Doug. "What then?"

"If you don't get the signal, you'll gather at the ORV, just like we rehearsed, and hustle your asses back to the hide. The next move will be up to you. But that won't happen. It simply can't."

I tried to put some conviction in my voice, for effect – everyone needed to believe that our raid would be successful. I was counting on the confusion a series of well-placed explosions would bring about. We had excellent concealment – our fire teams were portable and could shift their firing positions to avoid detection.

This *had* to work.

"Good luck, guys," I said, motioning for Sid and Cruze to follow me out of the depression and on to the next firing position. I didn't bother looking back, although I knew full well this might be the last time any of us saw each other. Strangely, I felt a wave of peace wash over me. I don't know why it happened – I should have felt terrified, but I didn't. It might have been because I knew what each person in the group was capable of when push came to shove – or possibly it was just a sense of relief at finally confronting Sunray's people. The prospect of a direct encounter had been hanging over us like a death sentence from the moment we set foot in Eden.

After a few minutes of walking, we rounded a series of boulders. Below us, near a modular tent in a thicket of poplar trees, I could see the glow from a large bonfire. We ducked down underneath a pair of logs that had fallen onto each other, forming a near-perfect A – beneath them was flat, snow-covered earth. I held out my hand and spread my fingers wide as I looked down into the coulee. This was as good a spot as any for Sid to set up the gun. I carefully opened the tripod, and the giant Newfoundlander inserted the receiver group. He handed me the five belts of linked ammunition, and I quickly laid them in neat rows with the projectile ends pointing down range.

Sid dropped onto his belly and opened the receiver group as I handed him the first belt. He placed the rounds inside, and then quietly closed the receiver.

"Ready," he said firmly, gazing down at the compound. "I've got a wide arc of fire here – I can cover the bridge, all the way to past the modular tent."

I pointed to the razor wire compound and the civilians as I handed him the night vision scope. There were all huddled, again, around a small fire. Behind them were the trio of creeps. "This is what we're up against," I whispered. "I wish I had someone to feed you belts of ammo, but you're on your own, Sid. I'm sorry about that."

He peered through the aperture. "*Jesus* ... what kind of place is this?"

"I don't know, man," I answered. "Maybe it's some kind of twisted new world order or maybe Sunray is just plain freaking insane. But you know what to do when the shit hits the fan. You understand now why we need to save those people?"

He flicked off the switch on the scope and handed it back to me. "Yeah – I get it. Don't worry – I'll make sure the covering fire works."

I nodded. "Good. You're the anchor for this action, Sid. Tell me I can count on you."

He cocked the gun. "You can count on me, Dave. And look … I'm sorry about how I've been the past couple of days. I'm sorry about everything … I truly am."

I was about to say something to make peace with Sid, but there wasn't time. Instead, I gave him a pat on the shoulder and motioned for Cruze to follow me. We ducked under the pair of logs and trudged on, being careful not to silhouette ourselves. We were going into the belly of the beast. Our firing position would be the closest of all three. After about 10 minutes of sneaking through the thick undergrowth, I spotted the main roadway as it snaked down the coulee, 300m to our left. It levelled out into an S-shape surrounded on either side by waist-high grass. Ahead, I could see the bridge, with a pair of sentries walking around the perimeter of the razor-wire gate, so we doubled into the grass and then leopard-crawled up to the edge of the river. The sound of the rushing water helped muffle any sounds we made as we set up the mortar. I carefully laid out a dozen 60 mm rounds on the ground next to the base plate and prepped them for fire as Cruze lined up the aiming line with our targets. She quietly dug the base plate into the ground as I peered out, using the night vision, to estimate the distance, then adjusted the increment charges on each bomb's tailfin assembly.

The entire compound was in front of us, with the light tanks smack dab in the middle. I watched in silence as half a dozen soldiers warmed themselves around the huge bonfire next to the modular tent. One of the Coyote light reconnaissance vehicles was missing. I peered up the road leading to the eastern edge of the coulee in search of tire tracks or movement, but there was nothing.

"They're down a recce vehicle since this morning," I whispered as I handed the scope to Cruze. She peered into the aperture.

"Six guys by the fire. Two on the bridge acting as sentry. I don't see anyone that looks like they might be you-know-who."

I nodded. "We hit them hard, and hit them fast. First rounds right onto that bonfire – if we're lucky, we can take out all six of them with a couple of shots. That'll get the guys on the bridge moving, but Sid can take them out. Once they're down, we'll double across the bridge and secure the other side. I'll send up the flare, and we'll try and use fire and movement down that track to the compound. You ready for this?"

Cruze gripped the mortar tube tightly and clenched her jaw. "Yeah. Let's go."

Eight soldiers were about to die. I didn't care – half a dozen civilians were trapped in a pen full of creeps. Sunray was nowhere to be seen, and we had the tactical advantage.

It was time to avenge Kate Dawson's death.

CHAPTER 28

I gripped the body of the high explosive round over the end of the mortar, and took one last look out onto the objective – as soon as the round fell in the tube, all hell would break loose. I knew that we'd take casualties; I knew there was the chance that I'd never see Jo again. And I knew that as soon as this round was in the air, everything would change. Cruze leaned into the mortar, forcing her body weight down on the base plate. In the distance, I could hear laughter coming from the soldiers, smoking and joking as they gathered around the bonfire to warm up against a cold night.

I glanced at Cruze and saw her eyes narrow through the holes in her balaclava. Her gaze was fixed on our target with laser precision. "You going to drop that thing?" she whispered, her eyes never leaving the men around the campfire.

I took one last look at the target as I released the bomb. "Round's away," I whispered.

A hollow metallic *thunk* filled the air as the bomb rocketed out of the mortar tube. I kept my eyes focused on the group of soldiers as I reached for another high-explosive round and dropped it in. Time seemed to freeze in place – though the sound of the mortar echoed through the coulee, not a single soldier huddling around that fire made even the tiniest attempt to take cover.

Seconds later, the round hit with a blast that shattered the silence. I grabbed another round and dropped it down the tube as a mixture of smoke and screams filled the air. Three of the enemies dashed for cover as the next round hit, blasting body parts in every direction. Then the shooting started. From the bridge, the sentries were firing on our position. Bullets cracked over our heads, but not for long; Mel's first round blasted a hole in the razor wire fence. Screams could be heard, both from the bridge and the modular tent, as I launched another 60 mm round that lit up in a ball of fire and molten metal. I watched with stone cold concentration as a soldier ran for the safety of the river, only to be cut down by a burst of machine-gun fire.

"Stand by," I said firmly as I grabbed my binoculars and scanned the area. Small fires were burning all around the tent as I searched for movement. Blood stained the freshly-fallen snow, where two soldiers lay dead. I panned to the right and spotted the civilians inside the compound, standing a few feet away from the fence. Another burst of machine gun fire rained down on the bridge, and I watched the tracer rounds screaming across the coulee, the ricochets bouncing high into the air over the tops of the metal arches. The sound of gunfire echoed through the coulee every few seconds, and I thought for sure I could hear that missing APC rumbling somewhere in the darkness.

"Something ain't right," I whispered to Cruze. "This was too easy. Way too easy. We cut them down, and we've got rounds to spare. Do you hear an APC?"

Cruze lowered the mortar and gazed out across the river. "Or it might just be a really frigging successful fighting patrol. Do you see anything?"

"Just listen," I whispered.

It was a faint hum that increased and decreased in pitch ever few seconds. A sound that could only come from a diesel engine.

"I hear it … if that vehicle is headed our way, we gotta move now!" said Cruze

There was another explosion as one of Mel's mortar rounds hit the bridge, lighting up the darkness with a massive ball of fire.

I peered through my binoculars at the scene in front of us. "All I see are the dead and the nearly dead," I said grimly. "I'll ready a flare. Have an eye for any movement."

She grabbed the binoculars and said, "Will do. Say the word, and we'll double across the bridge."

I nodded as I inserted the flare into the pen-sized launcher. I pulled back the plunger with my thumb, and then raised my arm in the air, releasing the flare. A neon green streak of light shot up in a high arc, signalling to the rest of the team to move across the bridge.

"Let's go!" I whispered as I stood up, carbine in hand. I pulled my weapon to my chest and, with Cruze in tow, dashed down a forward slope to the edge of the river. In seconds, we'd made it to the smashed fence in front of the bridge – there was a gap wide enough for an entire platoon to cross through. There were two small impact craters next to the body of one of the soldiers, lying on his side in the snow. He twitched a few times as we doubled past his corpse and onto the bridge deck. Cruze crouched low, her carbine pointed toward the compound a few hundred meters away. I raised my weapon to my shoulder and rested my cheek against the butt, my eyes scanning the area for anything that even smelled like a potential threat. After about thirty seconds, we'd made it to the other side, so we dropped down onto our bellies and waited for the rest of the team to arrive.

A deathly calm had washed over the coulee. In the distance, I could hear the cries for help from the men we'd hit with the mortar. I could make out three distinct voices, one of which was calling for his mother. After a few minutes, I heard the *clump clump clump* of footsteps as our team doubled across the bridge. I got up on one knee and gestured for them to hurry the hell up. Sid arrived first, his body covered with belts of ammunition. Somehow he'd managed to lug not only the machine gun receiver, but also the tripod. His carbine was slung across his back.

He dove into the snow next to me, panting heavily as I grabbed the tripod and opened its legs. Sid dropped the receiver inside and locked it as I pointed up the highway. "Kill anything that moves, Sid," I said.

"Yeah," he gulped for air. "I can do that. I got your backs."

Seconds later, Mel and Doug were on the ground next to Cruze. I motioned for both fire teams to get up and start our area clearance – individual fire and movement if the bullets started flying. Each of us would provide cover fire while their team member moved and we'd reorganize ourselves once we'd won the firefight. Only this time I was thinking the firefight might already have already been won. The lack of enemy fire from Sunray's troops didn't sit well with me.

"Nothing should ever be this simple," I said, before I motioned for each team to move forward. "Be extra vigilant. I got a bad feeling about this."

Cruze covered me as I dashed across the open ground, ducking down behind a mound. As soon as I'd dropped to one knee, I heard her footsteps clumping through the snow. She raced ahead about a dozen metres – out of the corner of my eye, I could see Mel Dixon and Doug hustling forward, their weapons at the ready. The brush next to the modular tent was on fire, and thick white smoke drifted across our field of view. I moved forward of Cruze until I spotted the blasted-out remnants of the bonfire, along with the impact craters from our mortar rounds. There was a pair of dead soldiers in front of us – one of them still clutching a plastic coffee-cup. His entire back was blown out, and I could see his exposed ribs sticking out like branches on a tree. The air smelled of blood and iron and smoke as I checked his pockets for intelligence, but there was nothing to be found. Cruze doubled past me and checked on another soldier, slumped over a battered oil drum.

"This one is still alive," she said firmly.

I nodded as I watched Mel and Doug checking the bodies of three other soldiers. "Is he conscious?" I asked.

"Not for long," said Cruze, as she stuck her finger in the man's neck to check his pulse.

The words had barely left her lips when a single shot rang out, hitting Cruze in the thigh. She made a gulping sound as she fell back, her carbine landing at her feet. What happened next was purely mechanical. I saw the wounded soldier clutching a Browning 9mm in his lap, the barrel still smoking – without even thinking, I raised my carbine and fired three quick shots into his chest. The gun dropped into the snow as he slumped forward.

"*Cruze!*" I shouted as I raced to her. She was lying on her side, clutching her right leg. A large blood stain had soaked through her combat fatigues and into her camouflage snow pants. I quickly pulled a field dressing out of my pants pocket and tore open the wrapping. I could see Mel and Doug about to run over to offer first aid, and barked at them:

"*Check the rest of the bodies!* I'll tend to Cruze!"

I pressed my hand against her leg, reaching underneath where the bullet had entered. I was surprised to feel an exit wound.

"*Shit!* I should have seen that coming," she cried out. "How bad?"

The bullet hadn't severed the artery, but it wasn't good. I pressed the field dressing against the wound and wrapped it on so tight the jolt of pain brought tears to her eyes. "You're not dead yet," I said. "Where's your field dressing?"

"In my other pocket," she said, wincing. "I'm really sorry about this, Dave."

"Don't be," I replied, as I ripped into her field dressing and placed the huge gauze pad against the exit wound. "That prick paid with his life."

Cruze reached for her carbine and grabbed it by the sling. She pulled it to her chest and clutched it tightly, like a child squeezing a Teddy bear. "You were right, this was too easy. I should have been more careful. I should have checked him for weapons."

I pulled the other field dressing tight around Cruze's now swelling thigh, creating a tourniquet to control the bleeding. She didn't cry out. Not freaking once.

"I need you to provide covering fire if the shit starts flying, Cruze."

"My leg – is the bullet still in there?"

I shook my head. "In and out – clean wound. Let's see if you can get up."

Cruze held her carbine out in front of her chest, and I grabbed onto it for leverage as I pulled her up to her feet. She bit her lip as she draped her arm around my shoulder. Ahead was the one remaining Coyote reconnaissance vehicle. The rear doors were wide open, and I helped Cruze slide into the back. With a huge effort, she pulled herself across the jump seats and climbed into the turret. Her head popped up through the hatch, and she spun the turret so that the barrel of the 25 mm chain gun was pointing toward the highway.

"Don't take all freaking day," she groaned. "Let's get those civvies and head the hell out of here!"

"I'm on it," I said as I doubled over toward Mel and Doug. They'd regrouped, and were lying in firing positions covering both sides of the river. I motioned for them to follow me, and we carefully made our way towards the wire compound. The pair of creeps was struggling against the chain in a desperate attempt to reach us. Perhaps they'd caught a whiff from our mortar attack, or maybe all the commotion triggered their need to feed. It didn't matter to me either way. I raised my carbine to my shoulder and fired a pair of shots into each creature's head.

Doug was the first to approach the wire compound, but the moment he laid eyes on the civilians, he stopped dead in his tracks.

He bristled, and then slowly raised his weapon to his shoulder.

"What the hell are you doing, Doug?" Mel snapped. "Get the wire-cutters and let these people out of there."

Doug shook his head and made a pointing motion with the barrel of his carbine. His voice was shaking. "This abattoir is something way worse than anything we could have freaking imagined. Look at them."

I shone my flashlight onto the group of civilians. One of them took a tentative step forward – a skeletal-looking man, with hollow eyes and a hastily patched wound on his neck. His skin was pale, and the whites of his eyes had turned yellow. He raised his hand and gestured for our group to stop.

"Don't come any closer," he said weakly. "We're dead already."

Mel shone her light into the compound. Together, we saw that each of the five people carried wounds we'd long ago become familiar with. They were the kinds of wounds that came from getting too close to the creeps.

"We're all infected," he whispered, as he dropped to his knees. "They put the living inside here with the creeps. It's our punishment for fighting back ... for trying to stop them taking over what's left of our homes and families. When someone turns, we're forced to fight the monsters with our bare hands. The two you shot ... those were once my sons."

"If you're infected and close to turning ... why chain up the creeps?" asked Mel. Her finger was on the trigger.

A woman of about forty placed a bloody hand on the man's shoulder in an attempt to offer comfort. He sobbed as she turned towards us, rolling up the sleeve of her sweater to show us the swollen bite wound on her left forearm.

"For their amusement."

I blinked. "Come again?"

"One of the soldiers took pity on us and tossed in a chain – the six-foot pickets are all around us to hold the razor wire. There used to be more than a dozen of us. Jasper here probably has a couple of hours until he becomes one of those things. You need to get the hell out of here, boy. You need to tell everyone ... tell them what they're doing to us. Tell them Sunray is a madman, and that he's got to be stopped! It's too late for us now. But you're all armed, just like Sunray's soldiers. Just do right by us before you leave. Do the right thing."

The man who'd been sobbing abruptly stopped. He raised his head and gazed at the three of us with a look of despair.

"Carlsbad Farms – it's across the border. That's where you'll find people who are willing to fight. They're starting a resistance – they're going to take back Eden. You need to get to Carlsbad Farms. It's off the main highway past Alsask. It's got running water and power. Sunray knows about it … he just don't know where it is. It's one of the reasons we're in here … to make our families talk. You gotta stop him!"

The other three gathered together and looked at us pleadingly. Each carried a wound, and each was counting down the hours and minutes until it was their turn to transform into the stuff of nightmares. I glanced at Doug and Mel for a short moment, and then said, "Cruze is in that Coyote. Scrounge as much fuel as you can and any supplies. Load it up, and get that pig started – we're going back to the hide, and we're going to find this Carlsbad Farms."

"What are you going to do?" asked Mel.

I spun around and roared at her. "*Just fucking do it!*

She didn't recoil at my outburst, and the look on her face told me that she understood. I spent the next few minutes learning as much as I could from the five infected until I heard the sound of the Coyote's diesel engine rumbling to life.

And I am going to hell for what I did next.

I am *so* going to hell.

CHAPTER 29

I sliced the tires on the two Cougar light tanks before we left. I'd have dropped explosives in their gun barrels, but I didn't have any with me, so immobilising both was the best solution I could come up with. We picked up Sid Toomey and crossed the bridge. He helped Cruze out of the turret and took his place manning the main guns as we pulled off on the west bank of the river. We took a short detour while I accompanied Mel back to her firing position and gathered the mortar and ammunition – we were back inside the Coyote within 15 minutes, and I crew-commanded the eight-wheeled monster up the serpentine highway until we were well out of the coulee.

Doug and Mel had been able to scrounge another five Jerry cans of diesel, and they sloshed about in the rear of the carrier as we ploughed through drifts of snow. It was shortly past midnight and the flurries had stopped, but the temperature outside the vehicle was enough to freeze your eyelids together if you faced into the wind. I hid behind the crew commander's hatch and scanned the horizon for signs of the enemy APC. I saw nothing.

Where had it disappeared to? They hadn't come after us with their guns blazing, as I'd expected. Were they another one of Sunray's roving patrols? I signalled for Sid to turn on the infra-red in the turret and scan the area. If we could cut off the patrol, we'd maybe gather some intelligence about Sunray, his strength, and possible whereabouts.

As we cruised down the highway, the slight resistance our patrol had met still tugged at me. I'd have liked to say it was dumb luck we'd only taken one casualty, rained death down on Sunray's troops, gathered valuable intelligence about why the abattoir existed and learned that a resistance movement was taking shape at a place called Carlsbad Farms.

But it was almost as if … Sunray *wanted* us to find out the truth about the abattoir.

I crawled back down into the Coyote and gestured for Mel Dixon. She scurried across the jump seat until she was within earshot.

"Take us back to the hide. You're in charge – I'm going to check on Cruze."

"Roger that," said Mel. I pressed myself against the engine panel to make room.

The inside of the Coyote was similar to our carriers, which made sense. They were effectively the same vehicles, save for the fact that the Coyote was newer and had eight wheels, whereas Ark One and Ark Two had six wheels each. There were modern radio sets, as well as more comfortable seating in the rear. Cruze was seated on the far jump seat, her wounded leg stretched out in front of her.

"We're going to have to do some painful medicine on that leg, Cruze," I said, peeking underneath the gauze field dressing. "It's still bleeding, and we need to cauterize the bullet hole. There aren't any doctors out here."

"No kidding," she said, grimacing. "Just do it."

"When we get back to the hide. I'll need one of the mountain stoves to heat something metal."

It was going to hurt like hell, and there was still the very real possibility that the wound might get infected. If that happened, Cruze's leg would swell up like a balloon and eventually turn gangrenous. We'd seen gangrene happen with another survivor back at Mewata. He didn't live through the trauma of having his leg amputated.

"We've got antibiotics in the medical kits – we grabbed a bunch from the armoury before we left. When we get back, you'll start taking them."

Cruze nodded. "Fine ... whatever. In the meantime, what happened back there with those civilians ... you didn't have a choice, Dave."

I clenched my jaw. "I don't want to talk about it."

She gave me a slight shove. "Well, maybe you should. Maybe you need to actually say that you shot all those people. They were infected, David. You were doing them a favour."

I grated my teeth as I changed the field dressings on Cruze's leg, binding both fresh dressings tightly. "There's a resistance," I said, changing the subject. "Some place called Carlsbad Farms – across the border. They've got running water and power – maybe they have a doc, and we can get your leg properly tended to."

She raised her eyebrows. "Resistance, huh? Sounds like occupied France during World War Two. Well ... the border is a couple of hundred kilometres away, if we stay on the main highway heading east. We could probably make it there by midday if we're extra stealthy. We'd need to ditch one of the carriers, though. We need every drop of fuel we can spare."

Suddenly, the carrier lurched sharply to the right, and then started bouncing cross-country. Cruze braced herself against the rear door and howled in pain. "Slow the fuck down!" she shrieked.

Doug Manybears must have heard her, because the Coyote slowed to a crawl.

"We've got slight advantage," I said, pointing to the radios. "We can listen in on Sunray – we've got two days worth of frequencies."

"And that might help us avoid him while we head east," Cruze said, finishing my sentence. "We should all load into this rig and disable the other carriers."

I nodded. "Yeah – that sounds about right. It'll take us a couple of hours to siphon the fuel from both APC's. Not to mention transferring all of our kit and stuff."

I slid back on the jump seat and listened to the rumble of the engine. The interior heating system of the Coyote was much more effective than the ones in our own carriers, and the warm air circulating inside wasn't tainted with the stench of diesel and motor oil. I exhaled heavily as I gazed at Pam Cruze. We'd made it through our fighting patrol relatively unscathed, Sid Toomey and I had made peace with each other, and we'd learned that other survivors out there were ready to band together to fight Sunray. Maybe there was a light at the end of the tunnel after all. Maybe we could take back Eden and somehow start over. It wasn't Sanctuary Base, but it was *something*. We were still fighting for our lives, but at least there was the prospect of fighting alongside people who wanted to rebuild this world and not rule it. The creeps would still linger, but if we were careful, if we took steps to defend ourselves in an organized way, maybe we'd somehow scrape by. Maybe Jo would get to grow up after all.

I allowed myself the luxury of a smile. My lips arched up into a grin, and I started to giggle. Naturally, Cruze looked at me like I'd just lost my freaking mind, and made a point of telling me so.

"What the hell are you laughing about, you moron?"

I raised a hand. "Nothing and everything, Pam."

She rolled her eyes. "You need to have some forced rest – you're getting all bat-shit crazy."

Our bodies pitched to the left as the Coyote made a sharp turn, and then the vehicle abruptly stopped, sending us sliding forward and pushing Cruze off her jump seat. She landed on the floor with an almighty yelp.

I crawled forward and tapped Mel's leg. She didn't respond, so I tapped her again and she dropped down from the hatch to stare at me wide-eyed, her face a ghastly shade of grey.

"What is it?" I asked. "Why are we stopping?"

"Holy shit," shouted Sid from the turret, cocking one of the guns.

I scrambled to the rear of the carrier and grabbed my carbine. I was just about to open the rear door when Mel made her way to the rear and threw her arms around me. She pulled me close and squeezed me, starting to sob.

"I am so sorry, Dave," Mel sniffled. "Just stay in the carrier … okay?"

I placed both hands on Mel's chest and gave her a shove. "What the hell are you talking about? Why are you freaking apologizing? You didn't do anything!"

She opened her mouth to say something, but Sid beat her to it. He dropped down out of the turret. *"The hide. Sunray found the hide!"*

I stared at Sid in disbelief.

"Jo …"

A wave of terror rolled through me. I flung open the rear door and jumped out of the carrier. Dozens of tire tracks meandered off in all directions. I raced around to the front of the APC, carbine in hand.

"Get back inside!" Mel shouted. *"The area isn't secure!"*

Ignoring her, I sprinted ahead of the Coyote, my feet ploughing through the snow. Thick black smoke billowed up from inside the tree line – the air smelled of cordite and burning rubber. Empty shell casings lay scattered in the snow alongside dozens of footprints, leading over a small ridge and into the wooded area where we'd camouflaged both our carriers. I stopped dead in my tracks as I saw what was left of Arks One and Two.

Ark Two was nothing more than a charred husk of blackened, smouldering metal. There was a basketball-sized hole just underneath the turret, from which oily smoke was wafting out, high into the air. It had been hit with an anti-tank weapon and brewed up. Ark One was nowhere to be seen. I followed its tire tracks deep into the woods until I spotted the carrier lying on its side in the bottom of a gulley. The hatches were wide open, and the bodies of three enemy soldiers lay face down in the snow – they'd been mown down from behind. I placed my weapon firmly in my shoulder as the Coyote caught up with me. Sid hopped out of the turret, carbine in hand and raced up to me.

He pointed to an obvious firing position, about 50m to my right: a thick stand of deadwood overlooking the gulley where the carrier had flipped over.

"Kenny wasn't stupid," he said. "Sunray must have sent in his armoured recce, but Kenny got his carrier the hell out of there once the shooting started – I think he rolled it in that gulley as a diversion."

"I'll go down and check the carrier," I said, trying like crazy not to call out Jo's name in case the enemy was still within earshot.

Sid shook his head. "No, you won't – just sit tight. I'll check it out."

I was about to protest, but Sid didn't give me enough time. He sprinted down the forward slope into the gulley, and then slowly circled the carrier. He poked his head in the open rear hatch and reappeared seconds later, shaking his head. I walked down to the first dead soldier and dropped to one knee, eyeing the deadwood stand. Sid was right – the bullet holes in his back lined up perfectly with a firing position hidden inside the broken, rotting timber. I scanned the area for signs of movement as Sid made his way back to me.

"No sign of anyone," he said. "There are no footprints in the snow around the carrier."

"Maybe he's still hiding," I said, trying to sound optimistic.

"Maybe Kenny and Jo and Dawn-Marie are waiting for us. It's still pitch black – he could be sticking to the shadows, waiting for us to get back."

The woods were dead silent, save for the sound of the fire burning in Ark Two. If that patrol was still in the area, they'd have engaged us by now. I didn't want to think about the possibility that my little sister might be dead. Surely someone had to have survived – Kenny, or Dawn-Marie, had killed three soldiers, using Ark One as a diversion. They had to be alive – they just *had* to be.

It was at this point that I heard a faint moaning, about 50 m away. I raised my weapon and followed the sound with Sid alongside me. We slowly made our way through twisted poplar and thick diamond willow as we carefully climbed a slight incline. There were footprints in the snow, big ones and little ones, but only two sets. Where was the third set of footprints? Kenny had gotten Jo out of the carrier. They both had to be somewhere nearby, but where was Dawn-Marie?

Sid placed a hand on my chest and dropped to one knee. He picked up a handful of snow and held it out for me to see.

"Blood," he whispered.

There were more drops of blood in the snow. They led to a deadwood thicket, where I saw him hidden under a pile of broken and dried-out branches. Kenny was still clutching his carbine, but he'd been shot to pieces. I ducked under the broken branches and loosened his parka to help him breathe.

"I'm so sorry, Dave," he gurgled. "I tried to protect them ... I tried to save Jo."

"Where are they? Where's my sister?" I said, as my throat tightened.

He raised a weak hand and touched my cheek. It dropped to his side like a stone. "Dawn-Marie was getting rations out of Ark Two. We were packing up your carrier, because mine was running on fumes. They hit us without any warning. In the distance, we could hear your mortars, and that's when they opened up."

"Where's Jo, Kenny? Where is she?"

He coughed up a mouthful of blood. "They took her, Dave. They took Dawn-Marie, and they've got Jo. I tried to stop them. I tried..."

Kenny's voice trailed off, and his head fell forward. Sid placed two fingers on his neck and shook his head.

Anger bubbled up in my chest. I scrambled out of the deadwood. Ahead were footprints leading out of the tree line – I sprinted forward, not caring if I was exposing myself to Sunray. They'd taken Jo. The bastards had found our hide. They shot Kenny and left him to die, and now they had my sister and Dawn Marie.

I just ran – that was all I had left. I ran straight through the tree line, following the footprints of a small group of soldiers. I followed them to a maze of tire tracks that ran in circles around me, eventually trailing off into single file out across a farmer's field, and back to the highway. Behind me, the sound of our newly acquired APC rang out, along with Sid's booming voice.

"Dave!" he bellowed. "Stay where you are, because we need to get the hell out of here now! I'm coming to get you!"

I slowed to a jog and then dropped to my knees, utterly defeated. They had my kid sister. The bastards had Jo.

CHAPTER 30

I crawled back in the carrier and took a seat in the corner next to the engine panel. Sid climbed in after me and closed the combat lock on the rear door. He glanced at Cruze and said, "Kenny's dead. They've got the chick, and they fucking took Jo. That APC we thought we heard ... the one that was missing from the coulee. It must have happened when we started our assault."

"Oh, my God."

We thought we'd taken every precaution. We were well camouflaged inside our hide, and Sunray had to know we were going to take out his people in the coulee. He fucking waited until the sound of our mortars exploding to launch his assault knowing that in the heat of battle, we wouldn't have heard his guns. And even if we had, there was no way we could have gotten back to the hide in time to stop him.

Mel dropped back down in the crew commander's hatch as a haze of static belched out of the radio. She was just about to fiddle with the squelch when a trio of loud beeps blared through the speaker followed by a man's voice.

"Three-Two Charlie this is Sunray, over."

She stared at the radio, unsure whether to respond or not.

"Three-Two Charlie, this is Sunray, over."

"Son of a bitch!" Sid snarled as he climbed over the jump seat and snatched the handset.

"This isn't Three-Two Charlie, you prick!" he spat.

The radio hissed again and then Sunray's voice filled the interior of the carrier.

"Three-Two Charlie – is the call sign of the Coyote you stole from me. Consider it a gift - or better yet, a fair trade. I admit that tracking you has been a challenge since the day you crossed over into Eden. Clearly, you reservists received exceptional training with your unit. I salute your effective use of strategy in finding what the locals refer to as the abattoir. I suspect you think me a monster, but I care little for how others see me. The world must be rebuilt, though there is no possible way to recover all that we have lost. Life in an unthinkable time must be met with unthinkable

measures, hence the abattoir. It is just one of numerous methods I have implemented by which order is established as we begin to start over."

I grabbed the handset from Sid and motioned for him to calm down. He ground his teeth and climbed back into the turret as I squeezed the PTT button.

"This is David Simmons," I said, forcing back my rage. "We're all that's left of the King's Own."

"I know who you are," he answered. *"The child told us your name. The King's Own was a fine unit before the end came, wasn't it? Nevertheless, you are trespassers in Eden. Our intelligence informs us that a resistance movement has taken shape, and that it has elements throughout the disputed territory. I don't need to remind you of the seriousness of your move into Eden and your unprovoked attack on the few survivors left in Dinsmore – it's why two of your people are now dead. Three, if you count the defector once we're done with her. Rest assured, however, that your sister is safe, and will remain so as long as you listen carefully to what I am about to tell you and do precisely as instructed."*

I could feel the bile rising in my throat. I squeezed the handset so hard that my knuckles turned white. "You think you've won a victory because you killed two of our people and blasted one of our carriers. Well, from where I'm sitting, your body count is worse than mine. We killed everyone in the coulee." *"A necessary sacrifice, but that is the nature of battle, isn't it?"* he replied. *"Still, I do applaud your efforts. Now, tell me what the infected knew about the resistance."*

I hadn't had time to debrief everyone about what we found. Cruze mouthed the word *resistance* and threw me a worried look. I raised a hand and motioned for everyone to remain silent.

"They had nothing to say because they were dead when we got there," I said, feigning innocence.

The radio spat out a haze of static followed by Sunray's voice. *"Don't play games with me, boy,"* he said angrily. *"You know there is a base somewhere not far from here. I aim to find out where it is. Remember that I have your sister. Perhaps you would like to talk with her."*

I ground my teeth together, and banged the handset against my head.

"What's he talking about?" asked Mel. "What's this stuff about a resistance?"

"Other survivors," I said. "A few hundred clicks away. He doesn't know where they are, and that's why he took Jo. He wants me to lead him to them."

"Well, you're not going to do that, are you?" asked Cruze. Her breathing was laboured. She had elevated her leg by placing it on an ammunition box.

"*I don't know what I'm going to do!*" I said in frustration. "He's got Jo. He'll kill her if we don't play his game."

The static on the radio disappeared and a wispy, terrified voice filled the airwaves. It was Jo.

"*David ... are you there?*"

An ache radiated out from the middle of my chest as my eyes began to fill with tears. "H-Hi Jo," I answered.

"*I don't know where I am,*" she said. "*I'm not supposed to talk about that. Is Kenny ... is he ... dead?*"

I squeezed the handset. "Yeah, Jo. He's gone."

What she said next broke my heart.

"*I'm sorry they caught me, David. I just couldn't find a good hiding place. I wanted so much to make you see that I was a good soldier too. Please don't be mad at me, okay?*"

I bit into my lip, trying desperately to keep myself from falling to pieces. "I'm so not mad at you, Jo. I'm never going to be mad at you. Ever. We all love you, and we're going to get you back. Somehow, we'll get you back to us again."

The radio went silent for a few moments inside our carrier. We'd failed her. *I'd* failed her, and now she'd been taken captive by a madman.

"*Tears the heart apart, doesn't it?*" said Sunray. "*I will allow her to live, so long as you find the location of the resistance. Do try and understand that I take no pleasure in using a child as a pawn, but I must neutralize them before they have a chance to mobilize more support.*

"*You have enough fuel inside that vehicle's tanks to see you through a day or so. I suspect you can scrounge up the remainder from what's left back in the coulee, but I'm going to give you a leg up. Prepare to copy the following information."*

I pulled my field message pad out of my pocket and flipped it open. Mel tossed me a pencil, which I caught with my free hand.

"Ready," I said grimly.

"Grid nine seven four three eight six. There you will find a fully fuelled G-Wagon, along with a trailer and a dozen or so empty Jerry cans. I recommend that you fill them with what's left inside the vehicles in the coulee. You'll need every drop."

I squeezed the handset. "And then what?"

"You'll find the location of the resistance and report back to me on the radio. Once I have confirmation from my recce elements that the information you have provided is accurate, I'll radio with a location for you to reunite with your sister. You have seventy-two hours – I suggest that you begin your search immediately. Sunray out."

The handset slipped out of my hand and bounced onto the floor as I stared at the grid reference on my pad. Mel had already opened her map and was looking for the G-Wagon's location. She held the map against an engine panel and pointed to a spot off the main highway, no more than 10 km to the east.

"Here," she said, pointing at the map. "We'll have to double back to the coulee and drain the tanks. Maybe we'll find some more Intel on Sunray once daylight comes. At the very least, we know he won't be attacking us this time. What do you think, Dave?"

I threw my field message pad across the back of the carrier. *"What do I think? He's got my freaking sister, and he's holding her hostage. He's using her as a bargaining chip!"*

Sid dropped down from the turret and slipped a hand onto my shoulder. "She ain't a bargaining chip, buddy. And he'll kill her along with the rest of us if you do what he asks you to do. To hell with finding this resistance – let's find this prick and end him."

I glanced at Cruze's leg for a moment. We'd have to cauterize that bullet wound soon, or she'd lose it. "Doug!" I shouted. "Get back here."

Mel Dixon made way for Doug as he crawled over the driver's seat and through the crew commander's hatch. "What do you need?" he said.

I pointed to Cruze's leg. "You once told me you and your uncle saved your cousin's leg after a hunting accident. You helped him cauterize the wound to stop the bleeding. Cruze has a bullet wound that went straight through – is there anything you can do?"

Doug crawled into the back of the carrier, lifted the blood-soaked bandage and gave me a grim look as he shook his head.

"I could have, about half an hour ago, but her leg is saturated now. Cruze needs to get to a doc ASAP."

I was out of options. Sunray had my sister, and Cruze was slowly bleeding to death. I searched the team's faces for a sign of hope, and each one of them stared straight back at me. Each was looking to me to come up with a plan.

I couldn't refuse to make contact with the resistance. I had a vague idea of they were located, and part of me wanted to simply grab the radio and spill the beans, but then what? Sid was right – Sunray was going to kill Jo whether we cooperated with him or not. We represented a glitch in his plans. We'd created losses. We'd destroyed the abattoir and killed his personnel – there was no way in the world he'd let us live after that.

Our team of survivors had dealt Sunray a blow, albeit a tiny one, but maybe it was enough to give other survivors living under his rule a measure of hope. If we could fight him, maybe they could as well. That left me with only one option: Cruze would come with me to link up with the people at Carlsbad Farms. I'd get her the medical attention she needed, and then my priority would be the rescue of my sister.

I exhaled heavily and said, "Some of our supplies and weapons are in the overturned carrier. There are probably some supplies that didn't get destroyed down in the coulee and somewhere out there are others like us – people who aim to take down Sunray. We've got seventy-two hours to save Jo, so team … put your thinking caps on."

JOURNAL ENTRY: 19 NOVEMBER 0337 HRS ZULU

I'm taking Cruze to Carlsbad Farms – that's the best chance she's got of saving her leg and hopefully her life. We're splitting up what's left of the team. Sid is now in charge, and his team is going to take that Coyote into a hide on the eastern side of the river. From there, they'll go on a long-range reconnaissance patrol. They're going to check all the grid references on that field message pad I took from the spotter who helped kill Kate Dawson.

They'll radio me information on Sunray's assets. I'm going to have to divulge the location of this resistance base. But what Sunray doesn't know is that Sid will be watching him mobilize. He won't come into Carlsbad without having conducted his own reconnaissance first. That gives me seventy-two hours to link up with the resistance and set up a diversion. Something to keep his recce elements busy while the resistance plans to attack Sunray's rear: that's where Sid's team will come in. Everything rests on Sid finding where Sunray is going to mass for his eventual attack. If we can hit him from the flanks when he's mobilizing, there's a chance we can save Jo and kill Sunray while we're at it.

He's expecting me to follow his orders to the letter, and that's what I'm going to do – I'll just feed him information that I want him to know. Enough to draw him into a kill zone so that we can take him out.

We've loaded Cruze into the G-Wagon, and I know that we're likely being watched – Sunray isn't stupid. He will dispatch a team to follow me from a safe distance – that's what I'd be doing if I were in his shoes. I'm going to have to figure out my next move once Cruze and I are on the road. In the meantime, we're going to head east. We're going to follow the highway across miles upon miles of empty, snow-covered farmland. We're going to make it across the border, and I'm going to find this resistance base called Carlsbad Farms. With a little luck, Cruze will survive the trip.

Less than a week out of creep the creep infested city and we've lost two of our people, we've lost both our vehicles, and my sister has been taken. Sunray is on our tail. We're out-gunned, outnumbered, and we're running out of time. We have to make this work. We have to find Carlsbad Farms.

Somehow we have to save Jo.

--- THE END ---

CHECK OUT OTHER GREAT ZOMBIE NOVELS

DEAD ASCENT
by Jason McPhearson

The dead have risen and they are hungry...

Grizzled war veteran turned game warden, Brayden James and a small group of survivors, fight their way through the rugged wilderness of southern Appalachia to an isolated cabin in the hope of finding sanctuary. Every terrifying step they make they are stalked by a growing mass of staggering corpses, and a raging forest fire, set by the government in hopes of containing the virus.

As all logical routes off the mountain are cut off from them, they seek the higher ground, but they soon realize there is little hope of escape when the dead walk and the world burns.

CHAOS THEORY
by Rich Restucci

The world has fallen to a relentless enemy beyond reason or mercy. With no remorse they rend the planet with tooth and nail.

One man stands against the scourge of death that consumes all.

Teamed with a genius survivalist and a teenage girl, he must flee the teeming dead, the evils of humans left unchecked, and those that would seek to use him. His best weapon to stave off the horrors of this new world? His wit.

CHECK OUT OTHER GREAT ZOMBIE NOVELS

RUN
by Rich Restucci

The dead have risen, and they are hungry.

Slow and plodding, they are Legion. The undead hunt the living. Stop and they will catch you. Hide and they will find you. If you have a heartbeat you do the only thing you can: You run.

Survivors escape to an island stronghold: A cop and his daughter, a computer nerd, a garbage man with a piece of rebar, and an escapee from a mental hospital with a life-saving secret. After reaching Alcatraz, the ever expanding group of survivors realize that the infected are not the only threat.

Caught between the viciousness of the undead, and the heartlessness of the living, what choice is there? Run.

THE DEAD WALK THE EARTH
by Luke Duffy

As the flames of war threaten to engulf the globe, a new threat emerges.

A 'deadly flu', the like of which no one has ever seen or imagined, relentlessly spreads, gripping the world by the throat and slowly squeezing the life from humanity.

Eight soldiers, accustomed to operating below the radar, carrying out the dirty work of a modern democracy, become trapped within the carnage of a new and terrifying world.

Deniable and completely expendable. That is how their government considers them, and as the dead begin to walk, Stan and his men must fight to survive.

CHECK OUT OTHER GREAT ZOMBIE NOVELS

CHECK OUT OTHER GREAT ZOMBIE NOVELS

900 MILES
by S. Johnathan Davis

John is a killer, but that wasn't his day job before the Apocalypse.

In a harrowing 900 mile race against time to get to his wife just as the dead begin to rise, John, a business man trapped in New York, soon learns that the zombies are the least of his worries, as he sees first-hand the horror of what man is capable of with no rules, no consequences and death at every turn.

Teaming up with an ex-army pilot named Kyle, they escape New York only to stumble across a man who says that he has the key to a rumored underground stronghold called Avalon..... Will they find safety? Will they make it to Johns wife before it's too late?

Get ready to follow John and Kyle in this fast paced thriller that mixes zombie horror with gladiator style arena action!

WHITE FLAG OF THE DEAD
by Joseph Talluto

Millions died when the Enillo Virus swept the earth. Millions more were lost when the victims of the plague refused to stay dead, instead rising to slaughter and feed on those left alive. For survivors like John Talon and his son Jake, they are faced with a choice: Do they submit to the dead, raising the white flag of surrender? Or do they find the will to fight, to try and hang on to the last shreds or humanity?

www.ingramcontent.com/pod-product-compliance
Lightning Source LLC
Chambersburg PA
CBHW031320170626
46807CB00002B/493